Praise for Ajay Close's ear

OFFICIAL AND DOUB

'Brave, vulnerable, intensely observant and articulate, packed with life'

John le Carré

'Her eye for the dreadful detail of contemporary life is acute, her pleasure in it is immense . . . she makes you glad to be alive and living now.'

Fay Weldon, *Mail on Sunday*

'With this novel Ajay Close stakes her claim to a deserved place in the pantheon of Scotland's exciting contemporary novelists.'

Val McDermid, *Scotland on Sunday*

'Remarkable prose which is polished and always vivid'

Carol Birch, *TLS*

'This is a very assured first novel. It is beautifully structured, written with a commanding voice.'

Carl MacDougall, *The Herald*

'This psychological thriller pulses with life and is riven with sharp observation. As the screws turn, the author's natural zest and intensity harden into a brittle tension to produce one of the most involving thrillers I've read.'

Daily Mail

FORSPOKEN

'She is a natural writer, with a rare gift of combining tartness and empathy, intellectual reach and an up-to-speed take on contemporary madness. Glasgow has a magnificent addition to its pantheon of fine writers.'

Candia McWilliam

'A book that engages at every level with questions of imaginative and spiritual depletion and restoration . . . Coloured, multi-dimensional, avid for experience'

Brian Morton, *Scotland on Sunday*

'Dense vigorous prose, alive with observation and shrewd intelligence . . . fate, coincidence, memory, romantic love, sibling rivalry, Scottish nationalism, city life – all are here.'

Literary Review

'Vivid, funny, touching and eerie'

The Herald

'Close's second novel is an exceptional one, firmly establishing the arrival of a major talent.'

The List

'A nutter of a book'

The Big Issue

TRUST

'Engrossing . . . the toughness and the edge that her prose achieves are perfect reflections of the content, and a boon to those who want to be made to think, both about men and women and the relations between them, and about the values we so often assume are shared ones.'

The Scotsman

'Dynamic, detailed and unsqueamish . . . Highly recommended.'

Morning Star

'Intelligent and uncompromising'

The Herald

'Blew me away . . . sharp as a blade'

The Weekly Worker

Born in Sheffield, Ajay Close took an English degree at Cambridge. She worked as a newspaper journalist, winning several awards, before becoming a full-time author and playwright. Her first play, *The Keekin Gless*, was staged at Perth Theatre in July 2009. Her second, *The Sma Room Séance*, was performed at the 2014 Edinburgh Fringe. She is the author of three novels, *Official and Doubtful* (Secker & Warburg 1996), which was long-listed for the Orange Prize, *Forspoken* (Secker & Warburg, 1998) and *Trust* (Blackfriars, 2014). All three books collected rave reviews. Ajay Close lives in Perthshire and is, always, working on a new novel.

A
PETROL SCENTED
SPRING

Ajay Close

SANDSTONEPRESS
HIGHLAND | SCOTLAND

First published in Great Britain by
Sandstone Press Ltd
Dochcarty Road
Dingwall
Ross-shire
IV15 9UG
Scotland.

www.sandstonepress.com

The publisher acknowledges support from
Creative Scotland towards publication of this volume.

ISBN: 978-1-910124-61-1
ISBNe: 978-1-910124-62-8

Cover design by David Wardle of Bold and Noble
Typeset by Iolaire Typesetting, Newtonmore.
Printed and bound by CPI Group (UK) Ltd, Croydon CR0 4YY

For Geraldine

'. . . a man whose blood
Is very snow-broth'

Shakespeare, *Measure for Measure*

ONE

Spring is here. I know it as soon as I wake. Not the pretty, pink-blossomy poet's season, but the petrol-scented spring of Earls Court Square. A sooty blackbird whistling on a chimney pot. The pistol crack of parlour maids beating their rugs. Any day now the typewriter girls on the underground trains will shed their ugly winter coats and the one-eyed costermonger on Derry Street will call out 'Give us a smile!'

'But London's so dirty!' Aunt Nellie wails, 'so noisy, so busy, so big'. Which is just what I love about it. Trains and motor omnibuses and electric trams, all the coalboats, barges and lighters on the river, and the workers spilling down Warwick Road like a sort of many-legged machine. Bill says there are two sorts of people in this country: the mousy, soft-voiced, unobtrusive types who like green fields, health corsets, scrambled eggs without pepper, and pitch-black nights so quiet a person could scream; and the other sort, the modern sort, who prefer Ragtime and gin punch and anchovy toast and scorching down to Brighton in Charlie Beevor's Austin, and a jolt of strong black coffee to start the day.

I love these mornings. Hot kidneys and buttery toast and the ironed-newsprint smell of Pa's *Times*. A lozenge of sunlight sliding down the wallpaper. Brewer bringing in the post. The murmur of half-distracted talk. Snippets of news from our letters, the price of copper, what everyone wants for lunch. No one really listening. A lovely desultory recitative of *mmms* and *ahs* and *pass the sugar* and *what about turbot?* Embellished this morning by a light descant of *good gracious!* and *Dot,*

1

you'll like this, as Auntie reads out Uncle George's gossip about the Bishop.

Today being the last of Aunt Nellie's visit, she and Mama are going to see the Assyrians, and maybe the Minoans if they don't get too tired. Auntie will take her sketchbook and Mama will trail along half a step behind, looking at the bluestockings' dresses. They're debating whether they'll need an umbrella, and wouldn't it be easier to take a cab, and is half past one too late for lunch, when Pa looks up from his paper and says to me 'You're very quiet'. Quickly, I fold the letter back into its envelope.

'Someone's rather furtive,' Mama says.

Pa leans across the table, 'That wouldn't be a proposal, by any chance?'

And now they're all ragging me about the sender. Is it William or Henry or Richard or Charles, or another young buck altogether? Even my sister Hilda joins in, though she knows full well who sent it. I caught her reading over my shoulder.

A whistle pierces the open window, not a moment too soon. I call, 'Just coming, Bill.'

Aunt Nellie's eyebrows shoot up.

Mama gives me a testy look (we do not shout out to the street in this family), leaving Pa to explain to Aunt Nellie, 'It's Argemone acting the goat.'

Argemone ffarington Bellairs is nearly six feet tall. Brown hair cut almost as short as Pa's, the frankest blue eyes I've ever seen, and a lopsided smile that saves her the bother of drawling 'I say, is anyone up for fun?' She is twice as clever as my brother and his Cambridge friends, fluent in French from her schooldays in Caen, and such a sharp mimic that I'm never sure whether to feel flattered or mortified. She knows everything worth knowing. Which hotel Sarah Bernhardt stays in when she visits London. Where Constance Collier buys her hats. The latest dance steps. How much to

2

tip a cabman in Paris. How to be served strong drink in a country hotel without causing a stink (cough delicately into curled fingers and order a whisky mac). She smokes, and bandies the Devil's name, and laughs like a stevedore, but you should see her play the great lady if the servant class gives her cheek. She is quite the most thrilling person I've ever met, and – how shall I put this? – my bosom chum.

We're kindred spirits: Do and Bill, quicksilver and gunpowder, brilliant and disputatious and loud. Mama can't understand it: Donella used to be such a dear sweet girl, perfectly happy with a window seat and an apple and a tome by Mrs Gaskell. Oh I could run like the wind on Torbay strand, but in company I was every inch the dutiful daughter. Until I met Bill, at a rectory tea party of all unlikely occasions, and Do was born.

And now we're never apart. When the doorbell rings, nine times out of ten it's Bill come to collect me for a game of tennis, or a lunch party, or a lantern lecture, or a jaunt down to Richmond, or a walk through Hyde Park.

Hilda says Mama is frightfully jealous, even if she doesn't show it: *she* would like to be the one walking arm-in-arm with her firstborn, and having the same thought, and both saying it at once, and bursting into peals of laughter. But how can Mama begrudge Bill my friendship? Isn't she always reminding us how lucky we are, compared to that poor motherless girl? Twenty-three and all alone in Bayswater, with her sisters and brothers scattered across the country and her father on the other side of the Atlantic. No one to put her to bed with an earthenware pig when she catches a chill. No one to tell her she would look so much nicer in a plain silk dress than in that awful grey serge. For two pins Mama would invite her to come and live with us in Earls Court. Only Bill doesn't live all alone. She shares a basement flat with that little witch Maud Jenney, two rooms

3

in a narrow white stucco house filled with the garrulous relatives of their Russian landlord, Mose Cohen. There's always someone rapping on the door to borrow an egg or a twist of sugar or the evening paper, or to borrow Bill herself to model a dress while the borrower circles her on hands and knees with a mouthful of pins. Nor is it all borrowing. As often they'll arrive with a bowl of borscht or a blini hot from the pan. I can't think of anything more splendid than living in that maelstrom of Yiddish and gossip and laughter and rages that blow over in the time it takes to thunder back upstairs.

'The garment workers are going to strike!'

Never 'Good morning, how are you, Mrs Atkins?' or 'Isn't it a lovely day?' Always some drama, a piece of news that bounces like a hot coal from hand to hand. A strike, what fun! That'll expose the hypocrisies of the bourgeoisie. Take away their finery and what do they have left? It's the skilled fingers of men like Mr Cohen that allow them to display their *soi-disant* good taste. Ha! Bill loathes taste. Taste is just the consolation prize for people with no intelligence, people who think choosing the right shade of brocatelle makes up for having no conversation, while honest, hardworking, clever people like the Cohens have to pander to their vanity, just to be able to eat.

And yes, I'm a bourgeoise, born and bred. Pa makes money, Mama comes from land. We have an account at Fortnum's. As one of that select group approved by the King as suitable brides for the better sort of families, I have a string of eligible admirers. All I have to say is 'I've had a letter from Johnnie Hetherington' or 'Aubrey Percival's invited me down to Cressley' and Bill will forget all about Isadora Duncan or the Mexican revolution or whatever she's blithering about, and get very hot under the collar indeed.

But something's the matter with Hilda. She clangs her tea cup back into its saucer and glowers at the tablecloth. Bill

4

winks at me. Pa glances across, then, wisely, returns to the *Times*.

Mama says 'Shall we ask some of the girls from school to tea, Hilly?' and I have to use my napkin to cover a smile. Hilda doesn't want to drink lemonade with her classmates. They're nice enough, as schoolgirls go, but she doesn't want a *nice* friend. She wants someone like Bill, and Mama knows it. Lately, she has taken to drawing me into the hall for these muttered confabs.

'Why don't you take Hilly with you?'

A long pause, followed by a sigh. 'If we must.'

So here we are, the three of us, strolling down Church Street on the first day of spring, glancing in the shop windows; looking beyond our own reflections, now and again. Hats, china, dresses, books, the usual clutter of propaganda in the Votes for Women shop. You see those green, white and purple brooches everywhere these days. At the bottom of the display, below a paper banner proclaiming *Holloway Corner*, five china dolls in little prison uniforms have been placed in miniature cardboard cells. A sixth doll is dressed in a doctor's frock coat and stovepipe hat. Someone has cut her hair off and inked a beard around her cherry-ripe pout.

'I suppose you think that's funny,' Hilda says to me.

'I do rather,' I admit.

She scowls.

According to Hilda, I have simply ruined her life. I have swiped the best of everything. Bill's friendship. Pa's witty turn of phrase and blithe assumption that of course people will like him – why would they not? Mama's charm and graceful carriage and lovely face. It's true I'm the spit of our mother, but Hilda could be quite a looker if she'd try smiling for once, and there's her talent for sketching, she's not completely null, just convinced she has been dealt a losing hand. Even in her birthplace. I was born in America.

I give off a whiff of the Iowa prairie and close shaves with red-skinned tribesmen, while she was hatched in Seaton, a one-horse town on the English coast with its gosh-golly red and white cliffs. She got boarding school, where they sent her because I'd been such a holy terror when I was fifteen. Not that she minded so very much, when she thought I was stuck in Newton Abbot baking macaroons for the Churchwomen's Guild. But the minute she was packed off to Tolmers Park, Pa took our house in town, so she got drumlins and algebra and Latin gerunds and February afternoons on the hockey field with a crosswind straight from Siberia, and the name Hilda, poor thing, while I got Donella, and ten minutes by train to the V and A and the Proms, and jaunts up to Cambridge to visit Gordon and his handsome chums, and gadding around London with Bill.

And I do see her point, life can be unjust: she's seventeen, with a nasty dose of the schoolgirl glums; I'm twenty-one and having a ball.

'Your pops was in a waggish mood,' Bill remarks as we saunter towards Kensington.

I decide to tease her. 'He's trying to get me married off, preferably to someone who'll put a bit of business his way.'

Hilda shoots me an accusing look, but there's more than a speck of truth in this. Four years since I was presented at court. Most of my fellow debs are wed. By the time Mama was twenty-one she had two children in tow.

'So put an end to his hopes,' Bill says.

'It's all right for you.'

'Because Pater's barking mad?'

Kenneth ffarington Bellairs has been a sheep farmer, newspaper editor, stock market savant, company director and bankrupt, and can currently be corresponded with care of Medical Lake Asylum.

I murmur, 'The situation has its advantages'.

'No one to horsewhip you?'

6

'You're the one who'd take the blame. I'm the perfect damsel.'

Hilda is listening very carefully.

'Look at that!' I say.

We've reached Throckmorton's Fine Art, which today is displaying a canvas by Samuel Peploe. A still life of a restaurant table late at night.

Bill's eyes are hooded. Her fingers stray towards mine, then, remembering, twitch away again. I know what she's thinking. I'm thinking it myself. The silver coffee pot beside the empty glass, the discarded napkin, that blown rose: it's a painting of us. What use have we for Nature? We're a new species, releasing our strongest scent in artificial light.

Her thumb strokes the pearl button at her throat. 'Half stupefied by meat and drink, the bitter aftertaste of coffee in my mouth—'

She's putting herself inside the canvas. It's a game we play when we're alone. I cough to remind her of our chaperone, but she takes no notice.

'—the throb of my pulse so alive to you, I can't bring myself to meet your look.'

Dinner at Mama's table is a cheerfully temperate affair, precursor to eight hours of soundly dreamless sleep, and yet my little sister says, 'I've felt like that'.

'I should hope you have not,' I say, sounding like Aunt Nellie.

'And why shouldn't she? She's old enough to provoke a glance. Or do you think they only have eyes for you?'

This is my cue to laugh, and reply *of course: one glimpse of me and they're smitten for all time*. Instead I say, 'She's too young for all that rot.'

Bill slides me a sidelong look, 'You weren't at seventeen.'

'Cheese it, Bill.' But it's too late, I can see Hilda wondering how, or rather with whom, I disgraced myself. The weedy aesthetes at Miss Burt-Cowper's dance classes? One of

7

Gordon's friends? The gardener's boy in Devon, with his strong brown hands?

It's almost eleven by the clock on the wall of Barkers department store when we get to Kensington High Street. I'm about to suggest we telephone Brewer with our apologies and have an early lunch in that place with the potted palms that does such delicious squab pie, when Bill catches my eye and directs a quizzing glance across the street. It's a perfectly ordinary Monday morning. A good throng on each pavement. Errand boys in their white aprons, ladies' maids in search of ribbons and stockings, chaps like Pa in bowler hats, a couple of fashionable gentlewomen rustling along in their whipped-cream skirts.

But now I do spot something. That tall girl. Dressed with a simplicity that graces her slender figure like a boast, her hair much the same colour as Hilda's and mine. She stands apart from the human tide, right against a shop window. All at once, as if she can feel my scrutiny, she turns and looks straight at me. A pretty face, though my first thought is not her prettiness. She seems terribly familiar.

And there is something in her hand.

Barkers' clock strikes the first of its eleven chimes and, with a tremendous cacophony of smashing glass, the perfectly ordinary Monday morning turns to madness. It happened on Saturday on Regent Street, I read about it in the paper, which makes the fact of it happening now even more dumbfounding. The cheek of them! To do it twice! All along both sides of the High Street women I had not noticed until this moment – women wearing mannishly-tailored jackets over shapeless skirts – are pulling hammers out of their sleeves and striking at shop windows. Other women, shrieking, cower from the splintering glass. Policemen blow whistles. The chaps in bowler hats wrestle hammers out of hands. Not five feet away from me, a chit of a girl in a green, white and purple sash has her arms pinned behind her and is frogmarched

8

towards a policeman. I feel so strangely filled and empty all at once, outraged and excited and even . . . privileged, yes, that's the word, privileged to be watching this, to have the breath snatched from my lungs and still to want it to go on and on. And strangest of all, when I look back, Bill has her arms around Hilda, who is weeping.

TWO

I was seventy-nine last birthday. I feel it in the knees mostly, and in the mirror. My neighbour's daughter calls me the leopard lady. She's doing the Victorians at school. Her mother sends her round to ask about chimney sweeps and long dresses. I tell her, when I was her age the little boys dressed just like little girls, and she laughs. But when I say 'Inside, I don't feel any older than you', she looks embarrassed for me.

I give her a biscuit and send her home. Perhaps she'll come back one day when she's old enough to sit and listen without her knee jiggling up and down. I tell her mother I've a fund of stories about the suffragettes.

'*You* were a suffragette?'

'No, but my first husband had a lot to do with them.'

In a little while, I shall tell you how I met him. How the very first time I saw him, in the garden, he seemed plucked from my dreams. How else could I have felt that recognition? Five months later, when he stood at the altar and looked me in the eye, I thought *ah yes, my love, my fate*. Well, I was right, and wrong, about that. He was drawn to me, but if I retrace the path that brought us together, taking it back to the very beginning, I find myself unknown, undreamt of, quite superfluous.

If you want to hear my story, we must start with a drama in which I played no part.

I think of her as I saw her that day in Kensington, while Bill stopped Hilda from using the hammer she had brought.

10

That swan-like beauty. Serene amidst shattering glass.

Have you ever really looked at a swan? Curiously self-conscious. They hold their lovely necks so stiff it makes my shoulders ache. But if you rile them and they go for you with their stabbing beaks, they're not so elegant.

I can't be certain it was her. But this is *my* story, and hers was the face that floated into my head when I finally put two and two – or should I say, two and one – together. Hers or another's, it doesn't really matter. She'll have felt the same blend of terror and elation. The suddenly-dilating capillaries. A kick-start from the adrenal gland. I went through something similar ten years later, the first time I performed an amputation, so I know how it feels to bluff your way through the unthinkable. And afterwards, to look in the glass and see the self you always hoped you'd become.

How could he not fall for her?

How can I not imagine myself in her shoes?

Arabella Scott.

Second sister in a brood of female brainboxes (with one petted baby brother) but, unlike so many other ambitious, intelligent Scotswomen, not a doctor. She can't have been squeamish about gore, given what she put herself through, so why follow the more conventionally feminine path of teaching? Why else but ego? All those young hearts in love with her. Or am I being unfair?

She was used to taking a lead. That was the difference between us. The whole country was her classroom. She would instruct, and so improve, us all. What a marvellous chance she was given: to shout and smash and insult and burn in the name of high principle. All the petty irritations, the boredom – and God knows, it was boring, being a young woman then – all of it rolled up into a great yell of injustice. She saw the opportunity, and grasped it, while I went about coveting other women's hats, and drinking myself lightheaded on Darjeeling, and flirting with young nincompoops, thinking myself quite the heartbreaker.

It starts at university. The old story. A new self. New friends. No one to pull you down, recalling that time the minister caught you watching his spaniel mounting Mrs Lawrie's pug. If you want to be the very embodiment of high-minded intellect, who is to gainsay you? Then there's the way your footsteps echo in the Old College courtyard, the freshness of your complexion against the grey stone, your crisp white blouse, the easy sway of your uncorseted gait, your waist so sweetly narrow in the cinch of your not-quite-ankle-length skirt. A bluestocking! A wholly new kind of woman – well, apart from lady novelists and Renaissance queens. The intellectual equal of any man, as rational and purposeful and far-sighted, but with an extra soulfulness. Born to show both sexes how far they fall short.

She has never given a thought to the vote, but now that it's been mentioned, of course she must have it. And the women who come to speak at the Suffrage Society are so much the sort of women she would like to be. So assured and passionate and imperious. And it's such fun, getting all dressed up to carry the banner, making speeches on a soapbox, heckling members of parliament.

It helps that she has her sister beside her. Dear Muriel. Clever, but not quite as clever. Courageous, but not in the same reckless way. She can't remember a time when Muriel was not looking up at her with that admiring gaze. And part of what dear, loyal Muriel so admires is her big sister's beauty. There's no getting away from it: a beautiful woman can do things a plain woman had better not attempt. If it's injustice that galls you, there's injustice. Why should one pair of eyes, one nose, one mouth, be more pleasing than another? And not just pleasing: more

12

aloof and unknowingly voluptuous, more like a ripe plum weighting down the branch.

Muriel is a solid little thing, her lips a little thinner, her eyes a little more bulbous. Touching in her true-heartedness, but not a beauty. They share rooms while studying at Edinburgh University. They walk to lectures together. They whip each other into a frenzy of indignation over the iniquities of our so-called democratic system. They admire the English heroines who get themselves arrested and starve in gaol, but their own roles are no less necessary. Chalking on pavements, handing out membership forms, waving placards at by-election meetings. In 1909 they travel to London to deliver a petition to the Prime Minister and are arrested for obstruction and sentenced to twenty-one days in Holloway Gaol, where they refuse to eat.

When they are released, they pour black dye into a postbox. Or rather, Arabella does the pouring and Muriel keeps watch. Postbox spoiling, window smashing, gouging holes out of bowling greens and golf courses. Since they are criminals now, in the eyes of the law, why not?

The newspapers call it wanton destruction, but there are rules. No person, however vile, is to be hurt. Humiliated, yes. Pelted with eggs, or flour, or pepper to make them sneeze, but not physically harmed. There must always be a clear message in the action. If possible, a witty one. So cricket pitches and other sporting places are chosen because the government is not 'playing the game'. A mansion in Perthshire owned by a prominent anti-suffragist is gutted by fire. (The Chancellor of the Exchequer is expected in Scotland. A postcard, found near the blaze, bears the words *A warm welcome to Lloyd George*.) When two women are interrupted in the act of trying to blow up Rabbie Burns' cottage, anyone with a head on her shoulders understands that their true target is popular hypocrisy. Why should Scotland celebrate the egalitarian principles of its national bard while denying women the vote?

That happens in 1914, when everyone has become so much angrier. In 1913 it requires no small amount of courage for Arabella, Edith Hudson and the elderly Thomson sisters to take their paraffin cans to Kelso racecourse. Muriel stays behind. After that spell in Holloway, their mother made them promise they would not be arrested together again.

The Kelso escapade is a disaster. The old ladies are game but not up to sprinting away from the fire. Arabella and Edith leave them in the taxi, with Donald MacEwan, a gardener sympathetic to the cause. Arabella insists on walking every inch of the stand to make sure it holds no sleeping cat or tramp sheltering from the weather. Valuable time is lost. When they start to pour the paraffin, it spills on their clothes. Stupid, stupid! Should they undress? No time. And think of the scandal: suffragettes arrested in undergarments. The best they can do is stand some distance from the cotton wadding they have soaked with fuel. The lit matches they throw at it extinguish in mid-air. Arabella lights one of the suffragette newspapers brought as calling cards. How quickly the flame races along the paper. She shrieks (more stupidity) and tosses it towards the wadding. Her aim is wide. It burns out on the wooden floor. Edith takes another, folding the cheap paper over and over. Her aim is better, but the paraffin seems to have missed that corner of the wadding. At long last, the cotton starts to smoulder. And now they face a dilemma: to run, or stay and make sure the fire catches, chancing a sudden blaze and the flames leaping towards their reeking skirts?

They run. Who is to say it is the wrong decision? But the fire does not take hold. Beyond a scorch mark on the floor no damage is done, and before they reach the taxi all five are caught. The case against Agnes Thomson is found not proven, but her sixty-five-year-old sister is sentenced to three months in gaol. Arabella, Edith and Donald MacEwan get nine months each, in his case for doing nothing more than ordering the taxi. Arabella learns her lesson. No more half measures. If she's in this game, she is in it to win.

Sent to Calton Gaol, she refuses to eat or drink and is out in five days, released under the Cat and Mouse Act, having agreed to return and serve the rest of her sentence once she gets her strength back. Of course, the mouse goes on the run. Visited by a supporter, she changes clothes with her and drives off in the other woman's car, under the noses of the constables standing outside. Sometimes the police get wind of her whereabouts, requiring hide-and-seek in busy streets and chases down railway station platforms. She has the most tremendous fun.

Re-arrested, she starves herself to weakness, and is released. This time, when the police track her down, she dons a false beard and her brother William's clothes and slips out of a back window. Again she is arrested, again released. She moves to Brighton and becomes a campaign organiser. For eight months she makes mischief there. They drag her back to Edinburgh. Once more she goes on hunger and thirst strike. This time they have to kick her out. She sits on the pavement, demanding that they let her back in to serve the remainder of her sentence. She has learned the great secret of political protest. None more frightening to the authorities than one without fear. The truth is, the government is quite happy to have her elude their grasp, as long as she keeps out of sight. Realising this, Arabella parades in her suffragette colours at a by-election meeting in Ipswich, under the eyes of at least a dozen policemen. Her placard reads 'Here is the Mouse. Where is the Cat?'

By now, she's a Scottish heroine. They hold a party for her at the New Café in Edinburgh. A female piper serenades her. A hundred women in white dresses cheer her to the rafters. She gives a speech and they stand rapt, eyes shining, wanting to be her. Oh yes, she knows how to move a crowd. How to balance her indignation with mockery, brandishing the metal

15

cell number she took as a souvenir of her stay in Calton Gaol, leaving them in no doubt that right and a certain aplomb will prevail. But the political situation is changing. The prisons are under increasing pressure to force-feed hunger strikers. Nobody in Scotland wants it, least of all the prison doctors. Call it chivalry, or Calvinist scruple, or deference to their social betters (as so many imprisoned suffragettes are): whatever the reason, they won't do it.

But there's a new medical officer they're transferring from Peterhead Gaol to Perth. Hugh Ferguson Watson. Ambitious chap: an asylum doctor by training, farming background on the west coast. Not quite one of us, you know. He's willing. And this Margaret Morrison or Edith Johnston or Ethel Moorhead, or whatever her real name is, has caused us such trouble. Refusing to pay her taxes. Smashing the glass in the Wallace Monument. Taking a dogwhip to a young teacher who strong-armed her out of a Liberal Party meeting. We're fairly sure she had a hand in the burning of those three Perthshire mansions . . .

This Watson fellow is brought to Edinburgh to feed her by stomach tube. Some of the milk goes down the wrong way, into her lungs. She gets pneumonia. Still, it's no less than the bitch deserves, eh what? And the message has gone out: the gloves are off. This happens in February 1914. Arabella is re-arrested in June.

She fights them all the way from London to Scotland, making them drag her, hanging on to lamp posts, smashing her head against door jambs and walls. Yelling at the unfortunate hansom driver '*Don't take me, cabman. They are taking me to prison to murder me*'. Two policemen and a prison wardress, three to one, and that one in handcuffs, and still she frightens them, going for eyes and testicles. In the train compartment, they lay her along the seat, holding her hands and feet, and still she almost hurls herself out of the window.

16

She's so violent – they've never seen anything like it. But even as she's screaming, her brain is racing ahead, spotting the next opportunity. It's a twelve-hour journey, you'd think she'd exhaust herself, but she's still roaring as they cross the border, and when they leave Edinburgh without letting her off, a new extremity colours her fury. For the first time she speaks to them. *Why* is she not being returned to Calton Gaol? It's as if everything so far has been according to a sort of plan and, even as she fought them, she was in control. But the news that they are bound for Perth shocks her. It's not hard to rally a crowd of supporters in Edinburgh or Glasgow, but Perth is many miles north. An out-of-the-way sort of place. Fanny Parker burned down their cricket pavilion last year, then held a public meeting to explain why she'd done it. Only the police saved her from a lynching. Not too many friends of women's suffrage in Perth.

They bring the cab on to the station platform and carry her across. It's not far to the prison. When they hear her bawling, the wretched inmates start up a charivari, knocking their tin cups on the stone sills of their cell windows. She is taken to the prison hospital. Eight beds, all empty. Eight wardresses. Before, she has always had a cell. They strip her and take away her clothes. Lay her on a bed, pinning her by the ankles, knees, hips and shoulders. A sheet is placed over her. Each time she struggles, it slips, revealing more of her nakedness. One of the wardresses says something she doesn't hear. They laugh.

For twenty minutes nothing happens. The wardresses pass the time by gossiping, backbiting, moaning about the bacon they were given for dinner. Someone mentions the prison doctor, a name she recognises. A part of her was expecting this. Once Ethel Moorhead was forcibly fed, the writing was on the wall. She knew it would be her turn one day. But still, she is afraid.

17

THREE

'I am Doctor Ferguson Watson, the medical officer here.'

I know what I saw, the first time I set eyes on him, two years later, but by that time his reputation had recovered. My aunt and uncle were aware of no stain on his character. There must have been people who shunned him still, but the war had intervened like a tide over a beach, sweeping the sand clear. In June 1914 he is notorious. Her dear friend Ethel has told her all about him. His abrupt manner, his choleric face, the complete lack of that courtesy she was brought up to believe innate in men's dealings with women. All this is already in her head. But what does she *see*?

How tall he seems from the bed, though no more than middling height. He was forty in March, but is built like a young man. Lean, athletic. Married life will put meat on his bones and widen his face, ageing him by twenty years, but in 1914 he eats his breakfast standing up. Blue eyes made for fervour, or fury. Skin that flashes from pallor to heat. The sort of sandy hair that the sun strikes into sparks.

Or is she so dehydrated and sleep-deprived she sees nothing beyond the equipment set out on the table?

He examines her. Pulse, temperature, respiration, heart-beat. As yet, he has not looked her in the face. He uncaps his fountain pen and writes on the chart. Later, in the endless opportunity for reflection afforded those in prison, she will wonder if there is something too brusque about his indifference. His manner says she is just another prisoner, one of several hundred under his care, but can this be true? The eyes

18

of the nation are upon her. He nearly killed the last one. He cannot afford a second mistake.

He is not a connoisseur of women. It may be hard to believe of any man of forty, let alone one who looks like him, but he has not kissed a girl in twenty-five years. He keeps a tight rein on his appetites. It has not always been easy, but he has his reasons, and after so long it has become second nature. So it may be that he, too, sees nothing. Only the ruby streak on her inner thigh. The vein to which he applies his fingertips. The sclera exposed when he lifts an eyelid. The heaving swell of her left breast as he listens to her heart.

No, I don't believe it.

She is no passive carcass under his hands. She has struggled every inch of the journey from London, it is now forty-eight hours since she last had food or drink, but somehow she finds her second wind. Spits out the thermometer. Flails and kicks at the wardresses who try to restrain her. Knocks the glass of milk to the floor. Ethel Moorhead was no less violent, but Ethel was a stringy harridan of forty-five. Arabella is twenty-nine, and lovely, and naked as the day she was born, screaming and twisting in his hands. So yes, he looks.

He says the minimum required in a level voice that for all his qualifications retains a trace of the Ayrshire farmyard. When did she last eat? Drink? Open her bowels? How many days has she been menstruating? She is tall but her physique is poor. He cannot allow her to weaken herself further. She will remain prone in bed for the good of her health, kept away from any source of excitement. This includes books, newspapers, visitors and letters.

She answers him with furious questions. Why has she been brought to Perth instead of Edinburgh? How is she to petition the prison commissioners if she is forbidden to put pen to paper? By whose order is she to be forcibly fed? Is he aware that she has been imprisoned and released repeatedly on this

19

charge *without* feeding? How dare he call himself a doctor, after what he did to Ethel?

She has been disrupting public meetings and resisting arrest since she was twenty-three. The decent types will restrain her as gently as possible. While she shouts, they hold their tongues. But there are others who will take advantage of the situation. Her breasts have been handled, her buttocks grabbed, hands jammed in her crotch. Less common, yet not *un*common, are the men whose secret desire is violence. Punching her, throwing her to the ground, dragging her by the hair.

What she has not yet encountered is a man who shouts back.

Even as he's talking to her in that infuriatingly even manner some instinct tells her he can be provoked. She's no snob, but this is war, and a soldier uses every weapon at her disposal. She can't help noticing the farmboy accent, and now she's enunciating more crisply, the righteous timbre of her voice close to patrician scorn. Her late father held the modest rank of captain in India. The doctor's father is a tenant farmer. Not the widest social gulf, but enough. He reminds her that while she remains in prison he is her physician, and she is his patient. This is the one remark of his she answers directly. He is *not* her physician. If he touches her, it is an assault. She knows all about him. The ambitious mad-doctor not content with torturing lunatics. So bent on advancement he is ready to do the government's dirty work. What a distinction: the only doctor in Scotland willing to defile his vocation.

That does it. His colour darkens. She is gratified, and terrified. It is a shocking thing, to have a man raise his voice to you. A man like him. When he opens his lungs, it's like a battering ram against the sternum, his breath harsh on her face, the roar vibrating in her bones. *He will not permit her to harm herself.* Either she drinks the milk

20

or he feeds her by tube. She has five seconds to make her decision.

Do your worst, she says.

Here my mind flinches. I have cut out cancers and severed gangrenous limbs. To break the sacred seal of human flesh with the point of a scalpel is to breach a taboo. By comparison, inserting a greased tube down the throat to the stomach is nothing. But a nothing I cannot bring myself to imagine. I know the wardresses will have pinned her down. I can list the equipment. Jug. Funnel. Vaseline. Rubber tube. And the gag, a deformed pair of scissors, designed to keep the mouth fully open. I can say what is used, and in what order. But then Arabella starts to resist with every last ounce of her strength, and the doctor puts all his force into overcoming her, and of course he is rough in the struggle, if she won't hold still it stands to reason that she will be hurt and cry out in pain and fear and call on her maker to help her, and his face will show . . .

I cannot.

When he is gone, taking all but one of the wardresses with him, the soaked bedding is removed. For subsequent feedings they will use rubberised sheets to save on laundry. She is dressed in a hospital nightgown and given a coarse woollen blanket. She shivers uncontrollably. The wardress seems to think she is pretending. Later it will occur to her that the woman feels guilty, even shamed, for her part in this, and that it is natural to turn such guilt into hostility, but at this moment Arabella is incapable of reflection. The moon streams bright through the uncurtained window. She turns her face away, draws her knees up in a foetal curl. The wardress prods her until she lies flat on her back again. Doctor's orders. Her stomach is ravaged with acid after vomiting up the rich mixture he poured down the tube. Her gums are tender. She tastes blood

21

in her throat. There are bruises all over her body from being pinioned by the wardresses. But worse than all her many pains is the violation. She will not give in to self-pity, but is this any better, this impotent anger?

When she sleeps, it colours her dreams.

And now it is the morning.

'Has she retained the feed?'

'Some of it, sir.'

When the thermometer touches her lip she flinches.

'Are you in pain?'

No answer.

'Prisoner Scott?'

The wardress tells him 'She's not said a word all morning, sir.'

He places the thermometer under her arm, lifts the other arm to take her pulse. He's finishing the count when she speaks.

'I am entitled to write and receive letters.'

Pulse: 90.

'Healthy prisoners are entitled, but you are sick.'

'It is my right.'

'You're very weak. Writing would weaken you further, and the mental effort would hinder digestion. As your doctor, I cannot allow it.'

'You are *not* my doctor.'

'If you eat, I'll think about it. '

He extracts the thermometer. *Temperature: 97.4.*

She raises herself off the mattress.

He pushes her back down. 'Sitting up promotes regurgitation.'

'*I will not be touched!*'

Her scream rings in the silence. The wardress looks unnerved.

22

He says, 'The examination is finished for now.'

But the prisoner is not finished with him. 'When Ethel told me what you did to her, I didn't fully understand. You could have killed her.'

He has been over this so many times with the Commission, he has the words off pat. 'She caught pneumonia by breaking her cell window and walking about in her nightdress, throwing water over herself . . .'

'It wasn't the water.'

'. . . behaving like a madwoman.'

'You drove her to it.'

'She was a prisoner, convicted of fire-raising.'

'A political prisoner.'

'A criminal.' But why should he explain himself to her? 'For the last time, will you eat?'

'I will not.'

'Then you'll be fed artificially.'

She sneers at the scientific term, 'You mean forcibly.'

'As you wish,' he says.

They put a man on the moon today. What a fuss. Beefy would have loved it. My second husband. Devoted to me, as I was to him. He would have relished the technical complexity. *'Ah but what about the hoojimaflip, will it withstand the stress of the thingimajig – have they thought of that?'* The Telegraph has been full of it for days, I've been doing the crossword and throwing the rest out unread. But come the hour, for Beefy's sake, I turn on the television. As I watch those giant maggots bouncing across the lunar desert, my thoughts stray to Australia. Is she watching this now, another widow rattling around a house too big for her, wearing her dead husband's dressing gown over her clothes, wondering if it's just the cataracts or did she put odd stockings on this morning? Thinking how strange that there should be men

23

on the moon in her lifetime, and yet how little it changes the things that really matter.

Is she, too, telling herself, I bet I don't live long enough to see a woman up there?

FOUR

Over the fourteen months since her arrest at Kelso racecourse, Arabella has been gaoled four times, but never for more than five days. She thinks of prison as a short-lived, necessary evil. The cold stone, the stinking air, the hard-eyed wardresses, the filthy blanket, the lice: all these can be endured because it will only be for five days. And after comes the triumph of liberation. The defiant speeches she will make. The letters she will write to the newspapers. The women in white dresses with their arms full of flowers. All of which depends on her being able to starve herself. If she takes food, there is no risk of her dying in prison, no reason for them to release her. Her stomach rejected most of what was forced into her last night, but some nourishment was retained. Her headache has gone. Noticing this, her heart sinks.

Yet she's no masochist. I've seen a few anorexics in my surgery. Those straight-A perfectionists with their ironed jeans and their hang-ups about Daddy, so proud of their oh-so-tiny wrists. Arabella is not one of them. There is a pleasure to be had from fasting, once you get past the hunger. The senses sharpen, the gap between you and the corrupt world widens. These physiological reactions help her towards her objective, but – and this is the big difference – she is doing it for the cause. In a just world she would eat her meals and smile at the mirror. She doesn't hate herself, or love herself so mercilessly that it amounts to hate. She doesn't want to suffer, but suffer she must.

The lower down the social ladder you look, the worse it

gets. Women work long hours in factories. If men fall sick or lose their jobs there is government help. Women go on the streets. It is said there are towns in India where British officers march whole regiments to the brothel to release themselves in the vaginas of white women. (To the sisterhood, in 1914, it seems worse that these women should be white.) On the rare occasions when a wife beater comes before the court, the sentence is derisory. The government could put a stop to all this, if it cared to, and the government would be made to care, if women had the vote. But Mr Asquith and his cabinet believe that women's brains are not as developed as men's, and must not be so, for this would drain vital strength from their wombs. Their superior tender faculties are best exercised in the home. Their role is to provide a steady supply of healthy children to serve the empire. They may rely on their menfolk to vote in their best interests.

Arabella and her friends would laugh, were the consequences not so serious. They will show the government their *tender faculties*. They will bomb and burn and, when caught, they will prove their courage by forcing the authorities to choose between releasing them and watching them starve to death. So far, this strategy has worked. Self-sacrifice has brought victory, weakness has been strength. But now the game has changed. Nine months. Two hundred and seventy days. No. She won't do it. She would rather die.

But would she? Would she really?

The campaign for women's votes reveals so many character defects in a newly-useful light. Neurotics make meticulous planners. The vulgar are happy to insult cabinet ministers in public. The obsessional streak that drove Ethel Moorhead to write thirty letters complaining about the loss of a brown travelling rug in Dundee gaol tied the prison bureaucracy in knots. There are women in the movement who thrill at the sight of their own blood. The English suffragette Emily

26

Davison attempted suicide in Holloway three times before she was trampled by a racehorse last year. Arabella can't get the thought out of her head: the jockey trying to pull up the panicked horse as the girl's soft flesh was mashed by galloping hooves. To her, it seems a desecration of the cause.

The way the wardresses jump to attention at the sound of the doctor's footsteps tells her that they, too, fear him. Freshly-shaven in the morning, by late-afternoon his jaw shows a gingery shadow. His breath smells of tea. She feels a little foolish, struggling after spending so many hours so passively in the wardress's company. The doctor is grim-faced. She will be fed twice a day. How that happens is entirely up to her. She can resist, and put herself through the experience she had last night and this morning, or she can eat and drink in the normal way. For her sake he hopes she will take the sensible course, but it makes no difference to him. Now, which is it to be?

She says 'The infamous Doctor Watson . . .'

His face shows a dismissal that undercuts the satisfaction of provoking him. 'Prepare the mixture. Three eggs in a pint and a half of sweetened milk.'

'. . . Doctor Watson, the hired brute and torturer of women . . .'

'Dr *Ferguson* Watson is my name.'

'You're just as Ethel described you. The face of an executioner . . .'

'If you resist, I shall have you restrained.'

'. . . a criminal sadist . . .'

'*I will not have you sitting up!*'

This is to be their pattern. The shouting match. His team of wardresses moving forward to hold her down while he puts on his long oilcloth apron. The greasing of the rubber tube. Her frantic, futile efforts to resist.

Morning and evening.

27

Her hair is soaked in vomit but he does not tell the wardress to bathe her, and she is too proud to ask.

It seems he is not the only doctor in Scotland willing to feed suffragette prisoners, after all. He has a medical assistant, Doctor Thomas Lindsay, a young man of around Arabella's age. His pores secrete grease as if he is still in the throes of adolescence. He has the adolescent's lubricious eye, too; the ready smirk, finding a prurient second meaning in the most innocent words.

Since that first night she has worn a nightgown at all times. Doctor Lindsay seems tantalised beyond measure by this garment. He stares as if his gaze would burn through the fabric. When she kicks, sometimes, her legs are revealed. Once, as she bucks and writhes in the wardresses' grip, the gown rides up to her waist. Doctor Lindsay's beady eyes nearly start out of his head. The awareness of his scrutiny is making her self-conscious. This is fatal to resistance. For all her advanced views, she was born in the reign of Queen Victoria and raised with the ideal of modesty. More than an ideal: a young woman's only shield. Compromise modesty in any way, even by the awareness of another's impurity, and your invulnerability, too, is compromised.

She grits her teeth and continues to struggle. Never more violently than when being fed. Her aim is to make them spill the mixture. Doctor Watson will only tell his assistant to prepare more, but the delay is a victory of sorts. The problem is, even with the rubber sheets, more often than not the mixture spills over her. Her nightgown is soaked. It might be June outside, but within the stone walls of the prison hospital the air is cold. Her nipples stand proud under the wet cotton gown. Doctor Lindsay's stare is like a spider's web holding her in its tension. She feels its loathsome silken touch on her skin, sees the bubble of saliva at the corner of his lips.

She is not certain Doctor Watson notices. Her great fear is

that one day he will absent himself, sending Doctor Lindsay in his stead. And then? Rape is what Zeus did to Leda in the guise of a swan, not a verb she can associate with herself. She does not care for the wardresses, but surely no woman would stand by and watch a man like Doctor Lindsay . . . So no, not that. But still, the thought of his hands in her mouth as he inserts the gag, his beady eyes seeking some acknowledgement in hers, is more than she can stand. Doctor Watson too is loathsome, but not like that. *Rather a poor physique.* His words have returned to her more than once in the endless hours since she arrived here. In her childhood she had rheumatic fever. Could it have marred her growing body in some way that is obvious to others, though invisible to herself? Or was the remark, perhaps, a tactic? This is her preferred explanation, though disturbing enough in its way. If it was said to undermine her, to attack her feminine vanity, then she should have challenged him. Failing to do so has handed him a victory. If he is capable of such a ploy, she has underestimated him.

Time flows differently in captivity, all the more so if you're fasting and may not rise from your bed. The wardress only speaks when she turns onto her side or raises her arms above the blanket. She drowses, crossing seas and climbing mountains in long complicated dreams, only to snap awake and find her keeper still contemplating her bunions. Hours seem to pass, but the shadows hardly move across the stone floor. The immobility is worse than the boredom. She is terrified by the thought of day after day without exercise, losing touch with her own limbs. Closing her eyes, she tries to name every part of her, starting with her little toe, moving along to the ball of each foot, then up to the Achilles heel, ankle, shin bone . . . Before she reaches her knees she has cramp. The wardress finds it funny, but it's more than her job's worth to let the prisoner walk it off. Ethel has the knack of turning her gaolers, persuading them to carry messages outside the prison. But the thought of sucking up to women paid to spy on her sticks in Arabella's throat. And besides, they are wary of her. She gave one of them an almighty kick in the face last night.

On the third day, when the sun is high enough in the sky to suggest it is close to noon, Doctor Watson comes back, dressed normally, without his apron and his posse of extra wardresses. She regards him with suspicion, but any distraction, even this, is welcome.

He draws a chair up to the bed. The wardress's face turns to stone.

He speaks in the level tone he used on the first night, but with a difference. A just perceptible softening. Nine months is a long time. He raises his voice to override her protest. *She will be in his care for nine months*. It would be better for both of them if they reached an understanding. Her unhappiness with the situation is a given. There is no need for her to demonstrate it continually. His position as her doctor – *as her doctor* – requires him to conduct regular physical examinations. She can resist him if she chooses, in which case he will summon the assistance of as many wardresses as it takes to subdue her, and she will tire herself needlessly. If he had his way, she would serve out her sentence quietly. Since she will not, it seems to him she would be better to offer resistance on a selective basis. No one, however strong, can put up a physical fight every hour of every day for nine months.

He sits back in his chair, awaiting her answer.

'And if I agree not to struggle when you examine me, what is my reward?'

He quizzes his eyebrows as if he doesn't understand her.

'Will I be permitted to write to my family?'

'No letters.'

'May I hear from them?'

'Reading interferes with the digestion.'

30

'Visits, then?'

'I will not have you excited.'

Two choices here. The words are already in her throat, *I'll tell you what excites me.* Or she can keep her voice low and her wits cool.

'So I get nothing. And you get your job made easier.'

'I don't barter with criminals.'

This is new. So far the traffic in insults has been all one way.

'I am a political prisoner.'

'A fire-raiser.'

'A political act. As you, here, feeding me, is a political act.'

'I am your doctor . . .'

'A hired thug.'

'. . . charged with keeping you alive.'

'Keeping me quiet, more like.'

'About women's votes,' he says dismissively.

'I pay taxes like you. Why should you vote when I cannot?'

'I don't vote—'

She is too surprised to speak.

'—They're all as bad as each other. Why would I vote for them?'

'Because I am ready to die for the right you discard.'

The decision is taken: she will educate him. If he can't be stopped, at least he will understand what it is he does.

Or it may be the intention is his.

This is long before the National Health Service. Doctors are small businessmen, in private practice. They acquire their patients by social connection. The poor get as sick as the rich, if not sicker, but they cannot be relied on to pay. As soon as he qualified, he threw in his lot with the mentally bereaved, whom everyone wants off the streets. The mad who can afford seventy-five pounds a year, or whose relatives think it a price worth paying to loosen the madman's grip on

31

his estate, receive moral treatment. Essentially a behaviourist technique. They are trained to say please and thank you and sit quietly at table and, if they seem sufficiently rehabilitated, they are released. The mad poor end up in the public asylums, where they are straight-jacketed or strapped to their beds or thrashed by their infuriated keepers and, should they become so crazed that they will not eat, they are forcibly fed. This is the expertise that has brought Doctor Ferguson Watson to his present position.

As well as treating Perth's convicts, he is in charge of Scotland's collection of criminal lunatics. Mad, bad and diseased are not so very different in his eyes. The thieves and killers and female alcoholics are all deplorable physical specimens. Many of them cretins, from birth or by pickling their brains in bad hooch. Ethel Moorhead might have spoken with a tottie-peelings accent, but she was just another menopausal hysteric.

Prisoner Scott as a type is new to him.

Her face is pleasingly proportioned, the features regular. Her hymen is intact. She holds a degree from Edinburgh University. She has a tendency to constipation. She is a school teacher. Her nasal passages are usefully wide, allowing the tube to be inserted in her throat without troubling her breathing. She set fire to a racecourse stand. She has a smaller heart than is normal due to *mitral phursis*. Her arguments are rational, her abstention from food and water is not. Her brain is overdeveloped at the expense of her reproductive organs, but she menstruates, which is a healthy sign.

He is an intelligent man. More so than most doctors. There were some who graduated with better marks, but they were not combining their studies with supporting themselves as a grocer's apprentice. Until now his grasp of what ails his patients has been swift and certain. Prisoner Scott is a challenge to his professional competence. He does not understand her. If she were ugly, or old, he would diagnose her easily, but

32

if she were ugly or old she would be a different woman physiologically. No less than her undergrown heart or her locked bowels, her beauty is a piece of the puzzle, suggesting she is well suited to breeding, and likely to attract the most virile mate. Why, then, is she not married? Neurosis? Inversion? Or an inferior pool of masculine acquaintance?

He is aware of the talking cure. Unscientific mumbo-jumbo, in his opinion, but he is pragmatic enough to scavenge the useful techniques of any bankrupt methodology. And after that harpy caught pneumonia four months ago, he needs nothing less than a cure: Prisoner Scott, sleek as a farm cat, emerging from prison after serving the full nine months. She must be made to see the limits of feminine intellect and brought to her true womanly nature. She will be grateful, in the end.

FIVE

The Scott family know nothing. Harriet is reduced to writing pleading letters to the Prison Commission, asking the whereabouts of her daughter. For all the good that does her. The answer comes from elsewhere. Perth Suffrage Society boasts barely a dozen members but it's a small town, word gets around. Muriel Scott packs her bag and boards the train. That night she addresses an open-air rally at Perth's High Street Port, the first of many in these long, warm midsummer evenings. The crowd is volatile. Supporters from Perth, Dundee and Fife are outnumbered by purple-palmed dye-workers, laundry maids, bleachers, distillery hands, insurance clerks, barefoot children, and a gang of youths there to make a nuisance of themselves. After the speeches they march through town and across the grassy common to the prison. A smallish crowd at first, but growing bigger as folk get to hear of the nightly entertainment. Muriel will become adept at putting down hecklers. She'll also get better at dodging flying vegetables. Feeling in the town is against the suffragettes, but not so much that the locals want the fun to stop. Doctor Watson is a blow-in – worse, a west-coaster – so they're not overly partial to him either. They're proud of Perth, and don't care to see its name dragged through the dirt with lurid headlines about cruelty to women. And when all's said and done, everybody likes a sing-song. *Scots Whae Hae, A Man's a Man for a' That*. What does it matter if the women change the words a wee bittie?

*

34

She hears sounds in the night, she tells him. Voices outside the gaol.

He says her mind is playing tricks on her.

Women's voices, she says.

He tells her hallucination is one of the symptoms of starvation.

But she is not starving, thanks to his torture, so why should she hallucinate?

She arrived at the prison in a severely weakened state. By feeding her he has arrested her decline, but she will not recover fully without rest.

Rest! He has her flat on her back twenty-four hours a day. She is rested enough. It is exercise she needs.

His mouth sets. They have been over this before.

She demands to see the prison rules.

He says the rules are written for healthy prisoners.

She is being denied her right to regular exercise. By refusing to let her petition the Prison Commissioners, he thinks to conceal this fact from his superiors.

He says the Commissioners fully endorse his actions.

But they won't like the presence of protesters outside the gaol?

He repeats, she is imagining things. Or dreaming them, perhaps.

Dreaming! How can she dream when she doesn't sleep? When she counts every second of the hours through the night?

He insists she is mistaken. She sleeps soundly. He turns to the wardress: is that not so?

'Aye, Doctor.'

She knows he is lying. Yet what if her longing could conjure voices out of the air . . .?

He tells her these fancies drain her strength. She must give them up.

In bed, prevented from reading or writing, every square inch of her surroundings scrutinised and committed to memory:

35

how is she to get through the days? The temptation to change something, anything, is overwhelming. But the only change within reach, to start eating, would be self-defeating in every way. Yes, she'd exchange the hospital for a cell, but who would visit her? They would say they understood, but they'd be so disappointed, and afraid of putting themselves to the test. She would become an emblem of failure, and they would shun her.

She doesn't know if she truly believes this. That's the worst of isolation. To escape the boredom and the hostility of her captors, she retreats inside her head. But cut off from the world of facts and proof, her head too is a perilous space. At school, after the family moved back from Dum Dum, her classmates would titter at her accent, mocking her when she forgot and said *ayah* or *memsahib* or *punkah wallah*. Within a month they had tired of tormenting her but, for a long time after, she was prone to the fear that this or that friend had turned against her. Surreptitiously she would watch them, noting the way they whispered, their glances brushing hers but not connecting. Minutes later, she'd be laughing with them, and the others would never guess the passionate, recriminatory speeches she had made to them in her head. She has not thought of this in years, and still her chest is hot with remembered hurt. She must resist such childishness. It is just what the doctor wants. She is to look on him as a father figure, acting in her best interests. Ha! The cruellest man she knows. His harsh voice, his pitiless hands, the way his jaw grits when she resists. The rage she senses boiling within him.

She will not think of him.

When he comes, instinct takes over. She fixes her attention on what he is doing at that precise moment, and how to thwart him. The same with his speech. She pinpoints the weakness in what he has said, how the words can be turned or mocked. It's a question of survival. There's never time to look at the whole man, to wonder *who is he outside this moment?* And yet, when he has gone, she finds every mole, every fingernail, every stitch in his clothes, the grain of his voice in calm and in anger, all of it committed to memory. She rehearses what she will say to him, new ways of pouring scorn on him, reminding him that he is the tool of an immoral government. To act as he does, suppressing another's freedom because he is told to, quite without political conviction, makes him the worst kind of slave. And in her head he replies that he has sworn an oath to keep his patients alive. As for her freedom: she knew the law. It was her free choice to break it. The argument goes back and forth until she defeats him, or until he leaves her tongue-tied and humiliated. Then the rehearsal seems less a preparation for ordeals ahead, and more a surrender to enemy occupation. Then she wonders if this, too, is part of his plan.

So she will not think of him. But she must think of *something*. It is too easy to let her thoughts trickle away, leaving a dull vacancy. Day, night, the same: abed but not weary, half in, half out of shallow sleep. Her dreams are as vivid to her as anything that happens while she is awake. Sometimes her body seems the prison. Some nights her soul slips free of its carcass to drift like thistledown in the air.

She compiles a list of all those who love her. Muriel, her mother, Isabella, Alice, Agnes, her brother William. Dear Ethel, Grace, Fanny, Annie, Janie, Flora . . . So many people. She must take heart from that. They admire her resourcefulness, the way she casts off her sober schoolmistress demeanour and makes herself such an infernal nuisance, with such a genius for righteous cheek. Her exploits are famous. That time she pulled the communication cord of the train taking her back to gaol in Edinburgh, then broke a window in the taxi, telling her captors to send the bill to the Home Secretary. She smiles at the memory. But it is lonely, being a heroine, obliged to generate an endless supply of witty and ingenious acts of defiance. Her fellow campaigners are sure she has the inner strength to withstand the feeding. Sometimes this thought lends her that strength. Other times she thinks: how can they sit at home with their mothers and sisters, their newspapers and letters and books, and think they *know*? She does not want them to worry over her, but their unshakeable confidence makes the loneliness much worse. In her reveries they place a hand on her shoulder, and even then she can't admit the truth.

There are hours when she fears she is going mad.

SIX

The Doctor sees Arabella three times a day. At 8.00 am and 5.00 pm to feed her, and once in between, usually mid-morning, when he comes in his black frock coat to take her pulse and temperature and sound her chest.

On the fifth day – or is it the sixth? Already she's not sure – she asks if she is supposed to pretend he is someone else when he comes in his frock coat? Does he think she will forget what he did to her this morning, clad in his butcher's apron?

He asks the wardress if she has slept. (She has.)

She informs him that from now on she will call him Doctor Savage, so both of them can keep in mind what he is.

He asks the wardress if she has opened her bowels? (She has not.)

She says, by rights, he should be serving a prison sentence himself.

He tells the wardress to fetch the calomel from Doctor Lindsay.

The wardress is surprised. Matron's instructions are to remain with the prisoner at all times. Matron and the doctor do not like each other. The Governor prefers Matron but is too spineless to back her in a fight.

For the first time since Arabella's arrival, doctor and prisoner are alone.

Outside it's a hot day. The north-facing windows show a cloudless blue sky, bleached by the invisible sun. The ward is bright. The mattress ticking on the unmade beds shows its stains very clearly. In her boredom, she has counted the shadowed indentations in the whitewashed walls. There is a smell of carbolic, to her ever-suggestive of the dirt it has been used to vanquish. The doctor takes the wardress's chair. His face has acquired a few freckles.

'You're a schoolteacher—'

What is she supposed to answer to that? He knows full well she is.

'—*were* a schoolteacher, I should say.'

'I've been put on the reserve list, after agreeing to leave militant action to others.'

He exhales, the breath making a derisive sound in his nose. 'And your word's worth so little?'

'Since Kelso I've done nothing illegal.'

'You were arrested at a by-election meeting.'

'Holding a political opinion is not yet against the law.'

She is waiting for him to make another derogatory remark about politics. Instead, he says, 'Your sister, is she a teacher?'

Instantly she is on her guard. 'One of my sisters.'

'The one you live with—'

It was in the newspapers, but still. She says nothing.

'—and she's of your mind, about all this?'

'She believes in votes for women.'

He takes the stethoscope out of his leather bag. 'Dull brown hair, not so tall?'

'You've seen her?' She is horrified. '*In here?*'

He places the chest piece inside the neck of her nightdress. 'Out there, on her soapbox.'

She is not going mad. The voices are real.

'How did she look?'

'Breathe in.'

She hesitates before complying.

'Like you.' His mouth forms a judicious shape. 'Less well-favoured.' He pauses to move the chest piece around her breast, 'And out.'

40

She breathes out. 'Would you . . .'

'No,' he says, cutting her off.

'Just send her my love.'

'I said no. And again: in.'

He would not have mentioned Muriel for nothing. It's a gambit. Well, she may give him what he wants, but only if he agrees to carry a message.

'And out.' He writes on the chart in his spiky, almost italic hand. 'You have a presystolic *bruit*, a heart murmur. Your sister is healthy?'

'Perfectly.'

'She wouldn't want you to put your life in danger.'

'That's exactly what she wants.'

'If she loves you . . .'

'She would have me remain true to my principles. That is what love means to us.'

'And if somebody burns to death, out of your love?'

'No one has.'

'Yet.' He tucks the thermometer under her arm. 'So I'm a savage and you're an instrument of love. For women.'

'And for men who would take women as their equals.'

Another derisive breath. 'You think men want to meet women as equals?'

'Some men.'

'They know you want to hear them say so.'

This stings as if she had a particular man in mind.

What is that smell? Something intimately foul. Too much to hope it might be him. What she wouldn't give for a tooth-brush to rid her mouth of this acrid taste. Or a bath. Even a bed wash. But what's the use? In a few hours he will feed her, and she will be drenched in vomit again.

Out of nowhere he says, 'Two sisters taught at the school I went to.'

'And were they supporters of women's votes?'

Snitting, Muriel used to call this sort of riposte when they

41

were children. But if he gives her less autonomy than a two-year-old, what does he expect?

'They opened the door to another world.'

Such a queer, wistful note in his voice.

She looks up from the filthy nest of her matted hair. He has cut himself shaving, a tiny nick under his right ear. Neat ears, for a man. Yesterday, when he turned in front of the window, the sun shone clean through the pink cartilage.

He says quietly, 'If you wished to write to her . . .'

Her face lights up.

'. . . I can't permit you to set pen to paper, but I could write a short note at your dictation.'

Why would it be this easy?

'You think she'll succeed where you have not, in getting me to eat.'

His face closes. 'As you wish.' He removes the thermometer, noting the temperature on his chart.

'I didn't say I didn't want to.' The words stick in her throat but she forces them out, 'It would be good of you.'

He has paper in his leather bag. Brought specially for this, or always carried with him? Don't ask. No more barbs. Not until he's posted the letter.

'So,' he says. 'Dear Muriel.'

'*My* dear Muriel.'

My dear Muriel, I know how anxious you must be without news of me, your imagination running riot . . .

His look says she is trying his patience. 'Stick to practical matters.'

But even *practical matters* are subject to censorship. He will allow no reference to the feeding. She wants Muriel to make arrangements for when she gets out of gaol, some sympathiser's house where she can convalesce. Her appearance will be too shockingly altered for her to go home. This sentence, too, he refuses. He lets her give details of how she came to be arrested, then a message to her mother, begging her not to worry too much. Talking to her sister, her voice softens, her carapace dissolving in the pity she will only accept from this one source. *Oh Muriel*. For a minute or so he writes at her dictation, the nib's scratch across the paper following her voice, his breathing audible with the effort of keeping up. She slows down for him. Such a strange feeling, the two of them cooperating like this. She wants a solicitor to challenge the legality of the feeding.

He has lost his temper several times over the past few days, but she still can't predict when he will snap.

'The letter is long enough.'

'It's hardly begun.'

'Don't overtax the Governor's goodwill. Or mine.'

Scolded like a naughty child. Was this his plan all along, this new way of making her feel small? Let it be a lesson, she thinks. No more truces.

The letter must be signed off. He suggests *yours sincerely*. She snorts. She is not writing to her bank agent. She wants *with love to all*, which he accepts, followed by *yours ever the same*. His eyes narrow. What does that mean? Exactly what it says: her affections are constant. It is how she always ends her letters, omitting it would strike her sister as most peculiar. Which is true, as far as it goes, but he's right to be suspicious. The phrase alludes to her commitment to the cause. Grudgingly, he transcribes it.

She notices the way he is bent over the paper. She is lying on her side to read the words as he writes. Their heads are almost touching.

The wardress comes back with the mercurous chloride. A laxative. To be added to her next feed.

A man and a woman conversing daily, mistrustful at first, but with increasing familiarity as the weeks pass. Anyone can see where this is leading.

And when the man has complete knowledge of the woman's

43

body, complete freedom to touch her mouth, breasts, genitals, anus? When he subjects her urine to chemical analysis, and forces her jaws apart with a metal gag. Where does *that* lead?

She hears the footsteps first. Two doctors, six wardresses. Up the stairs and along the passage. Every morning and evening, and still her heart lurches. She turns face-down on the thin mattress, clinging to the bed-rail, squeezing her eyes shut. Later she will wonder if she might have shamed him by looking him in the face, but when it matters she is powerless. Calloused fingers loosen her grip, their nails dig into her flesh, prising her hands from the rail. They turn her onto her back and pin her with their weight, their lousy bodies, their suffocating stink. She opens her eyes and there is Doctor Lindsay with his smirk to remind her how her nightgown gapes in the struggle. How the fabric, soaked by spilled liquid, clings to her form. But she will not acknowledge this because her task is to resist, and if she thought about the violation she would die of shame.

And then she sees Doctor Watson in his butcher's overall, greasing the rubber tube, and all rational thought flies from her head. He forces the gag between her teeth. She bites down on it, pitting tooth enamel against tempered steel. It prises her jaws so wide she fears the bone will snap. His fingers press on her tongue. He pushes the tube down her throat, grazing the sides. She retches and chokes, but still he pays it in, inch after inch, until it finds her stomach and she spasms. He pours the liquid down the tube. More and more of it – too much! – her stomach convulsing to expel it, so it burns a path down her nose. Quick fingers pinch her nostrils. Doctor Lindsay yanks out the gag and clamps his hand over her mouth.

'Swallow.'

Swallow her own vomit, he means. But there are things the body will not do, instincts stronger than the will, even the will to life itself. She cannot swallow. And she cannot breathe.

44

Panic beats its wings inside her chest. And then the man I will marry in two years' time says 'We will let you breathe when we see you going purple'. Her lungs are bursting. She knows she will die. And finally she looks into his eyes and

Oh God, I don't know, I don't know. I don't want to know.

SEVEN

Muriel never receives the letter. The Governor says a note in an unfamiliar hand would only inflame the family's fears, making them think Prisoner Scott too ill to write herself. The sister is troublesome enough as it is. Some damn fool let her into the Commission in Edinburgh the other day. She got into the Chairman's office. They're all writing to the gaol, the sister, the mother, that woman he fed in Edinburgh. *She* begs the Governor to be present at every feeding, to satisfy himself that it is done *with the least possible cruelty*. The words are underlined. What does Doctor Watson make of that?

The doctor says it's obvious. Lacking the grounds to make a formal complaint, she is trying to smear him by innuendo. Fortunately he enjoys the Commissioners' complete confidence. A sore point for the Governor. It is his gaol, the chain of command runs through him, he receives the Medical Officer's daily reports and forwards them to his superiors, but for all this, the doctor's presence undermines him. Twice their differences of opinion have gone all the way to Edinburgh. On both occasions word came back: Doctor Ferguson Watson must use his discretion. The Governor has given thirty years of his life to the Prison Commission, Doctor Watson has not yet one year's service. Who wouldn't suspect deals in back rooms stitched up over a dram and a sixpenny cigar? And yet the doctor's a nobody. You only have to look at him to smell the manure on his boots. Amazing how far he has got on a few Latin words, a university degree, and a grand opinion of himself.

Yesterday, the Governor learned that Doctor Lindsay had taken a day's leave: Doctor Watson did not require his presence. It is not Doctor Watson's place to decide when a member of the prison staff can take a holiday. The fellow needs taking down a peg or two. The Governor can't get a day's peace without Matron knocking on his door, chewing his ear off. *Himself* has doubled the amount of dirty laundry coming out of the prison hospital. *Himself* has hand-picked a team of wardresses to assist him. *Himself* draws up the rota, to make sure none of the other staff get in. When Matron catches them coming off shift and asks them to report, they tell her the doctor has forbidden it. To her face, they say it! Is she the Matron of this gaol or not? The Governor has some sympathy, but what can he do? And there's a useful side to the Medical Officer setting up his own wee fiefdom. When it all goes to hell in a handcart, it won't be the Governor's fault.

Those suffrage women are out on the High Street every night, ranting and singing their damned hymns. The King and Queen are due in town next month to open the new infirmary. The Provost calls him in, wagging his finger about not wanting trouble. To cap it all, they've arrested another one in Rutherglen, trying to burn down somebody's fine house. She'll be arriving on the six o'clock train from Glasgow.

Frances Gordon is four feet ten, a mouth-breather, sallow-skinned, small-eyed, pug-nosed. One of the moral purity brigade, destined to provoke variations on the same drawling put-down wherever she goes. *Don't worry, hen, you're safe with me.* She's no better at fire-raising than Arabella, but brave. Without that freakishly small nose, she could have stood the feeding. Made as she is, if you block her throat with a tube, she stops breathing.

The Doctor thinks she's acting. She is put in a cell. He doesn't want her anywhere near Prisoner Scott, the two of them giving each other the vapours. The Prison Commission needs a photograph. Half these women use aliases. Without a picture, it's impossible to keep track of them once they get out. But this one's full of tricks, screws up her face like a monkey the instant she spots the camera. He wants to give her chloroform, have Lindsay take the picture while she's out cold, but the Commissioners won't hear of it. Terrified of opening their morning paper to find that Prisoner Gordon is actually Lady something-or-other, a great friend of the King.

Whoever she is, she's no lady. They never had much to do with quality, down in the doctor's corner of rural Ayrshire, but he'd expect something more in the way of complexion and height, more like Prisoner Scott. If you're heir to half a county, why would you breed with a yellow-skinned dwarf? There's something about the woman, her ugliness, her English whine, her odd peppery smell of autumnal woods, and her evident horror of him, that scratches at his nerves. If she's going to resist: fine, resist. But this endless caterwauling . . . Aye, he shouts at her. It's the only way to make himself heard. If the wardresses don't like it, too bad. But next morning he has thought it over. He speaks in the tone he used on the farm, seeing a cow through its first calving. That's how he must think of her: a creature blundering against its own animal nature. In the days to come she will plead with him, her voice sticky on his skin, assuring him she is trying to co-operate; if the feed comes back up, she can't help it. Those mouse's eyes battened on his face. He'd almost rather have the screaming.

At least Prisoner Scott is healthy, he can count on her sound constitution. This one is a runt. God knows how she's made it to forty-five. He feeds her three times a day and she vomits back every fluid ounce. She's getting weaker, not stronger. Severely dehydrated, her lips crusted with dried saliva, her breath hellish. She asks if she can swill her mouth out with water and he braves the stench to bring his head down to hers and whisper 'Drink some, drink some – no one will know.'

You'd think he'd stabbed her. The wailing turns into a fit of hysterics, then she's gasping, hyperventilating, one hand clutching her heart. '*For God's sake, woman, get a grip on yourself.*' The wardresses look at him like he's the Devil. The fat one with the goitre raises her voice to him. 'She cannae breathe with that thing in her mooth.' Rank insubordination. If Prisoner Gordon is too far gone to exploit it, he can be sure Prisoner Scott will sniff it out. But he'll not lower himself to win over the wardresses. If it's a choice between ruling by love or fear, he'll take fear.

It has been at the back of his mind ever since he fed the Moorhead woman in Calton Gaol, a solution to the physiological difficulties. Sugars, amino acids and salt can be absorbed in the lower digestive tract without the enzymes secreted in the stomach, and the humiliation might prove helpful. It's not a queasiness he shares, the rectum is just another bodily part, no need for all this shame, but if others are fool enough to feel it then he'll turn it to use. In Peterhead there were hardened criminals he reduced to lambs with a single enema.

The wardresses pretend not to understand. Or perhaps they are so stupid they really can't see it. He spells it out: an Enule, otherwise known as a suppository, with enough prisoner's laudanum to relax the bowel. He resists the urge to slap that smirk off Lindsay's face. For a few moments the wardresses could go either way. If the fat one refuses, the other two will follow suit. He asks if they want the prisoner's death on their conscience? She won't eat, the feeding tube doesn't work: do they have a better solution? Look at her: skin and bone. She won't last the week unless they do something. Lindsay turns it, repaying the withheld slap. His silly grin reminds them of their wee brothers. They like to tease him about the sweetheart they know he doesn't have. The lad's a fool to let them take liberties, but that's his own affair. When he grips the patient's shoulders they move into position. On the count of three they turn her. Prisoner Gordon is screaming like a banshee. It would take so little force to stop her noise. He startles himself with this thought. Not that he'd do it. It's just the infernal racket getting to him. Lindsay parts her yellow buttocks, revealing the brown pucker of her anus and, below, the mouse's fur around her sex.

She is fed in this way thirteen times, over four days. Throughout, she suffers from extreme nervous prostration. The wardresses can't stand it. He allows them to administer the laudanum. It's the only thing that gives them any peace at all.

EIGHT

Arabella has found a new insult to vex Doctor Savage. He is her gaoler, plain and simple. His job is to keep her behind bars. She does not believe he is a doctor at all. What proper doctor would practise in a prison? She'll grant he's familiar with the basics, he can use a stethoscope and thermometer. Who couldn't, after ten minutes' instruction? Incensed by this goading, he reels off his qualifications. It takes some time to list them all. She has to bite her cheek to stop herself from smiling.

'All that studying,' she says, 'just to torture poor wretches in prison.'

He tells her he studied to heal the sick, and to understand those whose sickness is mental.

'If you mean me, you've still some way to go.'

'Oh I understand you well enough—'

She raises an eyebrow.

'—a neurotic hunger for attention. A classroom of children is not enough: you want the Prime Minister and all his cabinet hanging on your words.'

With anyone else I would call this a game. A ritual trading of insults. I've known married couples who did it all the time, loving married couples. But the doctor is not the playful type.

She tells him *the Prime Minister and all his cabinet* could ignore her forever if they gave her the vote.

That derisive push of breath down his nose. 'Twenty years ago it was the *right* to study medicine. Now it's the vote. Once you have that, it'll be the *right* to minister a parish, or

51

kill for your country. And you'll get those too, in the end, and none will satisfy you.'

On balance, she is rather delighted by this speech. So what would satisfy her, in his opinion?

'A husband.'

She laughs. 'Oh Doctor Savage, I had thought you would do better than that.'

'Nature seeks a balance. Masculine and feminine, virility and tenderness, brain and womb. Your body, a woman's body, is a part of Nature. Denied the balance of wedlock and motherhood, it must remain unfulfilled.'

'And what about you?' she asks softly.

'We are not discussing . . .'

She cuts him off. 'You are not married, I think. What of your fulfilment?'

He wants to talk seriously, without this persiflage, so he answers her question. 'I do what is needful.'

The mirth dies on her lips. If he is not referring to consorting with prostitutes, and already she knows him well enough to rule this out, then he must mean masturbation. She can say the word in her head thanks to Grace, who has a doctor's forthrightness about such matters. Grace says all men do it before they are married, all the cold water in the Firth of Forth couldn't stop them. They suffer needless guilt and worry about it sapping their vital energies. The whole subject ought to be dragged into the open. Arabella is sure Grace is right, but still, she is embarrassed.

He sees this and flushes, '*Potassium Bromide.*'

'Ah,' she says faintly.

And now he's furious. Did she think he meant vice? If she'd witnessed what he's seen in his career, she wouldn't have made that mistake. He presumes she has heard of the Wassermann reaction? (She hasn't.) A test for syphilis. He had a hand in developing it, under Professor Browning. A blood sample is drawn, serum extracted, a simple compound added. Agitate the test tube and you have your diagnosis. People with no symptoms who might not find out for years: now they can be told 'you are infected'.

'And they can be cured?'

'Some of them.' Without meaning to, she has taken the wind out of his sails. But he rallies. 'They can be prevented from breeding. We have a tool that could revolutionise public health policy.'

She wouldn't have called him an eloquent man, but on this subject he's unstoppable. His paper on unusual fertility in syphilitic patients was published last year. Locking up infected prostitutes is not enough. Every child born to foreigners here must be tested, the wandering of gypsies controlled. The tin cooking utensils they make and sell are a carrier of infection. Their habit of begging food from farmers compounds the danger.

She is sceptical. Just because rural people are poor, it doesn't mean they're unhygienic. He says he knows what he is talking about. He grew up on a farm. But surely, she says, his own family would not eat from unwashed dishes? He meets her look. She falters. He tells her he has worked in asylums in Glasgow, Lenzie, Paisley. In each place, the same story: one in seven lunatics tested positive. The politicians are fully aware of the scale of the problem: more destructive to the nation's health than tuberculosis or alcohol. But they would rather bury their heads in the sand and see innocent lives blighted, to spare their manly blushes. It is a scourge. A plague. It will not just *go away*.

She has not seen him like this before. Angry about the cruelty of the world, the short-sightedness of the powerful. Proud to be on the side of right. He reminds her of herself.

He tells her a woman whose husband dies of syphilis may remarry, remain clinically healthy, and yet bear syphilitic children. He has seen them, a few months old, already blind, or deaf, their bones weakened, their spleens enlarged. Others live for decades in apparent health, only to suffer sudden attack. These women may be blameless in their conduct – some of them – but they are a horrible danger to the community.

Women. Their fault.

'And what would you do about them?' she asks, acid-sweet.

'Test every woman admitted to a laying-in hospital. Those found to be positive would be sterilised, the children removed to an institution.'

'And the men—?'

He looks at her.

'—what is to happen to the men while these women are mutilated and their children incarcerated?'

His face shows a familiar exasperation. It is too serious a matter for rhetoric. He is talking about the opportunity to wipe out cretinism and disease, to eliminate a significant source of human misery. If every country adopted such a system they could weed out the breeding stock and improve the entire human race.

Again she asks, 'Why take no action against the men?'

'Syphilis is not a notifiable disease. The government favours a voluntary approach.'

'For men.'

'The women will be in hospital anyway.'

'So women are to pay?'

'Half measures are better than none.'

Always she has this sense of rival perspectives within her. Feminine, masculine. Her own true judgement, and the order of things outside her, the prejudices the world calls common sense. Men are not split in this way. They sense our inner division and call it neurosis.

'Thank you,' she says.

He knows he shouldn't ask. 'For what?'

'Confirming my principles. Women are to be tested because we're more biddable, and our unjust treatment will continue until we become as violently unreasonable as men.'

54

She has long known this, it is what pushed her into militancy, so I wouldn't accuse her of insincerity. She means every word. But unlike him, she understands that they are also playing a game.

'How are you sleeping?'

'The bedding could be cleaner.'

'But the sleep itself?'

'Too many dreams.'

'Of what?'

She turns onto her side. He will allow this sometimes, pretending not to notice. 'Are you an admirer of Doctor Freud?'

'That charlatan.'

'Maybe. But it's intriguing, no: the idea of an unconscious life whose proof is its invisibility?'

'A fool's paradox.' He looks at the wardress, who walks out.

'Have you never suspected you might possess a hidden self?'

'No.'

She smiles as if at some private joke, 'I sense him.'

'Do you?' he says sarcastically.

'A gaoler who envies the lawbreaker's freedom.'

'Claptrap.'

'You're sure of that? Only, the strangest look just crossed your face.'

'And I suppose you envy the racegoers whose stand you set fire to?'

Again and again he comes back to this. The flames didn't even take hold, and still he can't forgive her.

'The fire was intended as a cathartic. We live in diseased times. That's why I'm in this hospital. And you, for that matter. Our sickness is symptomatic.'

'I'm not sick.'

55

'Not even at heart? When you push that tube down my throat?'

'I do what has to be done.'

'But what do you *feel*?'

'Feelings don't come into it—'

She gives him a long look.

'—And what do you feel when . . . when you are fed?'

'I feel powerful—'

He laughs, a short sharp bark.

'—you can imprison my body, but there is something within me stronger than my flesh.'

'You are *doing yourself harm*, weakening yourself in ways you may never recover from. You don't understand the risks.'

'I think I do.'

'Then you belong in a lunatic asylum, not a prison.'

'You're too afraid of weakness.'

This takes him aback. 'Every man fears weakness.'

'But not like you.'

When I meet him, two years hence, Hugh Ferguson Watson will be charming, good natured, quietly humorous. Admittedly, a heaviness in his silences, an occasional rush of blood to his face, will suggest he might be otherwise if I cross some invisible line. This masculine edge of danger will only make him the more attractive to me and, in so far as he is aware of it, he will seem pleased. But in June 1914, he is not a man who cares overmuch how others feel towards him. He applies judgement. Approves, rather than likes. His step quickens when he goes to meet the person who stimulates his intellect, but this is not the same as forming an attachment. Relations with his parents are strained by disappointment on their side and frustration on his. None of the Watsons understands why an eldest son with first claim on the farm would choose a trade that depends so greatly on the practitioner's affability. His teachers have impressed on him the vigilance required if he is to rise to a social distinction matching his intellectual gifts. The first question he asks in any situation is not *how do I feel?* But *does this demean me?* And, *how can it be turned to use?* Every impulse but one is filtered in this way. The exception is irritation. The portcullis of his intellect lifts. That country boy's body unbends. Heart pumps, lungs fill, muscles flex. This is his only indulgence.

Lord knows, he's provoked to it. There's a case of tuberculosis in the men's hospital that could yet turn into an epidemic. Summer is always bad for contagious diseases. A housebreaker has shingles. In the upper ward, a wife-killer lies baw-faced with parotitis and a baker who used adulterated flour is sweating his way through scarlatina. Half the criminal lunatic department has gone down with enteric. On top of that, he must deal with the thirty or so women the last damn-fool Medical Officer weaned off gin with prisoners' laudanum. He has enough on his hands without having to worry about healthy women trying to kill themselves for the vote.

An MP is asking questions in the Commons about his treatment of Ethel Moorhead. There's a procession of busybodies trying to get into the women's hospital: chaplains and town councillors and freemason solicitors, respectable matrons who lick envelopes for women's suffrage. The Governor forced his way in last night. What's the point of writing daily reports if the old soak doesn't trust him? He'll be turning the Prison Commissioners against him, passing on tittle-tattle from Matron. Careful how he does it, nothing that puts him out on a limb, but the Commission secretary can be relied on to read between the lines. Why else would Dunlop be here? Doctor Dunlop has been a friend to him in the past, but he's another who has not risen so high without knowing how to hedge his bets. 'Just a flying visit,' the Governor says, as if you can introduce the Prison Commission's medical adviser into a situation like this without stirring up a byke.

57

The wardress is instructed to give Prisoner Gordon an extra dose of laudanum, which should keep her quiet, but one glance will show Dunlop she's not gaining weight. Thank God for Prisoner Scott. A complete vindication of the feeding policy, if only she would behave. But she has a genius for sensing what he wants of her and doing the exact opposite. She knows something's afoot, and puts up an extra struggle against the morning feed. Not that she's ever passive, but today she's like a demon. Lindsay has to straddle her. The milk that comes back up is pink with blood and gritted with chips of tooth enamel.

At eleven he comes back and tells the wardress to bathe her and comb her hair. She wants to know why. He puts on a show of changing his mind and her face falls, but she won't beg him. So now neither of them have what they want, unless he can think of a way of getting her washed that won't look like weakness. He's sounding her chest when she announces she has heard screaming. This seems unlikely: the hospital and the female cell block are separate buildings. Has the wardress been gossiping, or is she fishing for news? He says her ears are playing tricks again, but the blasted woman is like a terrier with a rat: *she knows* there are other suffragettes here. Why are they not in the hospital? He tells her she should be able to work that out for herself. The hospital is for the sick. They are taking their meals and serving out their sentences. That shuts her up.

She passes the empty hours by ranking all the people she hates in order of precedence. Before she began campaigning for the vote she would have been shocked by the thought of hating anyone. It was ignorance that made people do hateful things, they just needed help to see the light. She knows better now. She has been mocked, and insulted, and called obscene names by men who dine with bishops and professors. She has been shouted down by rich men's wives who couldn't care less about their destitute sisters. It is hard to decide whom she detests more: the society women who use the position they have gained through marriage to deny other women a more honest influence, or the men who find the idea of women voting too killingly funny. Today she hates neither as much as she hates the prison functionary who doesn't care enough to form an opinion on the question.

He is behaving oddly this morning. When he examines her, her nostrils detect the usual tobacco and shirt-collar starch, mingled with a new scent of sweat, though the air feels no warmer than yesterday. She is given a bed bath, after all, and her hair is brushed and plaited. Her heart leaps. Is it possible that by tonight she will be held in Muriel's arms? She composes a pithy, defiant, witty speech for the women at the prison gate. If her appearance is truly unaltered, as the doctor claims, she can go home. Mother will make her cloudy lemonade with the perfect balance of bitter and sweet. She will climb Arthur's Seat right to the top, looking out over all Edinburgh, feeling the wind that blows up there on the stillest of days; or take her sisters to pick wild strawberries by the water of Leith, find a patient toad on a shady path, touch a fingertip to his dear dry back to make him jump.

Early in the afternoon, when the sun burns a patch of whitish-gold on the floor just beneath the window, they come. The doctor's tread and less familiar footsteps. The door opens. She last met Doctor Dunlop in Calton Gaol. Older than Doctor Watson, short and stout, with mutton-chop whiskers and a better cut of frock coat. The sort of roguish uncle who offers you a sip of whisky behind Mother's back. She sits up, ignoring the wardress's command, and smiles at him. He does not reciprocate. So now she knows: she is not getting out.

Doctor Watson's face turns beetroot when he catches sight of her. He rasps at the wardress to *get her down*, then, in a new, unctuous voice, tells Doctor Dunlop that the prisoner has gained two pounds since arriving at the gaol. The calomel has sorted out her bowels, which moved twice overnight.

It is intolerable to be spoken of like this, and the disappointment is worse, having come so close to freedom in her head. Tears prick her eyes, but she won't weep.

Our mothers brought us up to exercise self-control. Our brothers might lose their tempers, but it was the duty of we women to exert a moral influence. We were not always angels but, year by year, the habit of restraint became more entrenched. It was for men to make their mark in the world. Women's sphere was internal, a space which must remain spotless. Socially, we existed as a stillness: a half-warming, half-blinding glow from our corner of the room. To raise your voice or, heaven forbid, your hand, to throw back your head and show your teeth in a laugh – or even a terrible glimpse of tongue! – to be present as a creature of flesh-and-blood and impulse and error, was to become at once conspicuous and invisible. Outcast. Arabella knows women who suffer agonies just stooping to chalk a meeting place on the pavement, dreading the chivalrous gent who will see a swooning maiden and rush to her aid. In the beginning, she managed the embarrassment by creating a sort of shame spot, a blur on her left side she was forever looking away from. But here, now, there can be no looking away. She lifts her head, fills her lungs, and roars.

Are the Commissioners aware her treatment is in breach of their rules?

Doctor Watson forces her head back against the mattress.

When she cries out at the indignity, she sees Dunlop wince. She tells him Doctor *Ferguson* Watson is a disgrace to his profession, and to the Commission. Needlessly brutal. Quite without regard for her modesty.

The doctor bends over her, blocking Dunlop's view. His jaw is tight, a whitish margin around his mouth within his florid face. Behind him, Dunlop mutters something about not wanting to undo *all your good work* and for a split-second the doctor's glassy stare sharpens to check her reaction. It doesn't take her long to work it out. He has been boasting of winning her confidence, dropping nuggets of intelligence into his reports. She has told him nothing that matters. What difference can it make if they know about her early rheumatic fever, or her mother's disapproval of militant action? Nevertheless, to have told him anything now seems an error of judgement. This too is more than she can bear.

She fights him, really fights him, trying to sit up. The wardress can't get close enough to help him and Dunlop doesn't try. Doctor Watson warns her she is growing excited. This agitation is not good for her. She must lie back so he can sound her chest. His would-be calm demeanour fools no one. The tendons in his neck are taut, his breath smells violently metallic. She too is out of her depth, past the point of histrionics, revolted by what he has done to her, the talking no less than the feeding, all that cant about cowardly politicians at odds with the public good. The cynicism of it rises within her, filling her throat.

She vomits over his legs. Considering the length of time since her last feed, the quantity is remarkable.

He shouts, *'You did that on purpose!'*

'I wish I had!'

His face contorts in rage and disgust. 'You are out of order.'

'Take your hands off me!'

'Will you *lie down!*'

Is Doctor Dunlop reminded of anything, as he watches this scene; might he even feel a pang of exclusion? How like it is to marriage, the uninhibited passion in their voices, the murderous vigour in their limbs. Neither hears Dunlop's cough, his *sotto voce* warning. The medical officer handles her as roughly as he would a man, using all his might to overpower her.

She screams at him, 'You're hurting me.'

'And *you* are putting on a show for the company.'

She sinks her teeth into his hand.

'Damn you!' he roars. His arm draws back. Not the flat of his hand, but a fist.

'Doctor Watson! Calm yourself.'

The arm drops, the blow unstruck, a cloudiness in both their faces, as if wrenched out of a dream.

Dunlop takes over, despatching the doctor to change his sodden trousers. A wardress arrives to help, but by now Prisoner Scott is docile. She reclines on the mattress, a fetching colour in her cheeks.

That afternoon, when Dunlop has departed and Doctor Watson is absent on his rounds, Arabella gets out of bed. Immediately, the wardress is upon her, dragging her back. No matter. She has stood on her own two feet again.

With me, he sulked. Silent days, weeks, months on end. When he spoke at last, I had to smile as if it were a day like any other. As if his moods were as unchallengeable as the weather. If I dared to remark on the change, he withdrew again. I could not rouse him to violence, or any other passion.

NINE

The doctor believes the prisoner's resistance may be dietary in origin. He will try three tablespoons of sugar, not four, in the pint and a half of eggy milk, plus regular soap-and-water enemas. The wardresses grumble about cleaning her up, but she's always quiet after, purged of the irritability that so disturbs her rest. He goes over the Governor's head to the Commission and gains approval for two wardresses to remain with her at all times. Any movement seems to excite her, jeopardising her health. There will be no turning a blind eye when she rolls onto her side. Even in sleep, she will obey doctor's orders.

He sees now he has been too lax with her. What he called humanity was weakness. He won't make that mistake again. She is a criminal serving a prison sentence. She has forfeited her right to the respect other women enjoy. Day after day so civilised and ironical and then, for the one hour that matters, to turn hellcat, spitting and clawing, making all his successes look like empty boasting. Well, he's not done with her yet.

Each day he follows a fixed routine. Urine samples are taken early, enemas administered late. The feeding takes around two and a half hours. His part is over in twenty minutes, but until the liquid has been absorbed into her system Lindsay and the wardresses must sit it out, clamping a towel over her mouth, fingers ready to close her nostrils. They do it in relays: it's tiring on the arms. Only when the contents of her stomach have passed into the small intestine can she be left to sleep.

63

So far, the physical examination has been a relatively dignified affair. He has touched her with a formality that is almost a seeking of permission, and she has anticipated each gesture, lifting and closing her arm over the thermometer, offering her wrist, unbuttoning her nightdress and averting her face a moment before the stethoscope touches her skin. There has been a trace of satire in her movements, it is true, but also grace, and physical collusion. A rhythm. As if they were dancing.

For him to deviate from this protocol, to grasp her chin and push the thermometer into her mouth, is not much less shocking than a blow.

Twenty-four hours have passed since Doctor Dunlop's visit. He ignores her wrist, a finger on her neck the way a stockman checks a cow. She is tempted to spit out the thermometer as she did on the first night, but what if he is trying to provoke just such a reaction? If she obliges him, he will be free to vent the anger boiling inside him. She is afraid of this anger. She doesn't know why. What could he do to her that could be worse than the feeding?

He will not speak, and she cannot with the mercury in her mouth. At last he removes it, checks the reading, writes it down.

'Silent today?' she says drily.

He closes his bag and moves towards the door, nodding at the wardress to indicate that he is finished here.

The wardresses complain about the stink. Her stink. By now she barely notices it. The window has a small casement to allow the circulation of air. Although suspicious of her suddenly breaking silence, they decide it can do no harm. Once the glass is pushed open she hears the singing, faint at this distance, but evidently a crowd. Florence, the stout one, slams the window shut. She assures them she will not tell. Besides, Doctor Watson has admitted these nightly gatherings take place. They exchange glances. Jean (thinner, with the beginnings of a moustache) says, 'Ach, open it, afore we're poisoned,' and Arabella spends a pleasant hour feigning sleep, straining her ears to pick out Muriel's off-key mezzo.

Two days since Dunlop's visit, and still the doctor holds his tongue when he comes to examine her. His thumb remains bandaged. She must have bitten deep. He behaves as if she had betrayed him. As if she were not his prisoner, but his friend. If she has shamed him in front of his employers, he has only himself to blame: she did not ask him to bring Doctor Dunlop to see her. Though she's glad he did. The visit has left her with a new sense of power, new insight into her captors. Now they have someone to gossip with, the wardresses have Christian names and personalities. They like to gang up on Doctor Lindsay, teasing him, sometimes so roughly that his cocksure grin slips. He reminds her of the boys who sit at the back of her class laughing at Willie McKelvie's jokes: if you call out their names, they're petrified.

She knows she can beat them: Lindsay, the wardresses, Doctor Watson, the Government, all of them. The trick is to make the most of the cards that are dealt to her. No knowing when opportunity will present itself. She must watch and wait and keep herself ready.

Today, after the morning feed, one of the wardresses sponges her face. When Doctor Watson enters the hospital, he is accompanied by a tall man in an exquisitely tailored coat. She can't help comparing him to the doctor. Softly fleshy where the other is lean. Both of them white-skinned but, where the doctor's pallor calls to mind a switch stripped of bark ready for a thrashing, the visitor's is milky, with two faint spots of colour that, in a girl, would be called rosy cheeks. A lack of definition around the jawline, those boneless-looking hands. But Councillor Stewart is man enough to notice that she is a woman. His little eyes seek hers, his pink lips pursing and parting like some creature anchored to the seabed. She meets his look, feeling her eyes grow large and sorrowing like those portraits of Arthurian maidens so popular when her mother was a girl. He introduces himself as a representative of Glasgow Corporation, surprising the doctor by bending over the bed to take her hand. Though his touch is clammy, she doesn't pull away. The doctor's face reddens. She can well imagine the objections he raised with the Governor. Interesting, that he can be overruled.

Councillor Stewart says she must not think herself forgotten. The Lord Provost himself awaits news of her. This will be Janie Allan's doing. Her father is one of Glasgow's wealthiest citizens. He has pulled strings with the Corporation, or perhaps Janie persuaded the councillor herself. Either way, his presence here proves him a friend. Yet the air between them is charged with something more than simple friendship. She looks into his eyes, and sees the roses in his cheeks shade into a blush. Every cell in his body is attuned to hers. The heat of this knowledge spreads through her like brandy. She fills her lungs and lets the breath out in a shuddering sigh. His grip on her fingers tightens, his gaze quite naked. Her eyes bore into his, sensing his longing to change places, to lie prone as she looms above him. She tells herself she does not understand this intuition, but some demon inside her extends her tongue-tip to her lips as she complains of thirst. Councillor Stewart murmurs a faint 'dear lady'. The doctor's voice is loud as he says it is her own free choice not to eat or drink, his face showing the immense effort of will that keeps him from breaking their hands' clasp.

Councillor Stewart asks if there is anything that could be done to make her more comfortable? A bath, she says. The doctor replies that she is washed according to prison regulations. Her lips form a fleeting *moue* as if to say *you see how it goes with me here*. Doctor Watson's eyes flash, but what can he do? She holds the power now. She asks the councillor to arrange for her to petition the Commission. She cannot expect the doctor to breach regulations, but if she could address his masters directly, she is sure they would exercise compassion. Councillor Stewart says she may consider it done. At last she smiles at him. The blush spreads to his ears. Rather rudely, the doctor says they must move on. He steps aside at the door, allowing the visitor to go first. She knows he means to follow without a backward glance, but he can't help himself. His head turns. She raises her eyebrows at him before he closes the door with a slam.

Next morning he informs her that she may dictate her petition to Doctor Lindsay.

Prisoner Gordon is still losing weight. She screams in her sleep, dreaming of the feeding tube. Awake, she is never less than hysterical. She flinches at the mere sight of the doctor. He tells himself he'll give her something to flinch about, but he won't. Her nearness disgusts him like matter under his fingernails. He prescribes liquid bismuth to stop the diarrhoea that is making rectal feeding so problematic. It tightens her bowels, but makes no difference to the unspeakable odour she gives off from every orifice. When Doctor Dunlop visited, somehow she summoned the strength to insult him. This remarkable show of vitality gave the medical adviser a misleading impression, and it is not the doctor's place to introduce doubts into his mind. He was appointed as a firm hand in a faint-hearted profession. He cannot show weakness now. He must continue with the regimen and hope the minuscule traces of nourishment she retains will get her through her sentence.

He thought the disruption caused by Dunlop's visit would put paid to further interference, but no: that ass Stewart must be given the run of the gaol and touched to the shallows of his sentimental Weegie soul by Prisoner Scott's comely suffering. So now her hopes are raised by this damn-fool petition. After all he has said about the inadvisability of such a step. In his

67

daily report to the Governor, he writes 'She told me after-wards that the man did not show any sympathy'. He surprises himself with this fiction, but it cheers him up.

Matron continues to make trouble. She waits until he is across in the criminal lunatic department, and barges her way into the women's hospital. Prisoner Scott complains about not being allowed to sit up, giving the meddling hag just the ammunition she is looking for: where's the sense in taking six wardresses off the rota, leaving her short-staffed, merely to see that Prisoner Scott lies flat on her back? The Governor requires him to answer this point in writing, which means the Commission has been informed. The doctor explains, for the umpteenth time, that sitting up brings on sickness, in which case he is wasting his time feeding her, they might as well let her go now. He understands the Commissioners wish her to serve the full nine months, or is he mistaken? 'That remains to be seen,' the Governor says.

After due consideration, the Commissioners refuse Prisoner Scott's request for early release.

She looks stunned when he tells her. Her eyes darken with the threat of tears. He says he knew it would come to this, he tried to protect her from needless disappointment, but she would have her own way. She screams at him to get out. The wardresses stare at the floor. He says he will return when she takes a more rational view.

But that doesn't happen. She sinks into a decline, her lustrous eyes dull, the ripe push of her lips pinched with misery. He hates this shrivelling, as he hated her triumphal glow after Dunlop's visit, both ways of getting back at him. When he examines her, she yields like a sleepwalker, absent, unseeing. She even submits to the evening feed, then cries out, complaining of heart pain. He examines her, finding an apex beat one inch inside the left nipple line. He could tell her this heart murmur is aggravated by distress, what she calls pain

68

is actually fear, she is in no immediate physical danger. But explaining anything to her is a waste of breath, she'll only find some means to turn it against him, so let her lie there and worry.

The night of the storm, a wardress comes to his door just as he's sitting down to the cold tongue supper his housekeeper has left for him. It's Thompson, one of the relief staff transferred from Dundee Gaol. Prisoner Scott is very bad, sir. Talking queerly. He must come quickly. He leaves the meal on the table, quits the house in his shirtsleeves. The air is dense with electricity, thickly humid, the sky like a sheet of lead. And now, in a flash, magnesium white. Thunder grates above him as he crosses the prison yard. The first fat drops of rain spatter his white shirt. He takes the stone stairs two at a time, bringing the smell of outdoors in with him, the unearthed charge. She looks up from the bed and the current jumps between them. He wants the wardresses out. Impossible. There would have to be a reason, and even he does not know why. But they seem to catch his mood, backing away from the bed.

'What's the matter?'

He asks the prisoner, but it is Cruikshank, the other wardress, who answers. 'She says she's in pain, sir.'

'Where?'

In a listless voice, as if speaking of someone she hardly knows, Prisoner Scott says, 'My chest.'

Cruikshank says, 'Her heart, sir.'

He ignores her, addressing the prisoner, 'Palpitations?'

She nods.

He sits on the side of the mattress, touching the back of his hand to her brow. Her skin is sweaty, but not fevered, her pulse uncharacteristically faint. The energy kindled by that sprint up the stairs still fizzes in his chest. He takes out his stethoscope. Thompson moves to help him but he waves her away and unfastens the nightdress himself. There is no question of indelicacy, a doctor's hands are God's instruments, yet

69

some breach is involved in this act of undressing. A compromising of professional detachment.

As ever, the hospital is several degrees cooler than the air outside. Gooseflesh rises under his damp shirtsleeves. He raises the stethoscope pad to his mouth and breathes on it, as he was taught to do at medical school, not a courtesy he observes habitually. The metal kisses her skin.

The wardresses open the casement windows. The warm air smells of wet earth. Lightning flashes, followed by an almighty clap of thunder. The prisoner's face pales. Fasting purifies the complexion, and artificial feeding has not changed the blemishless gleam of her skin. How lovely she is, stretched out on the bed like this, her body soft and unresisting. He cannot allow himself to think this, not here, not now. But a shiver passes through him.

She says, 'Does this gaol have a lightning conductor?'

'I expect so.' His eyes follow the stethoscope's progress over her breast. 'Are you afraid of the storm?'

'I'm praying for it to strike me dead.'

One of the wardresses tuts.

'Come now,' he says in a bluff voice, 'the pain's not that bad.'

She turns her face away from him. At temple and nape, her hair is damp. His tongue prickles with the taste of salt.

The stethoscope tells him nothing new. And yet he doesn't like this listlessness. He has seen patients let go of life, their heartbeat weakening, their lungs refusing air. He has closed their eyes and signed the death certificate with no medical diagnosis, no reason but despair.

She asks, 'How long have I been here?'

'Almost two weeks.'

The eyelid visible to him flutters. 'Is that all?'

'Thirteen days.'

A memory surprises him, surfacing from a quarter-century ago. His sister Jane playing keek-a-boo. The silky-gingery

70

back of her head. She is only just walking. Tottering, really. She will drown in the cattle trough before she is old enough to talk.

'Sister, let me see your face—'

He starts. Out of the corner of his eye he sees the wardresses' hands touch. He hates their superstition as he hated his mother's, feeling its tug within him. The prisoner's eyes stare up through the ceiling.

'—I go home. Past the cracked tile in the close mouth. Up the stairs. Through the storm doors . . . ' Her voice drops to a whisper, 'There she is, at the window. But she will not turn round.'

How to cut a path through the thicket of another's mind without destroying what we would reach? Yet to enter the tangle unarmed, ducking and twisting through the thorns, is to risk being lost forever.

He asks Thompson if Prisoner Scott is often like this.

'It's the loneliness, sir. A night-time thing. It comes and goes.'

'With the palpitations?'

They all hear the urgency in his voice.

The wardress shrugs. He turns his back on her. 'Have you pain elsewhere?'

Prisoner Scott's eyes roll towards his, then away. When Dunlop came she was an Amazon. He wants to shock her into life, put the spark of fury back in her voice, but to speak harshly to her would be like kicking a dead thing. At once monstrously cruel, and useless.

'How am I to help you if you won't tell me?'

At last she turns her gaze on him. 'There is nothing you can do for me.'

He touches her cheek. 'Never say that.'

The wardresses are watching.

The lightning comes again, the thunder immediately after. She moans.

71

'Arabella?'

He has never spoken her name before.

A sudden wind drives a volley of rain against the window. Her eyes close. She is beaten. What else has he striven for? And he can't bear it.

TEN

The crisis passes. Next morning she resists the feeding again. He envies her capacity to recover. For forty years his body has been a tireless and uncomplaining servant, now it nags at him with aches and pains. He cannot remember when he last felt rested. His mental stamina, too, suffers. Nothing that others would notice, but a slackening in his former rigour. He knows he can cure Prisoner Scott, but how can he give her the attention she needs? Three new suffragette prisoners are about to arrive, all hunger strikers. There is so much to keep control of, one emergency after another. He is losing weight, too preoccupied to taste the food he puts in his mouth. A couple of bites are all his clenched stomach can take. He works every hour he is awake. Past midnight he returns to his tied house outside the prison gate, falls into a dead sleep, and opens his eyes at dawn, unrefreshed, to begin the next day.

He falls into the habit of visiting the women's hospital at night. The wardresses think he's trying to catch them sleeping on the job, but it's Prisoner Scott's sleep he comes to watch, her humid skin and softly-rasping breath. Experience has taught him that the more guarded the patient is by day, the more helplessly exposed at night. Sooner or later, she will give herself away. She's a sleep talker, but in scribble, like infants just on the threshold of speech. Her noises have the tantalising rhythm of adult conversation but, no matter how close he brings his ear, he can make no sense of them. Sometimes she laughs, sometimes whimpers, or writhes or flails her arms

73

or thrashes her legs like a dog that dreams of running. It is maddening, to be shut out of this night-time world of hers, this secret life of mirth and sorrow and flight.

Next morning, he will use the force required to feed her, no more, no less. If it involves bruises and blood and broken teeth, that's her decision. She has the wherewithal to end it. But in the night, bending over her sleeping form, squinting with the effort of trying to read the movement of her lips, he has this feeling. A tunnel opening inside him, a flower blooming. No. Even at night, these are not his thoughts. He reminds himself to avoid cheese for supper.

One evening she opens her eyes. His skin jumps.

'You should be asleep.'

Her expression says this is too fatuous to merit a reply.

'You need rest.'

'Why? Am I gaunt with fatigue, jittery with exhaustion?' She looks up into his face. 'Like you.'

'I'm not sleeping much,' he admits.

'Troubled by a bad conscience?'

Both wardresses are slumped in their chairs, mouths agape, dead to the world. At mention of the Doctor's conscience, one of them snorts. Doctor and prisoner smile. Then realise that the other, too, is smiling.

'What day is it?' she asks.

'Monday. July sixth.' For a moment his face belongs to another man.

'What?'

'It's Glasgow Fair next week.'

She smiles, 'I always wanted to go, when we lived in Dunoon—'

He had forgotten that she, too, hails from the west coast.

'—is it as thrilling as they say?'

'I only went the once.'

'Something happened to you there?'

74

This catches him off guard. For a moment he stares at her. And then it is too late to deny it.

'Something bad?'

Perhaps it's the tiredness. He answers honestly, 'I didn't see it like that at the time.'

She slides to the edge of the mattress. He sits down.

'Begin at the beginning,' she says.

It's going to rain. Every woman who's ever hung her washing out knows it, the same as every farmer's son, but still they say 'Braw day, the day'. Their smiles sharper than the wifies back in Ochiltree, as if they're in on a secret. A gang of keelies down the street who'll snatch his cap and call him teuchter. A dipper waiting round the next corner to take the pennies from his pooch. He slides his hand in there to touch the coins, and saliva fills the hollow under his tongue the way it did when he was wee and put a ha'penny in his mouth. An old ha'penny, browny-black and worn, with the head chopped off at the neck. Not like the shiny new bun penny his teacher has given him to spend at the fair, the copper so fresh-minted he can see the pleats in the Queen's coil of hair and the plump breasts pushing out of her dress.

Glasgow Fair. Every summer of his twelve years he has heard the words spoken and, just after, seen this secret look between his father and his uncles. Like they ken fine it's a parcel of rogues, with the cheapjacks' gold rings that turn your fingers green, and African princesses covered in boot-black, and counting pigs, and a six-fingered hag who says you're to meet a bonnie black-eyed lassie, and still the Watsons can't wait to have the wool pulled over their eyes. So here they are, his uncles and cousins, with that hawk-fierce Watson stare in their pleasant country faces. And, now that he's old enough to find his way back to the railway station if he gets himself lost, Hugh is with them.

On the journey, they drew straws to decide who'd keep an

eye on him. It's his big cousin Robbie he's trailing. Thirteen and holding down a man's job in the fields this past year, with yellow callouses on his palms from gripping the scythe in the haymaking. Hugh's big for twelve and can look Robbie in the eye, but he doesn't have his wide shoulders or the curly brown hairs his aunt trims with the scissors every few days to save his soft chin from the razor. The other cousins laughed when Robbie drew the short straw, but he doesn't seem to mind Hugh tagging along, if he keeps a couple of paces behind. Close enough to clamber into a swing boat with him, but not so close that folk can see he's minding the wean. This mix of company and solitude suits Hugh well enough. He's a singular one, his teacher says, not of the common herd. Thinking of her smell of lavender, the blueish underside of her wrist, the way she will lower her voice when she draws him aside after class, he feels a flutter behind his ribs. He has done his last sum at Ochiltree School. Once the harvest is by, he's off to the big school in Ayr. Ten miles there and ten miles back every day, and the townies making fun of his accent, and his father having to get by without the extra pair of hands he was counting on, and the uniform to be paid for, and his books, even with the scholarship money. But he won't think of that just now, because the crush of merrymakers he's caught up in – men, and women in their Sunday hats, and undergrown weans with old-looking faces – this river of folk is now past the tenements and bursting upon the Green.

Robbie has agreed to make a circuit of the whole fair. Hugh is tempted by the crazily-painted helter skelter, but he can't fritter his money on bairns' rides. He needs to go home with a story. A tattooed lady, an Indian swami, a dragon from across the China seas, something to make his brothers gasp. And that's only half the challenge. He has to make the right choice, distinguish himself from this crowd of country bump-kins, justify his teacher's faith in him. So he takes his time, breathing in the smell of gingerbread and frying sausages and the sweetness of trampled turf, filling his eyes with the gaudy painted booths, the striped canvas, the flashes of gilt on the steam carousel's prancing horses, the wee monkey in his red jacket collecting pennies from the crowd around the hurdy-gurdy. What a din! Like a fiddle bred with the bagpipes. And all tangled up with it, a dozen bands playing different tunes, and bells ringing, and girls on the sea-on-land screaming, and barkers calling through speaking trumpets, promising three murders and a ghost in the theatre tent.

He passes boxing booths where bookies' runners and tailors' apprentices are queueing to shed their jackets and take a swing at a chisel-faced professional. Thimble-riggers slide cups to and fro across fold-up tables. The stereorama tent promises views of Venice and Paris. A moustachioed dwarf in a chimney-pot hat beckons him in to meet the amazing blood-less man and the world's strongest woman. Daft laddies hurl wet sponges at their pal in the Aunt Sally. There are jugglers and tumblers, coconut shies and shooting galleries, cages of goldfinches and canaries, a menagerie with leopard and tiger and laughing hyena. And, tucked between the Cabinet of Curiosities and Doctor Darwin's Missing Link, a dancing booth with a fiddler sawing away inside, and a barefoot lassie tossing her long black hair, her skirts changing colour when she turns her hips to the music, swinging her arms to make her chest shoogle.

'Hello there,' she calls in her foreign-sounding lilt, 'will you take a turn with me?'

He looks into her laughing eyes. His heart is racing. 'Kitty,' he says.

The laughing look turns confused, and wary.

'It's me,' he says, 'Hugh Watson from Cawhillan Farm.'

And now she knows him. 'Hugh,' she breathes, 'you're a ways from home.'

Kitty, the tinker lassie who calls at the farm twice a year with her father and half a dozen raggedy weans. It's one of his earliest memories, the painted wagon drawing up with a rattle of tin cooking pots, and the weans with their snottery faces and their black-soled feet, and all the farm dogs barking. For years Kitty was just another urchin, the oldest like him, but they'd join the rest in a game of tig, shrieking as they chased round the farmyard. Until the year Kitty turned up with a clean face and her hair brushed, and gave the wee ones a telling when they startled the hens. He was shy of her for a couple of minutes, until he got used to the idea. Her father never changed: that brown and grey beard, the fleshy pink pearl on his cheek. Ma always bought half a dozen bone buttons, and a pair of boot laces, and his father got the sickles sharpened, and if any of the aunts had a birthday coming up, the tinkers left the lighter by a string of glass beads and a yard or two of ribbon or lace. But before they went, they'd sit down to a plate of stovies, and pass on the gossip from Cumnock or Sorn or whatever place they'd been last, and the tinker da would take up his fiddle and the red-headed wean his penny whistle, and Kitty would sing a mournful song about men who lose their sweethearts in her surprising singing voice. Like a heartbroken old woman elbowing the girl aside. This happened not four months back, and will surely happen again in another few weeks. Hugh doesn't care for the tunes, but he likes to watch the throb of her smooth white throat as she draws out the keening notes. And there's always the moment when she gathers up the plates and passes them across to him, looking into his eyes as he takes their weight. She's a year or two older and used to be taller but, as he closes the distance between them, he finds he has an inch on her.

'I'll jig with you, Kitty,' he says, 'if you've no one else. But are you not meant to be watching the front of the booth?'

She laughs and says her daddy won't mind, if it's a friend of the family, but he'll need to give her a penny. He frowns, not understanding, and she lays a hand on his arm. 'They pay me to dance, Shuggie.' And even though he's never been called Shuggie in his life, he gives her his penny, and she draws back the heavy canvas.

Loose boards have been laid on a frame above the grass to form a dance floor. Nothing nailed down. The racket from the couples clumping to and fro across it almost drowns out the fiddle. A dozen dancers. Country boys like him, and a couple of farmers old enough to have a wife of their own to jig with. The tinker lassies all barefoot, all pretty, in dresses of some filmy stuff that's hardly there, with their long hair flowing loose and their shoulders bared, and hectic spots of red on their cheeks. It's hot in here, with so many bodies. Tilley lamps hung from the roof cast flickering shadows. The burning paraffin catches in the back of his throat, half thrilling, half sickening.

Up close, Kitty smells of something stickily, saltily delicious that he knows is forbidden, without knowing what it is.

'Are you not worried you'll get skelfs in your feet?'

Again she laughs. Is everything he says so funny? But it's not cruel laughter. And he likes the way she puts her head back, offering him her white throat. He trusts her. Even if she doesn't remember Cawhillan Farm and passing him the tin plates, she knows him. He has the feeling he gets with his teacher. Only Kitty's knowledge is different.

He has danced the Gay Gordons the night after the harvest, and the Dashing White Sergeant, and a furious headlong Strip the Willow with his cousins all vying to see who can birl the lassies round the fastest. Waltzing is new to him. She says she'll teach him, taking one of his hands in hers, laying her other hand on his shoulder, waiting for him to do the rest.

'Here?' he says, finding the dip where her back tucks in so neatly.

'If that's comfortable,' she says.

He was right about the dress. It's hardly there. He can feel the heat of her skin, slightly damp, through the material. He slides his hand down, and down again. 'This is comfortable,' he says, and they both laugh.

He thought it would be the leopard man, or the Highland Seer, or the cannibals from the Amazonian Jungle. But this is the tale he'll take home to his brothers. How he met a lassie he'd known since he was wee, playing tig around the farmyard, and they stepped into a tent.

Afterwards his father will give him a row. Robbie was frantic with worry. His uncles and cousins had to leave off enjoying themselves and help with the search. They've been all round the Green twice, combed every inch of the fair, got themselves soaked to the skin in the downpour. They thought he'd been ambushed by a pack of thieves, and left for dead behind some booth. What the hell has he been doing? How come he's bone dry?

His cousins, too, are furious. He has spoiled their day. When they go for cold beef and pickles and all his pennies are gone, no one treats him. But he can't take the smile off his face.

It's a sweet tale, and sweetly told, sparing with the details. Arabella can fill in the gaps. His first kiss. The press of young bodies, licensed by the dance. It could easily have been no more than this.

She does not guess there is a coda to the story. And yet he feels strangely lightened. As if she knows it all.

His mouth is dry after so much talking. He stands, jarring the nearer wardress's chair with his foot, jolting her awake. He could do with a cup of tea. Is it the sudden longing in the prisoner's face that puts it in his mind? Doctor Lindsay is away. He would rather not feed her without assistance. If she will take a cup of tea then he will suspend the procedure tonight. Suspicion narrows her gaze. Just a cup of tea, he says: a fluid ounce of milk, four of five of hot water, some leaves. If she wishes to starve herself, it seems to him that foregoing her usual three eggs in a pint and a half of sweet milk would be a victory.

'And you would hand me victory on a plate?'

He smiles. That loose crimp of his lips I will see two years later from the far side of Aunt Nellie's parlour. And seeing it, I will feel his soft lips brush my neck, and after, the grind of five o'clock whisker. So sweet and sharp that my breath will catch. All this from across the room, before we have been introduced. So I know that smile and what it can do.

You would hand me victory on a plate?

'In a cup,' he says.

She drinks the tea.

ELEVEN

On his way back from the hospital he meets a wardress come to tell him that Prisoner Gordon is dying.

His thoughts are still with Prisoner Scott. It takes him a moment to understand. That thump in his lower abdomen, the rush of blood to his face. *Get a grip on yourself, man.* Every cell on this corridor is occupied. Twenty-three bored women. They can see nothing, but they know his tread, and they have a feral instinct for trouble. They call out to one another: 'Doctor's here', 'He'll no be pleased', 'It's the minister she needs'. He pushes open the cell door and sees the guttering candle, a wardress dabbing at the prisoner's brow with a wetted cloth. The other wardress wringing her hands, not even enjoying the drama. That's how bad it is.

He sends Lindsay to fetch the Governor. A wardress goes with him to retrieve the prisoner's clothes. She must be liberated tonight. As soon as possible. The Governor protests there are procedures. He needs authorisation from the Commission secretary, who will have to contact the Chairman, who will have to contact the Secretary for Scotland. The doctor has to spell it out: the woman will die here, in his gaol, unless he gets her out right now. Is that what he wants? As it is, she may not survive the journey. There is no creditable outcome, it is a question of the least damaging course. Another half-hour might make all the difference. If they wait until morning he will not be answerable for the consequences. The Governor is not such an old fool. He knows he's being threatened with the blame for a mess that is not of his making. He reminds Doctor

Watson that his authority has been flouted at every turn . . . The words die on his lips as the flaring lantern catches the doctor's expression.

So Prisoner Gordon is given a hasty bed bath and dressed in her own clothes. Only ten days since she wore them last, but the blouse hangs off her. The skirt has to be pinned, lest it drop from her shrunken hips. She looks like a rag doll propped in a chair. The wardress tries to make her tidy but has to stop when the comb comes away with clumps of hair. The Governor scuttles off to send his telegram. To have done everything that could be expected of him. Lindsay is on the street, trying to find a cab. The wardresses take the excuse of carrying away the reeking bedlinen, the pail of dirty water.

The doctor is alone with her.

The noise from the other cells has subsided. It's so quiet, he can hear her shallow breathing. He waits for the rattle that will surely come. If not with this breath, then the next.

'You are being released.'

Does she hear him?

'Prisoner Gordon. Frances. You are a free woman. You are going home.'

Those mouse's eyes open. She is listening.

'You will leave here tonight. In a few minutes.'

What is she thinking? Or is she beyond thought?

'You will wake tomorrow among friends. You will take a cup of tea, a little milk, for breakfast. Some toast, if you can. Not too much at first. Until you grow stronger.'

The eyes know he is lying.

'Sit by an open window, but be sure to keep warm.'

She is dying. Even the Governor could see it.

'It's a couple of hours by train to Edinburgh. Doctor Lindsay will go with you.'

What's that? A groan, a bubble of trapped air? Surely she cannot be *laughing*?

She stops breathing.

He is on her in an instant, one arm under her shoulders, the other under her thighs. Lifting her – so *light* – to lay her on the mattress. His ear to her chest, his mouth on her mouth, the air in his lungs poured into hers. Turning his head, waiting to feel her breath on his cheek, watching for the rise and fall. Nothing. Use the heel of the hand to compress the lower third of the breastbone by one third of the depth of the chest, taking care to avoid snapping the ribs. One hundred compressions a minute. Thirty for every two breaths. Compressions, breaths, watch, wait, compressions, breaths . . .

Her chest moves. Weakly, but it moves. Her heart beats. That's my girl. That's it. In and out. Come on. *Come on.* He lifts one rag-doll arm and chafes her cold hand. Her hold on life remains tenuous, but she is breathing.

Lindsay comes back. The hansom is in the yard. There's a train to Glasgow leaving at ten o'clock. The Governor has sent a telegram. Her friends will be waiting.

Prisoner Scott is still awake. She shows no surprise at seeing him. The wardresses are despatched to quell the excitement in the women's wing.

When they're gone she says nothing. It is exactly what he needs from her. A minute's peace. His breathing slows, his heart settles. Such a relief to close his eyes. It may be that he dozes for a few seconds. He dreams he is lying down while she sits upright in the chair. Her face is grave, but her eyes are warm. He feels the touch of her lips on his brow. He opens his eyes. She has not moved from the bed.

He asks her, 'Do you pray?'

'Of course. Don't you?'

'Not since I was a boy.'

She receives this without comment.

He says, 'What words do you use?'

*

84

Do they know? Or are they too preoccupied by how the world sees them to notice what's happening inside? In his case, I can believe it. But in hers?

I want her to have toyed with him – oh, entirely justifiably, wielding the only power she has left. Dropping confidences like bait: longings, betrayals, small defeats. Encouraging him to reciprocate, drawing him out, every switch from purring intimacy to shrieking insult coldly premeditated.

Is it too much to ask: for the one true passion of his life to have been a hoax?

I have lived in the shadow of a gaol. I have felt trapped and alone, and suffocated by a man who could not tell the difference between love and hate, but I have never been watched as she was, every micturition and defecation, twenty-four hours a day. And I have always eaten, or not eaten, of my own free will.

So I have to admit the possibility that Arabella is in no condition to manipulate her captor. The immobility, the stale air, her crusted lips and parched mouth, sore gums and chipped teeth, the hives from the itchy blanket, the constipation and the enemas, the cramp, the psychosomatic heart pains, the boredom and yet the agitation caused by the slightest departure from routine, the fighting and talking, talking and fighting . . . I have to concede, the strain of all this might break her spirit. For a while.

But she is the resourceful type, and she *is* being fed. Her young woman's body is metabolising the eggs and sugar and pints of milk into hair and fingernails and blood and tissue, renewing the dead cells, doing the miraculous business of living. Her ovary releases its monthly egg to slip down the fallopian tube and burrow into its cushion of blood. The scent given off by her skin changes subtly. A subtle change, too, in sensation: a warmth down below, a tension across her stomach first thing in the morning, anticipation in her throat. That suspended moment when everything is *just so*. It would be delicious, if she paid attention to it, but Arabella is

85

not a sensualist. Her curiosity is strictly above the neck. She has never sniffed her own bloomers, never wondered why she leaned forward when her father sat her astride his horse, never fingered the nubble between her legs. And yet, when the doctor arrives in the hospital, she notices the way he pushes through the door. Despite the frock coat, she knows exactly what her hands would find if they came to rest either side of his waist. That muscular solidity. She watches the deft way he turns up his shirtsleeves, the glinting ginger hair on his arms, the freckled back of each scrubbed hand. These too are *just so*, as purely and unmistakeably him as his jaw or mouth or eyes. All this noticing is her body's doing, but sooner or later her head will catch up.

The morning after taking that cup of tea, she is furious. When he comes to feed her she demands to see the prison rules. This again! How many times have they been over this? She cannot see the rules, she is too excited, as her doctor he cannot sanction it. But he is *not* her doctor, and she is entitled to exercise. For a sick person, in her condition, it would not be wise. Wise! Oh he's *Solomon* now.

He tries to catch her eye with a look that asks 'why are you doing this? Were we not friends last night?' But she will not acknowledge his glance. So be it. She had her chance. He feeds her by tube. Which is what he was going to do anyway.

In the afternoon she gets out of bed and makes a dash for the window.

The wardresses are caught off guard. Cruikshank grabs her round the middle. Thompson blows her whistle. MacIver arrives to help wrestle her back to bed. As their bad luck would have it, the doctor witnesses the end of the struggle. What's the matter with them? Don't they understand orders? The prisoner is to remain in bed, prone, at all times. MacIver is tasked to remain as a precaution. He is *not* having this again.

*

I spend that summer in Italy with my sister Hilda, who is nineteen and head-turningly lovely: hair, lips, eyes, blazingly vivid. I am twenty-four and pale as tripe, trailing after her through the streets of Florence. The sun bleaches me to transparency, like a photographic plate. To the men who call out to her, I am invisible. At least once a day some bent-backed crone will compliment me on *la bella*, as if I were her mother.

Bill is with us – *Billy*, as Hilda has taken to calling her, to her manifest pleasure. She swaggers alongside us in a cream linen sack suit from the Empire Stores, with a starched shirt and pink Leander Club tie. Street children run after us, calling 'Signor, Signorina' and laughing, but the hotel staff don't turn a hair. To them, it's one of the milder strains of English eccentricity.

We tour the Uffizi and the Pitti Palace, promenade on the Ponte Vecchio, light candles in Santa Croce, drive up to San Gimignano. But what gives me most pleasure is creeping out of bed alone before dawn and climbing the four hundred and sixty-four steps to the top of the Duomo. There I watch the sun rise over the Apennines, the dark rock turning smoky mauve, the sky lightening to transparency before blushing rosy-gold. Deep blue shadows stipple the red pantile roofs. A breath of incense drifts up from the cathedral below. When I get back to the hotel the concierge is awake. The smell of coffee almost detains me, but I return to my room. Passing Hilda's door, I hear a sound. Low shared laughter, and a long busy pause with no words spoken, and a sudden sharp cry. Two voices, my sister's and Bill's.

I want to go back to London. But how can I suggest it? We are staying in one of the most beautiful cities on earth. We have Medieval palazzi, Renaissance basilicas, Giotto, Botticelli, Michelangelo, Fra Angelico, the divinely-scented shade of cypress groves. At dinner we eat lamb that has grazed on rosemary and drink wine that tastes of the sun.

And if I had insisted on returning? If I had swapped Italy

for the handkerchief-white sky of home and the sort of wan light that shows women like myself to modest advantage, would I have taken a train north to stay with Aunt Nellie? Would I have seen the crowd of women gathered at the High Street port, and stayed to listen, and followed the procession, and sung hymns outside the prison wall? And if I had done all this, would I still have married him?

TWELVE

Maude Edwards is the one I met.

Mama bought all my underthings at Dickins and Jones. The saleswoman had your measurements at a glance. It was Maude's job to wrap the purchases in tissue, and then brown paper, tied with a specially printed ribbon. You sent the maid to collect it later. Maude was a cack-handed wrapper. You could see her wrestling with the whalebone, muttering under her breath, getting pinker and pinker, then she'd look up and catch your eye and grin. Among the dozens of girls who served me in shops across London, she's the one I remember. She had an engaging dauntlessness, but she was not my idea of a suffragette.

Despite which, she had the courage to march into the Royal Academy in Edinburgh and stick a hatchet in the King's portrait.

The court case is a triumph, or a farce, depending on your point of view. When the charge is read out, she cries 'I will not be tried. I am not going to listen to you or anyone whatever.' In the public gallery, her supporters find this hilarious, and raise a cheer. The Sheriff orders the court to be cleared. There are twenty policemen, and thirty-odd suffragettes with no wish to leave. It takes three men to shift Doctor Grace Cadell alone. When order is restored, the Sheriff addresses the Clerk of the Court. Maude answers him. The Sheriff says he was not talking to her. 'But I am speaking to you,' she replies, 'and that makes all the difference.' The jury files in. 'Blimey, mate, what happened to your hair?' Bald spot, hooked nose, wally eye, double chin: no defect passes unremarked. For the next half-hour she keeps up a barrage of cheerfully offensive backchat to the jurors, the Sheriff, the court orderlies, the policeman who arrested her and the witnesses attempting to testify. ('You old liar.') She makes so much noise that the jury cannot hear the evidence. They convict her anyway.

Three months in gaol.

She arrives at Perth Prison in a state of elation. She has always been a comedienne, but never before has she brought the house down. Even the jury was laughing. Removing her supporters made no difference. Clapping, cheering. Much of it unfriendly, responding to those moments when she stumbled over a word or had to pause and clear her throat. But still, Court One was like a music hall, and she was top of the bill.

She has thought it all through. She gave up her job at Dickins and Jones with some cock-and-bull story about a sick aunt. Mr Hunter has promised her a glowing reference should her aunt, *ahem*, 'should you need to seek a position in future'. The train fare up to Edinburgh was an investment. The case won't make the London papers. And even if it does, who's to say there are not other Maude Edwardses in Scotland? Prison holds no fears. She'll skip her meals and be out within the week, to be greeted as a heroine by the Edinburgh suffragettes.

'Hello. Who are you?'

An impertinent question, delivered in a self-amused English chirp. The doctor has only just entered the cell and already he is irritated.

He turns to the wardress. 'Undress her and put her to bed.'

'Yes sir.'

'*No*, *sir*. I go to my bed at eleven o'clock and not a minute before.'

'You are in prison.'

She makes a pantomime of looking about her. 'So I am! And here's me thinking it was the Ritz.' She offers her hand. 'I'm Maude, Maude Edwards—'

He returns his most forbidding look.

'—And your name is . . .'

'I am the prison medical officer.'

She smiles to herself, yet not *for* herself. It's all a performance. '*Oh,* the forcible feeder. Well, you won't need to trouble yourself with me.'

'You will eat normally?'

'Oh *no*. But there's not a thing you can do about it.'

The timing couldn't be worse. He has not slept. The adrenaline which carried him through Prisoner Gordon's departure has now ebbed. The woman is out there, beyond his control. Whether she lives or dies, she will cause trouble. He will tell them he doubted she was a suitable case for feeding from the start, but he could not say for certain without making a careful trial. If only he had been more circumspect in his written reports. The one consolation is that the Commissioners, too, are incriminated. They read his words and did nothing. Dunlop saw the woman with his own eyes. Still, he knows he has not heard the last of Prisoner Gordon.

And now here's this other one.

The Governor has received a certificate signed by one GF Fleetwood Taylor MBChB, claiming Maude Edwards has a heart so weak that forcible feeding could prove fatal. It explains why she was so sure of herself. Smirking and mugging. You'd think she'd won a watch, not been sentenced to three months in gaol. That glint in her eye reminds him of Kitty.

If he is attracted to her, and I don't rule it out, he buries the impulse very deep. She is a shopgirl. He is a doctor. He'll stand no nonsense, and that includes a medical opinion referring to forcible feeding written long before the prisoner's arrest.

He lowers the stethoscope.

'What?' she asks.

He is pleased to hear the chirp is gone from her voice.

'Is something wrong?' she prompts him.

He gives her imagination a few seconds to explore this possibility, then: 'Doctor Fleetwood Taylor wouldn't be a lady doctor, by any chance?'

'And if she is?'

He hears impudence in this retort. Without it, he might have been moved to pity her.

'Ah, well, I don't attach much importance to her opinion. I am your doctor now.' He tells the wardress, 'Bring the equipment.'

'*What?*'

'You have a weak heart, but I don't agree with Dr Fleetwood Taylor that it rules out artificial feeding. Starvation would be more dangerous.'

He can see her meagre wits trying to think their way through this.

'But the doctor told me it's not safe. I was on my back for four months last winter.'

'I can't allow you to hunger strike. The chances are you'd be an invalid for life – a chairbound invalid. You'd never lie flat in a bed again.'

She cries out.

'You cannot starve yourself and expect to thrive.'

'But the feeding'll see me right?'

He has her on the hook, it's just a matter of reeling her in.

'The feeding carries its own risks. It's less dangerous, if you co-operate, but I wouldn't call it safe—'

Her breathing grows laboured.

'—Or would you rather eat normally?'

'I can't,' she says in a new voice. Candid, broken. 'I don't want to let them down.'

'But you don't want to die.'

'*Die?*' She presses both hands to her chest.

92

'Starvation places a strain on the heart. Artificial feeding places a strain on the heart. Your heart is already weak. Do you think you're immortal?'

He doesn't notice the revulsion on the wardress's face. And it would make no difference, if he did.

All he has to do is turn that unblinking stare on her, and she starts to whimper. He finds himself drawing out the seconds, letting her work herself up. It is curiously gratifying, watching the boldness drain from her eyes, her lower lip start to quiver. When he breaks silence, he can feel the relief flooding her chest.

'There is another way.'

Strange that this glimmer of hope should render her more abject than her terror. She is beyond speech, but her eyes plead *'Anything'*.

'We could administer the sweetened milk by feeding cup. Your hands will not touch it. The wardress here will bring the cup to your lips. You will still be fed, but by the least hazardous means.' He pauses, to let her take this in, 'Do you agree?'

She nods, 'Thank you, Doctor.'

THIRTEEN

Three wardresses now sit with Prisoner Scott. Jeannie Thompson, Florrie Cruikshank and Lizzie MacIver. MacIver's the malicious one. The most easily, and dangerously, bored. She likes to talk, and she doesn't censor herself on the prisoner's account. Thanks to her, Arabella learns about the screamer ('Gone now and good riddance'), and the new one with the heart, *Miss Maudie* (she cups a breast, pulls a lewd face). Though initially diverting, this chatter soon becomes oppressive. There is no end to MacIver's grievances. The smell in the wardresses' sleeping quarters. The laziness of the other relief staff brought in from Dundee. Matron's favourites and her pet hates, her efforts to cheat the three of them out of overtime payments. After a few hours of this, Arabella is desperate. Being in gaol is bad enough, without being locked inside her gaoler's head.

MacIver asks, 'Wha's on with wabbit Maudie the nicht?'

'Jessie Cole,' Thompson says.

'Lucky besom. Maudie's a good girl.' MacIver puts on a Cockney accent borrowed from Marie Lloyd, 'Yes doctor, no doctor, *oooh* doctor—'

They laugh.

'—echt hoors sleep on watch, then aff hame: that'd do me.'

'If Doctor Watson didnae catch you.' Thompson is less afraid of MacIver than the other wardresses.

Cruikshank says, 'He's gone by ten.'

'That's where you're wrang. I've had him creep up on me past midnicht, when I'm resting my een.'

94

'I wish I'd seen that.'

'It wasnae funny at the time, I tell ye.'

MacIver raises her eyebrows, 'Ye think he's putting in the overtime wi' Maudie?'

'Oh aye,' Thompson says, 'Maudie'll be the dawtie noo.'

MacIver moves her hand in an obscene gesture. 'He must like 'em flat-chestit. You cannae say he's no had a keek at the goods.'

Cruikshank glances at the prisoner. 'Wheesht!'

'She needs to know.' MacIver turns to Arabella, 'You want to watch Miss Maudie, or she'll steal the doctor frae under yer neb.'

Abruptly they fall silent. Doctor Watson glowers from the doorway. She is glad to see him, glad to catch the whiff of tobacco on his coat and hear his baritone voice after hours of feminine jabber, but she is mortified that he has heard the wardresses' innuendo. She would like him to rebuke them, but what could he say that would not be repeated behind his back, to sniggers and suggestive looks?

He asks if the prisoner has slept.

She interrupts Cruikshank's reply, telling him she has not lost the power of speech since their last meeting. Nor has she gone deaf. He may address his questions to her.

There is no softening as he turns his gaze on her. He is still sulking about her defiance this morning.

'I can't breathe, never mind sleep,' she says. 'Four of us – five now – inhaling and exhaling the same air. Is this a new torture?'

He tells her he'll have no suicides in this gaol.

She almost laughs. Is *that* what he thinks she was doing?

'You swallow neither food nor water, then you hurl yourself at the window.'

'Did it not occur to you I might just want to look outside?'

'I can't read your mind.'

Does she say it? *And I can read yours so easily.*

The wardresses exchange glances. She notices him noticing, his upper lip tightening.

'Send them away.'

'You must be watched.'

'Then you watch me.' She looks up, into his face. 'Just for an hour. So I can breathe more freely.'

He has many more pressing things to do in the next sixty minutes, but he says, 'One hour, then they return.'

'One of them returns—' Her voice so sly she hardly knows herself.

He hesitates.

The wardresses are watching their knees. Perhaps to stop themselves from smirking.

'—you have my word I won't move from the bed.'

'And you will take a cup of tea?'

So that's what he's after.

'One cup of tea,' she says.

Because really, what does it matter? And she gets to sit up again. The sheer physical relief, after so long on her back. The miracle of stretching her spine, raising her arms up and out, all the little bones crunching with pleasure. To pull her shoulders back and look him in the eye.

'They gossip about me?'

'As you heard.'

'And about my other patients?'

'Hardly at all—'

A pause while each hears again the ribald voice. *Ye cannae say he's no had a keek at the goods.*

'—you'll just have to tell me yourself.'

Silence.

'Or not,' she shrugs, 'as you choose.'

'It is not a situation of my *choosing*.'

'But what is, in life?'

'Plenty, for those with the wealth and social standing.'

'And the right sex.'

'Aye, women can always marry into money and position—'

They smile to themselves, pleased by this fencing.

'—How is it you're not married?'

She looks up, surprised. 'I could not decide between my many suitors.'

He thinks she means it, so now she has to clarify.

'I have received one proposal, if you can call it that.'

'What else would you call it?'

'A case of mistaken identity.' She waits for him to laugh. Perhaps the joke is too feminine. 'We met at a Liberal Party meeting in Edinburgh. Mr Lloyd George was speaking. Muriel and I had chained ourselves up so they couldn't eject us when we asked our questions. The stewards had to unscrew our seats from the floor and carry us out, seats and all. It was quite a comedy. Frederick took exception to the men who lifted me, though in the flurry of the moment I don't think they knew where they'd placed their hands. He waited with me while they fetched the wire-cutters, to make sure there were no further outrages against my person.'

'And then?' A strangulated note in his voice. He needs to know everything, and at once. Does she recognise this as jealousy? Is that why she says, in a maddeningly inconsequential tone,

'We went for a cup of tea—'

The suddenness of their connection. This stranger who stepped out of the crowd taking her arm so naturally to escort her across the street.

'—we spent most of that summer in each other's company. Plays. Concerts. Out of doors, visiting ancient sites.'

'But you refused his offer of marriage?'

'It was not me he asked, but a doll with my face. So I disappointed him early, to save him from graver disappointment when it was too late—'

He has no idea what she means. She is tempted to explain:

97

how insulting it is to be adored by a man who refuses to know you. But already she has said too much.

'—And you? Have you ever proposed?'

His face stiffens. 'I have not been in a position to support a wife. My father's a tenant farmer. I qualified late, before that I worked as a grocer's apprentice.' He watches her reaction closely. 'I had brains, but no private means. I had to find employers who offered board and lodging. Asylums, prisons. My classmates had the money to buy themselves into a practice. They'd sneer at me. As you sneered just now. As any woman looking for a husband would sneer.'

She flushes, feeling the injustice of the accusation. 'I was just surprised.'

'That a tradesman who might have sold your kitchen maid a pound of sugar should now lay a physician's hands on you?'

She imagines Effie placing her shopping basket on the counter. What is she supposed to say: that his origins make no difference? But they do. To rise so far, exchanging the grocer's apron for a frock coat: she could believe it of Lindsay, just about. He has a tradesman's manner. But she cannot picture the doctor in a shop.

She smiles to herself, finally understanding that, for all the freedom she has lost, she still has a choice. 'Was it the beasts gave you the idea?'

'The beasts?' he echoes coldly.

'Calving, lambing.'

'You confuse doctoring with veterinary science.'

She can cling to her gentility, horrified by this shameless, sordid, locked-in world. Or she can match its shamelessness with her own.

'You don't want to marry,' she says.

He does not contradict this.

'You study the human body, yet deny your own—'

He looks at her.

'—the bromide.'

'I've given it up,' he says. 'It dulled the mind.'

Twenty years ago, Arabella and her sisters played a game they called Grandmother's Footsteps. One turned her back. Inch by inch, the others crept up on her. When Granny turned to look, they had to appear frozen. The delicious tension worked both ways, the terror of being hunted by stealth mirrored by the terror that the quarry would turn round and find you moving.

And now, Arabella and the doctor. Hearts in their mouths. Neither sees the other encroaching. Each fears being caught mid-step. Exposure and rejection. The dread of it alive on their skin.

Three years later, newly married and living thirty yards from the prison gate, I will discover that, for Doctor Hugh Ferguson Watson, professional obligation always comes first. Before love, kindness, even common civility. Will we manage fifteen minutes' talk a day? Certainly no more.

How different he is at work.

When he comes to examine Prisoner Scott in the middle of the day, the wardresses know to retreat out of earshot. After catching his eye once or twice, they also turn their backs. Matron would be scandalised – and delighted – to learn that they are being paid to gaze out of the window, but imagine telling tales, only to discover he is acting with the Governor's approval. He would skin them alive!

The prisoner has taken tea on two occasions. He tells the Commissioners he is confident of persuading her to give up her fast, but she will need careful handling. No representative of the outside world is to be permitted inside the women's hospital. Not chaplains nor prison visitors nor Commission officials. He changes the wardresses at the first hint of intimacy. She has a woman's instinctual need of friends. If she turns to anyone, it must be to himself. He remembers his classmates in Glasgow havering about the importance of bedside manner, the soothing murmur, the professional advantage of blue eyes. Finally, he has a use for all this.

They have been talking daily since she arrived, but with a sense that every minute brings them closer to the evening feeding. When she is tube-fed only in the morning, it alters the whole day. They still talk at eleven, when he comes to examine her, but more casually than before, saving themselves for six o'clock – the hour he will return home to me, as a married man. What is it that makes these evenings of theirs so pleasurable? His visible relief, as he sheds the cares of the working day? The stories they exchange? The caffeine flooding their veins? The echo of all the men and women who have raised a cup together since time began?

All of these, and something else. The golden key to his heart. And, fortuitously, to hers. He is sanctioned by duty. Every glance, every thickening in the air between them, the sudden dryness in their mouths, the throbbing and the vortex, all these symptoms of growing attraction might also be a ploy, the latest twist in their power struggle. How intoxicating it is, this meaning it and not meaning it, at once overcome by feeling and ruthlessly calculating, wide open and helpless and cold-bloodedly controlled.

What a mistake I made in loving him.

Sometimes, with the taste of blood still in her mouth from the morning feed, she will be sarcastic. He schools himself to suffer these barbs, but not with too much forbearance. She hates his implacability most of all. If she scores a hit, he shows it, and may hit back. She will reveal herself to him, but only reciprocally. He must woo her, seduce her, for the sake of her health. He won't use these verbs, even to himself, but what else is he doing? And in order to seduce her, he must also be seduced.

This is where it starts. Daydreams is putting it too strongly:

they're no more than idle thoughts. Of taking her out of this unclean place. A sea voyage, surrounded by indifferent strangers. Hour after hour to talk, and watch the swell, and see her grow plump on sea air and the sweets he will bring to her lips. And at night, *at night* . . . Even in the privacy of his bed, he cannot bring himself to picture it.

My poor Hugh.

FOURTEEN

The first day Prisoner Edwards is fed, he stays to talk her through it. When the wardress tilts the cup too much, making her cough, he takes over, holding it to her mouth himself. Next day he is busy and leaves the procedure to the wardress. The prisoner blocks the feeding cup with her tongue. Most of the mixture ends up on her nightdress. The doctor is called back to feed her by tube. This happens again and again. She will only take milk from the cup in his presence. The price of her compliance is his constant attendance. She seems to enjoy provoking his intervention, then sinking into a warm bath of masculine reassurance. Well, he too has a trick up his sleeve. He reports to the Commission that she shows congestion of the stomach due to cardiac dilation. Let's see her make doe-eyes at him when she's being fed through her backside.

I feel for her, this young woman assaulted from both ends by a man who seems now cruel, now kind. She thought they understood each other, that he'd found a compromise between his duty and her convictions, a way she could keep both dignity and health. She nearly died last winter. Doctors are life-givers, their word is second to God's. When he barks at her to lie still and forces the gag between her teeth, the unfairness stuns her. The *needlessness*. It dawns on her that he offered her the feeding cup to test her resolve. He has no interest in compromise, only victory. He thinks, because she has given in once, she will always give in. She begins a thirst strike.

The doctor reports that Prisoner Edwards is fed by tube

twice a day and by Enule four times a day. She flushes before-hand, but he talks to her to gain her confidence. She is giving no trouble. There is not the slightest chance of causing her death by feeding as long as she cooperates. If she resists, he will stop and report back. Since the feed is liquid, her thirst strike is irrelevant. She seems set to serve every day of her three-month sentence.

Against all expectation, Frances Gordon survives. After five days in a nursing home, she is strong enough to receive visitors. One morning the doctor is summoned to the Governor's office. The Governor's face has a yellowish tinge. His eyeballs, too. Some days his skin reeks of last night's whisky. If he were the doctor's patient, he would take the pledge.

'Ah, Watson,' he says, 'what do you propose to do about this?'

The doctor takes the newspaper, folded to the relevant page, and scans the contents.

'Well?' the Governor says, before he has finished reading.

'It's a suffragette propaganda sheet.'

'It's not true, then?'

Even by the Governor's standards, this is an idiotic question. Of course it's *true*.

The Governor thumps his desk. 'For God's sake, man, they're going to crucify us.'

The revelation that Miss Gordon's treatment included injections into the bowel causes national outrage. Headlines in all the papers, letters to the editor, questions in the House. Coming close to killing his patient is as nothing to *submitting a lady to this most degrading of obscenities*. It does more to win support to the suffragettes than any number of banners and processions. By noon Doctor Ferguson Watson finds himself the most reviled man in Scotland. But he will never admit he is wrong. Not in 1914, and certainly not when he

103

is married to me. Criticism merely strengthens his determination. His first act after leaving the Governor's office is to feed Prisoner Edwards by rectum.

The doctor sits at his desk, writing a point-by-point rebuttal of Doctor Mabel Jones's allegations about Prisoner Gordon's treatment. As if he doesn't have enough to do. The Commissioners have his daily reports, what more do they need? Something to release to press and parliament, seemingly. Something *tailored to the situation*. Face to face with Dunlop he could have said it: you're asking me to lie. But they're canny enough to keep him at arm's length.

Far from being drugged in prison, Prisoner Gordon arrived at the gaol showing evidence of systematic drugging to induce continual retching. The Enules used to keep her alive contained a very small dose of institutional opium to secure rectal tolerance, as has long been standard practice in hospitals and asylums. At no time was the prisoner stupefied. Nothing but very great patience was observed with her. Her only complaint was that the tube had a bitter taste. She left the prison in a healthy enough state to sit up and talk with Doctor Lindsay all the way to Glasgow.

It is not easy for him to write this. He is a truthful man. He can only do it in a bitter fury with his employers. He delivers his statement to the Governor, who reads it through and nods. So now they are bound by a falsehood. Evidently this troubles the Governor less than it does himself.

Arabella does not understand how it is possible to resist, and surrender, hate and need, now cleaving like soft butter, now impregnable as steel. To fight her enemy in the morning, and open her heart to him at night.

She hates herself for those evening cups of tea. And yet he's right: they hold less nourishment than a feed. Unless the energy she expends in fighting the tube cancels the calorific benefit, in which case a cup of tea taken placidly is more perniciously sustaining. When did her thoughts become this pendulum: yes, no, good, bad, this, that? She knows when. That first sip. To hold out for so long, refusing to eat or drink, was no small achievement. And she just threw it away, gave him a victory at the very moment when he must have been close to despair. Why did she do it? Who would have guessed that character could be shrugged off like an ill-fitting dress, leaving her naked, a shape-shifter who can take a hundred forms, all of them true to this moment and false to the next?

She prays, reciting the comforting words she has reached for since childhood. *Our Father who art in Heaven. The Lord is my shepherd. I lift up mine eyes unto the hills. The song of songs which is Solomon's . . .*

Her mind is rudderless, her body assailed by sensations. An oily feeling in her stomach, breathless, dizzy, lightheaded, the pain like a stone in her chest, this fluttering in the base of her throat, her racing pulse and pounding heart. Terror. Elation. Terror. A dropped glass shattered into a thousand shards.

Such hubris, to think she could endure a prison sentence. The justice of the cause, the debt of loyalty she owes her comrades, the love of family and friends are just words to her now. They belong to the iron-willed Arabella Scott, not to the nameless creature she has become.

He walks into the hospital. The hinge of his jaw. His Adam's apple. His blue eyes. He washes his hands. Even immersed in water, the ginger hair on his forearms won't slick down. The slither of his soaped palms. The fastidious way he plies the linen towel. The thousand fragments reassemble, she can breathe again.

At school, he basked in the approval of his teachers. Such discipline. No other pupil came close. He was thirty-two when he enrolled at St Mungo's College to study medicine, a man among boys. His classmates were callow but quick, their wits not dulled by grocery, their minds impressionable as wet cement. More than half his year were born overseas. India, Ceylon, Jamaica, Trinidad. Sureswar had seen the treasures of the ancient world. Madan had watched great actors, heard celebrated orchestras. Phiroga had eaten at the same table as famous scientists and philosophers. His first chance to learn from his peers. Another man would have sought out common ground. Not Hugh. The more he coveted their knowledge, the more he shunned them. But they're still there, in his head, holding their brilliant conversations, giving their names to new diseases. For a farmer's son, he has done very well for himself. But when all's said and done, he is forty years old and treating criminals and lunatics.

He is capable of so much more.

A pulse jumps at his temple. Arabella remarks on it. These days she mentions everything she would once have pretended not to notice. *Pert*, her mother calls women who do this. Meaning, too eager to draw masculine attention.

He says it is an effect of the heat.

She supposes the ladies are all walking around Perth in their summer whites.

He has no idea. He has not left the prison precincts since she arrived.

'Then we are both imprisoned here.'

Sometimes his neat ears redden when she takes this ironic tone. Today he looks disapproving. Her stomach shrinks, her shoulders brace for a fight.

'You have to start eating,' he says, 'I cannot justify fore-going the nightly feed for a cup of tea—'

She remembers last night, after he had gone. Awake in the dark. Her promise to herself.

'—I am answerable to the Commissioners. They want to see some progressive increase. Even a piece of toast.'

'No.'

106

The vein jumps. 'Do you want me to go back to feeding you in the evenings?'

'Yes,' she says.

Thompson, sitting by the window, glances towards them.

'Get out,' he barks. It has happened a couple of times since he overheard them joking about Maude Edwards. Thompson and Cruikshank depart, closing the door behind them.

He takes off his frock coat, laying it on the chair, waiting for her to move across the mattress, making space for him to sit down. Under the blanket, she digs her fingernails into her palms. After a moment, he brings the other chair to the bed.

'What's the matter?' he asks in the voice he uses when they are alone. It takes her like a drug, diffusing through her blood. Her eyes close. She forces them open again.

'I am on hunger and thirst strike—'

He quizzes his eyebrows. She knows him so well, she can hear his thoughts.

'—This has nothing to do with my bowels, or my menses, or an imbalance of bodily salts. Our interests are irreconcilable. It is in my interest to remember that.'

'You had a bad dream last night,' he says.

'*I'll have no more cups of tea.*' But she cannot leave the question unasked, 'You were here?'

Their eyes lock. An outrageous breach of privacy, and yet, this stirring inside her.

'You spoke in your sleep—'

Rise up, my love, my fair one, and come away.

'—you were panting, clutching at the air.'

Her body burns inside her skin. 'What did I say?'

'I caught your hands. It seemed to calm you.'

'*What did I say?*'

He moves from chair to bed. The horsehair mattress creaks. Her body slides into the dip made by his weight. Four layers of cloth between them, but each feels the other's heat.

107

He peels back the blanket, unbuttons her gown. Usually she averts her gaze, but today she watches his face.

How many hundreds of breasts has he seen as a doctor, reading the fatty tissue for clues to the fascinating machine within? Now it is the surface that fascinates, the curve of pearly skin, the rosy pucker that is not rose-like at all, but a delicate shade of coral. His fingers rest on the stethoscope pad. He does not tell her to breathe in.

'Are you often here, in the night?' she asks.

Let him kiss me with the kisses of his mouth.

'It's the one place I can get peace.'

'No more cups of tea,' she says.

'Why?'

'We are not friends. You have made me—' careful now '—an enemy to myself.'

'I'll not let you die.'

'You must do what you're paid to do.'

His eyes flinch. 'You think I like it?' His voice barely a whisper, 'It's worse for me than for you.'

She stares at him, dumbstruck. Did he really say that? She sits up in bed. Worse for him? Disbelief turns to fury. Worse than a dozen hands pinning her to the mattress, MacIver's fingers digging into the tender crook of each elbow, Thompson's iron grip on her legs, Cruikshank's dead weight on her breastbone, Doctor Lindsay's popping eyes roving across her flesh? Worse than having her head forced back, the tube scraping away the lining of her throat, the gag reopening the cuts in each corner of her mouth, a scalding wave passing through her body as she fights for breath, spasms in her throat, a blinding pressure in her skull? Worse than the chorus in her brain: Oh God, save me! Oh God, let me die! Let me live to kill him with my own hands?

He grabs her by the shoulders, his hands on her skin. Her breasts swing free of the gaping nightgown.

108

Now. Do it. Kick the blanket aside. Lie down with her. For once in your life, let passion be your master.

Maybe it happens, and they spend the rest of their days pretending it did not. Maybe this is the key to everything. To the tragedy of his life, and mine. Or maybe what gives it such power is the fact that it doesn't happen. The lifelong regret.

'You said, "The tiger is coming".'

She laughs, disappointed. 'We used to say it as children.'

'You and Muriel?'

'All six of us. The house in Dum Dum had a tiger-skin rug. When we were naughty Father used to tell us it would eat us.'

'You lived in India?'

'For a few years.'

The fearful, tantalised look on his face. Blazing sun, babbling tongues, strange gods. When he finally leaves Scotland, he will go north, to Norway, a land even colder and more costive than his own. But that is years away. Tonight, in this prison hospital, anything is possible.

'The government would send you to Canada.'

'To *Canada*?' It's the first she has heard of it. 'As breeding stock, you mean? I hear they're short of wives, but surely not so desperate as to risk me giving birth to a tribe of pyromaniacs.'

Why is he not smiling?

'It could be arranged,' he says, 'if I gave them assurances.'

'What assurances?'

A suspense in the air between them. Her nipples stiffen.

'That I would conduct you there.'

That evening she eats a slice of toast with her cup of tea.

To Canada.

She has a life outside the gaol. Home, friends, family, a job. Her reputation. The campaign. All these are hers still, however remote they feel right now. He must know she would never give them up. And yet she can picture it. The snowbound village by the frozen lake. Her days in the schoolroom, his in the surgery. The rosy-cheeked children exhaling clouds of vapour. Evenings by the fire in their log cabin. The stitched furs covering their feather bed.

Or is it just the journey he has in mind? *I would conduct you.* Ten lost days neither here nor there. Sun-sparkle. Salt spray. Laughing gulls riding the air. The rocking ship on the rolling waves. Cut off from the world like a prison, but free.

HILDA

No white bread, no butter, no butcher's meat, no front or back garden without its jungle of spuds, and no Billy.

If Hilda found Newton Abbot a drag before the war, it's a thousand times more moribund now. Caleb the gardener's son is boxed. And Tommy Hithe, and Peter Baxter, and Charlie Cavendish, and so many of those boys she danced with and fended off in cabs (with varying amounts of pep) the summer she came out. Ancient history now. She still sees three or four of her fellow debs, but they drink watery tea, not fizz, and the talk limps along to the pother of needles because they're all knitting toe bags for the troops.

Argemone ffarington Bellairs is at the Front, pulling shrapnel out of wounded soldiers. Out there, everyone calls her Bill. *It's dangerous of course but by God we're alive*. Hilda would have given her right arm (or at least a little finger) to go with her, but the Ancestors wouldn't wear it. About the one thing they've agreed on since the war started. Hilda told them 'Billy will look after me', and Pa snorted and mumbled something she couldn't hear, but it didn't take a genius to twig the gist when Mama shot him that cyanide look. So then Hilda and Mama went down to the shore to gather seaweed to dress the vegetable beds, and had a little chinwag about how worried Pa was with Gordon in Flanders, but with a son there's no choice. Hilda could make bandages with the old biddies of the Townswomen's Guild, or stand on the station platform handing out gaspers to the sailors on their way to Dartmouth, or even nurse the wounded Tommies in Paignton if she really had a vocation. Was it fair to put Pa through all those sleepless nights just so she could have an adventure? And if anyone needed nursing, it was her own sister.

So that was that.

Perhaps it's just as well. Hilda's not sure tending the sick is her cup of cocoa. This last year has been an absolute penance. Dodo off her chow, getting feebler by the day. Pop your head round the door and there she is, her cheeks that ghoulish bluey-white, mushroom shadows around her closed eyes. A goner, Hilda's sure of it. She'll lean right over the cot, put her ear to those papery lips. Nothing. And when she touches her: cold as croak. This grisly feeling in Hilda's chest, as if her ribs are made of chalk. And suddenly she's blubbing like a babe and pleading with a God she hasn't prayed to since Sunday school. But even as she's offering up her spiffy future as a femme fatale and famous painter, she's in such a bate. What the hell is Dodo playing at? All those years she blazed like the sun in Hilda's sky: hotter, wittier, more dazzling. And then the clouds closed in. At first Hilda was tickled pink – who wouldn't be? – to find the chaps all staring at *her*. To find *hers* was the laughter Billy looked for when making a joke. But what's the point, if Dodo's not green with envy? A bit of honest competition, is that too much to ask? The fabulous Atkins sisters, the toast of fashionable London, the subject of endless debate: which one would *you* marry? But it's not like that at all.

Appendicitis. Poor Donella. *She nearly died, you know.* One day Hilda wakes up to find her elder sister resurrected as a saint. And how is she supposed to compete with that?

For thirteen months Mama hardly leaves her bedside. She's worn to a rag. Pa's clothes are hanging off him. All those suits he had made in Burlington Arcade look like hand-me-downs from a happier man. Hilda's practically an embarrassment, with her peachy cheeks and silky hair. No one throws parties any more. There's no reason to get all dappered up and drink too much and flirt your eyes at the best-looking buck in the room. The best-looking bucks are all at the Front getting themselves boxed. That's social success these days. Hilda can't say any of this out loud. Even thinking it, she feels like a monster. But that doesn't mean it's not true. And even more monstrous, and every bit as true, is the thought that Dodo has hit the jackpot. Everyone admires a plucky invalid, especially during a war. The peakier she looks, the less she smiles, the more they adore her. It drives Hilda mad.

So when a plan is hatched to send Dodo up to Scotland to convalesce with Aunt Nellie and Uncle George, and to give Mama a break from the sickbed, Hilda's not sorry to see her go. She could have gone too, but what's the point of swapping the old biddies of Newton Abbot for the auld wifies of Perth? For the first month or so it seems she has made the right choice. Dodo's letters are gratifyingly yawnsome. She spends her days trailing Aunt Nellie from the Girls' Sewing Guild to the Red Cross Hospital where she stains her mitts making war dressings out of sphagnum moss. But in July there's a twinkle of gold amid the epistolary dross. When Hilda gets back from the tennis court, Mama is at the bottom of the garden picking greengages, humming to herself.

Only Dodo could travel to a one-horse town in Scotland and bump into the last eligible bachelor in the kingdom.

FIFTEEN

I didn't mind the boredom. The thing about nearly dying at the age of twenty-five is you emerge no longer young. You have knowledge you don't want but can't unlearn. All those war casualties didn't shock me. I counted myself lucky not to be among them, but I wasn't alive like Hilda or Gordon or Bill. I felt older than Aunt Nellie, with her sketchbook, her sewing-guild musical review and her sweet, girlish love affair with Uncle George. *That* was shocking to me. Kissing the top of his head when she found him at his desk. The poems he left in her workbasket. The feverish notes of a Mozart sonata leading me to discover them side by side at the piano, pink-cheeked, nimble-fingered, breathless with laughter.

I had been visiting Perth since I was three years old. Hilda and Gordon and I had crawled around on Auntie's rugs, played house under her piano, shod her cat in walnut shells, tickled each other with the ostrich feathers she had worn to bob her curtsey to Queen Victoria. Of the town itself I knew almost nothing. The River Tay. The big cathedral where Uncle George had married my parents. The flat stretch of common where the men played golf and the women hung their washing. On previous visits this had seemed enough. But now I was twenty-six. I had come out at court, attended the balls, danced with more amusing young men than I could remember, eaten kedgeree break-fasts with their mothers, clinked glasses with my own kind on the French and Italian rivieras and, receiving no offers

114

of marriage, had almost died. It was time to make the best of things.

I borrowed Auntie's bicycle and explored the Tay, drinking air sweet with the first hay crop. I watched the chuntering ducklings learning to fly, the swan patient on her nest. I saw an old man upto his thighs in cold river, casting and waiting and casting and waiting but never, so long as I stood on the bank, hoisting the silver salmon, and I thought: he has hope, but it doesn't mar his pleasure in this moment.

Some days I accompanied Auntie to her good works. I met Lady Georgina Home-Drummond and Lady Cheyne and Miss Murray MacGregor of MacGregor and we talked about the young men they knew, my old dancing partners, now married or dead, or both. I tried to look too dignified to allude to a dead fiancé of my own. Better to be pitied for that than as an old maid. It may not be fashionable to talk like this now, but I didn't make the rules. Women had all sorts of freedoms in that war. We took over the jobs the men had done, raised our hemlines, shed our underskirts, smoked, drank, but we all knew this time would come to an end. You had to be married. Only then could a man and a woman get on with living their separate lives.

I think now that the summer of 1916 was the happiest of my youth. The sun shone. The birds sang. The dust motes swam in the light streaming through the morning room window while the old cat purred on my lap. I had my aunt's extensive circle of acquaintance and the run of my uncle's library. They didn't care whether I was married or not. The only bone of contention between us was my poor appetite.

And then Aunt Nellie came home all fired up about some act of rudeness at the war dressings.

As if Doctor Ferguson Watson did not have enough to do treating Scottish convicts and criminal lunatics, Perth Gaol now doubles as a camp for German prisoners of war. And with so many of his peers away at the Front, there's a shortage of doctors in the town. He spends a couple of mornings a week treating the aches and pains of Doctor Stirling's patients, and another afternoon at the Red Cross hospital checking for gangrenous wounds. One Tuesday, he casts his supervisory eye over the volunteers making surgical dressings.

He has not paid much attention to the stories about cowards being presented with white feathers. When the woman plants herself in front of him, he thinks she is going to ask him to look at the cyst on her neck. She is holding something, offering it to him. *Ah*. Now he understands. Conscription applies to men between the ages of eighteen and forty-one. He is doubly exempt, being forty-two (though looking ten years younger) and employed in a reserved occupation. Not that he wears his *King and Country* badge. He is not going to explain himself to anyone, least of all this sour-faced besom. 'Excuse me,' he says, not particularly civilly. The woman thrusts her feather in his face. '*Excuse me,*' he says again, more distinctly. She remarks that better men than him are dying in Normandy.

He raises his voice, 'For the third time, madam, will you let me pass?'

She throws the feather at him and stalks out of the room.

A grey-haired matron jumps to her feet. Wearily, he turns his gaze on her. These confounded do-gooders think they run the country. She says he must not think such rudeness typical of their town. If he will do her the honour of coming to tea on Saturday she will introduce him to as pleasant a selection of people as he could hope to meet. He laughs. He has been living in Perth twenty-seven months. This is his first invitation.

Aunt Nellie has held a couple of tea parties at Balhousie Bank since my arrival. I've cut cake for the diocesan ladies and passed the sugar to wounded soldiers and, frankly, my expectations of amusement that afternoon are not high. But I change into my periwinkle silk and get Aggie to dress my hair. Then I stand at the upstairs window, watching for the first guests so she'll know when to put the kettle on.

It's one of those blazing June days, the sun reflecting platinum off the pitched slate roofs, the silk dress sticking under my arms. How cool it looks down there in the garden, a faint breeze stirring the leaves. He slips through the gate. The boyish swing of his stride. His face flecked with shadow as he passes under the silver birch. 'Dashing' I will write, describing him to Mama, but the word I use to myself is 'beautiful'.

Lady Cheyne and her thick-waisted daughter follow him up the path. The maid admits them all together. Already he regrets coming. Half an hour, then he'll plead an ailing patient. There's a long moment of silence after the introductions, before the cleric with the receding hairline takes charge of the conversation. Music, the servant shortage, the Somme.

Someone asks about the prison. Lady Cheyne's nostrils flare, but she's as curious as the rest of them. Does he have to do with murderers? Child-killers? Poisoners? Do they really deserve his cure? How can he bear to touch them? What's the point in treating a man who's going to hang? All these good God-fearing folk, so sadistically avid. He feels like telling them to go to hell. Across the room, his hostess catches his eye, her brows lifting. Up and down, so quick, no one else sees. It occurs to him that she has invited these people expressly to meet him: the first act of unambiguous kindness he has received in this town. So he tells them about prisoners flogged with the cat o' nine tails in Peterhead Gaol, the knotted ropes wrapping twice around their stomachs, the roars heard as much as a mile away, the permanent scars and the lifelong deterrent. He's

117

never known a prisoner risk a flogging twice. In fact, there was one man so terrified . . .

He stalls mid-sentence.

I have been downstairs, fetching more hot water. As I enter the parlour, Aunt Nellie inclines her head to draw me towards her. He stops talking. I can feel him staring at me, my hair, my brow, the way the light strikes my face. I leave my aunt and cross to the window. He is sweating. The guests smile politely, waiting for him to continue. He excuses himself.

'Arabella.'

He takes my hand. I turn to look him full in the face.

'*I beg your pardon.*' We say it together.

He drops my hand, gives me the most desolate smile. 'I thought . . .'

'I was somebody else—?'

He can't take his eyes off me.

'—Are we so very alike?'

'In profile.' Still he stares.

Behind his eyes, his brain starts working. Any moment now he'll return to Lady Cheyne.

'I'm sorry I startled you.' *Touched me*, he means.

I think about her, this woman I do and do not resemble, this fascinating person who knew how to make him fall in love with her. My colour heightens becomingly. I can feel it happening. As if I'm turning into somebody else. My eyes glitter, my lips soften. I smile.

'I'm Donella,' I say, 'Nellie's niece, up from England. Though I was born in America.'

He is the last guest to leave. Reaching the garden gate, he looks up. The big house looms against the evening sky, the windows too dark to see in. What is he thinking? Does he know I'm watching him? He suspects, just as I suspect he is letting himself be seen, but we could be wrong. It's the possibility of error that makes it so delicious. He has never taken a girl out to the theatre or a concert or even for a walk, unless you count his cousin Jeannie when they were students at Glasgow and living in her father's house, but he knows he will court this woman he has just met. Does he fight the return of these feelings he thought dead? Does it occur to him to spare me? How completely I match his desires. Young, intelligent, spirited, yielding, with that dark-haired, white-skinned loveliness that tears at his breast. The odds against our meeting dumbfound him. A gentlewoman, presented at court, my home five hundred miles away. His first invitation in two years. He has no time for superstition but, all the same, it feels like fate.

So much like fate that he sees no need to engineer another meeting. When a week has passed with no word, I accompany Aunt Nellie to the war dressings. He doesn't show. I sit there, rolling sphagnum moss in my best frock. So much has happened since I met him. When I leave the house the recruits being drilled on the North Inch follow me with their eyes, no matter how the sergeant major yells at them. Twice a week I help out at the patriotic barrow in the railway station, distributing tea and buns to the troops. They whistle. The bolder boys shout *give us a kiss!* It's not just that I'm using Vaseline on my eyelashes, a little rouge on my cheeks. I'm alive again.

The following Friday there is a charity night at the theatre in aid of the Red Cross. During the interval Aunt Nellie and I sell refreshments in the little bar off the grand circle. Tea and coffee threepence a cup. Quite a scrum in here. No matter how quickly we fill the cups, the queue never seems to shrink. A man's hand holds out a pound note. I take my time looking up, enjoying the secret thread that stretches between us. Admiration in his blue eyes, along with something keener-edged. 'I'm not sure I can change that,' I say, demure and provocative. He says he doesn't need change, as it's for a good cause. How badly he wants to impress me. A whole pound! He could have me for sixpence. But the last thing he wants is a bargain.

Look at us, laughing at nothing together as the bell rings to call us back to our seats. Are we so different from other couples? Don't they all have this double vision: the man in love with a slightly different woman, and the woman so eager to please?

The next week the family comes north, renting a house around the corner from Balhousie Bank. They all know about my sweetheart, as Uncle George has taken to calling him. I welcome the teasing at first. It gives substance to a courtship that can seem, in the cold light of morning, mostly air. Having been in love with Bill, I recognise the symptoms. I lose what little appetite I've had, ignore the people around me and think about him all the time. The trouble is, I have so little to go on. What do I know of him? My aunt's account of his dignity when handed the white feather, and three conversations: one when I did most of the talking, one plagued by interruptions from thirsty playgoers, and one managed without speech, as he lingered by the garden gate and I watched him from the window. My uncle and aunt are astonished to learn he has been living in Perth for two years. He belongs to no club or congregation, doesn't bat or bowl or cloister himself with the Freemasons. The only person who seems to have heard of him, Miss Fairlie of the Sick Poor Nursing Society, gives me a narrow look and changes the subject. Which, I decide, could mean anything.

The mercury rises to eighty-five degrees. All day his house cooks. He gets Mrs Hendry to strip his bed of blankets but, even with the windows open, the night grips his chest in its sticky embrace. One evening he retires without pyjamas and, waking in the dark with a raging thirst, twists to retrieve the glass of water at his bedside. The linen sheet brushes his engorged member. He waits. Some nights it subsides of its own accord. St John's bell chimes the quarter, and then the half-hour. Groaning, he turns to lie on his belly. Against his will, his mind conjures a nightdress, soft white skin, a cloud of dark hair. Mine? Or hers?

Next morning he decides to have nothing more to do with me. I know it. I wake up feeling such a fool. All this fuss over nothing. How Hilda will mock. When Uncle George makes some harmless joke about my future as a doctor's wife, I snap at him. A walk along the river. *No, I don't want company.* I suppress every thought of him, but they're like ants: kill one and another ten arrive on its trail. Nine days since I last saw him. If I were a man, nothing would keep me from my loved one's door. *Quod erat demonstrandum.* The prison is on the other side of town, by the South Inch. Not far. Why should I not take a look, since we are nothing to each other?

The size of it. Towering over the landscape. Like a city within its high walls. The sun beats down on the soot-blackened cell blocks, the windows little more than slots. The sight darkens my spirits like news of a death. How can he spend his days in this place and it not leave some mark on him?

Edinburgh University awards him a diploma in public health. For a day or two he sinks into despondency. It's always like this when he gains the longed-for qualification: this hollowness, after years of endeavour. A day out in his hired gown, a chance to shake the vice-chancellor's hand, his fellow diplomates taking their wives and mothers and sisters to lunch while he slinks away to the museum in Chambers Street. Studying has been the best part of his life, filling his empty weekends, helping him rise above the sordor of the prison.

He is aware of me in Balhousie Bank. I exert a magnetic

pull which grows stronger if he ventures into town. Uncanny, meeting me at the theatre like that. First time he'd been inside the place. I was flushed from the heat of so many bodies, my colour deepening when I saw him. But what's the use? I'm here on holiday. By the autumn I'll be home again, dining with Lord This and Lady That, flitting between the ballet and the opera and hunt balls and weekend house parties, telling my friends about this *funny little Scotchman* I met.

This feeling he wakes up with in the mornings, the nameless residue of his dreams. Prisoner Lennox is the only patient in the women's hospital. A recurring blood disorder. Matron has put her in the middle bed, facing the window. There's no physical resemblance but, walking in yesterday, seeing the summer light strike her form under the blanket, he almost cried out. It has been two years. For weeks at a stretch he won't think of her. Then suddenly every moment brings some fresh reminder. Where is she now? The suffragettes have disappeared from the newspapers. The government offered them an amnesty when war broke out. They're driving ambulances, nursing in field hospitals. Safer than fighting, but not without its dangers. Or is she still in Edinburgh, keeping the home fires burning? And if she is, might their paths not cross again?

Three days later he has a change of heart. I have a hundred theories. He wants to reconcile with his parents. It will further his career. Boredom. Sexual frustration. Fear of growing old alone. We are staying in Pitlochry for a fortnight: Uncle, Aunt, Pa, Mama, Hilda and myself. We sketch and bicycle and walk up Ben Vrackie and every second of it I am talking to him in my head. One afternoon we go boating on the Tummel and return around six, weary and dishevelled and rather damp. The doctor is waiting on the grassy bank outside the station master's cottage we have rented.

SIXTEEN

Already he seems part of the family. He dines with us, joins our walks and expeditions. When we cycle out to Moulin, where my great-grandmother was born, he asks all the right questions, setting the Richmonds' decline in shame-free perspective. The wealth they amassed by canny use of drainage and potash. Borrowing to farm more and more land once the railway arrived to take produce to London, leaving them that much more vulnerable to cheap imported American grain and the dead hand of the Depression. Despite himself, Pa is impressed. I'm pleased about this, and at the same time put out. So far, I have been the doctor's principal interest. My eyes, my hair, how well I look in red, my love of cornflowers and yellowhammers and wire-haired terriers. No doubt I play a part in his engagement with Mama's family history, but I'm beginning to realise it is *ideas* that move him. Not the sort of ideas Bill and I could debate late into the night, about art and feeling and whether the new age of machines will change the human soul. The doctor – Hugh, as I learn to call him – will listen to such talk in silence, before moving on to the more comfortable ground of facts.

But this is a small thing beside the way his eyes follow me when I move away from him, and how readily he laughs at my jokes and teases my aversion to spiders, and the heart-stopping moment when he catches me up in his arms and carries me across a patch of bog. The feeling of being held by him, helpless and protected and womanly. The startling discovery that every simple thing you are is mysteriously

123

precious to someone else. As his manliness is precious to me. Oh God, his shoulders. The timbre of his voice, the way it roughens when he speaks of Ayrshire. The two of us strolling between the hedgerows at dusk, with the flittering moths catching the last of the day's light, and the air cooling, and the heat of his body held in the lining of his jacket when he slips it over my dress. His smell. Hot chestnuts in newspaper, and saddle leather, and empty train compartments on long journeys, and potatoes just pulled from the black earth. And none of these, really. He smells of himself.

He loves to hear me talk about America. The endless corn fields. Clapboard churches whitened by the scouring wind. Homesick Scots curling on the frozen lake in winter. Saturday-night socials held in tin huts, the women dancing with each other because the navvies have poured so many surreptitious slops of rye into their tea they can barely stand, let alone steer a girl around the dirt floor. They called Emmetsburg the new Edinburgh. Pa went out at twenty-four, to be secretary and treasurer of the Scottish American Land Company. There was money to be made building houses along the new railroad. Mama couldn't bear the vulgarity of the place, so Pa brought us back to England, but my Uncle James is still out there. And my Uncle Thomas, who gave his last five hundred pounds to a swindler and spent three years as a cowhand with the Muskatine Cattle Company before he'd saved enough to start his own ranch.

It's after I finish this story that Hugh asks 'Would you go back?' I say *yes, one day*, although I've never really thought about it. Hilda is in the window seat with her nose in a book but, I now realise, eavesdropping. 'She can't remember it. She left when she was three.' Which is mean of her because I never claimed to be speaking from memory. And this is when he says, 'I'd go.'

So far he has said nothing of his intentions. Mama dotes on him with the fondness a woman five years older can afford to show a future son-in-law. Hilda has been driving me mad, humming Mendelssohn's wedding march under her breath whenever she walks past us. While we can't deny it is in the air, we do our best to ignore it. It's funny: I have spent the past two years daydreaming about a man – any man – asking me to marry him, and now I'd quite happily postpone the moment. But *is* he working up to a proposal, or just making a whimsical remark? There's no way of finding out, with Hilda here. My sister and my suitor do not care for each other. Though preferable to the alternative (Hilda is a very pretty girl), this brings its own difficulties. And will bring more.

He has taken a week's leave from the prison. Usually he arranges locum work on one of the Hebridean islands, treating consumptive adolescents and liverish crofters pickled in home-distilled potato spirit. He has never spent a holiday in idleness before. He takes the precaution of packing some medical periodicals. We make gentle fun of him for arriving at a celebrated beauty spot only to bring out the latest copy of the *Journal of Mental Science*. He came here hoping for an afternoon walk, maybe an invitation to tea, but every evening we ask which would he prefer tomorrow, croquet or cycling, a picturesque church or ruined towerhouse? If it were just the two of us it might be a strain, keeping me amused for hour upon hour but, in a group of seven, it is only polite to fall into conversation with my uncle, or my aunt, whose good-natured cleverness he finds so congenial. Mama often walks alongside him, enquiring about his family, admiring his mother for bringing up six children when she found three quite exhausting. Pa is warier, but has talked with him enough to ascertain that he has a tied house and seven hundred pounds a year. Considering Hugh had not met half the party a week ago, he is remarkably at ease with us, so long as he ignores my younger sister.

The days slip by. Every so often he catches one of the

family studying him. To hell with their expectations. And yet, if I return to London and he hears word that I'm engaged to somebody else, he won't like it. On Thursday he excuses himself from the general expedition: he'll go back to Moulin and see the crusader grave in the churchyard. I offer to go with him. There's a brief pause in the conversation, as everyone weighs the advantages of privacy against the notional impropriety. We set off after lunch, on the hottest day so far in this blistering summer, cycling side by side. Wonderingly, I remark that there are at least three different heats in the day: the fiery burn of the sun on our shoulders, the thick warmth adjacent to stone walls and metalled roads, and the hot wind. When he begins to explain the physical principles at work, I interrupt him: 'I understand there's a reason, but sometimes the thing itself is enough.'

Reaching Moulin, we lean our bicycles against the church wall and inspect the flat stone carved with a sword. He can see at a glance it's no earlier than sixteenth century. He is ready to climb back on his bicycle and join the others in their hunt for wild raspberries, but I want to visit the castle where I played as a child. We pick a path through a field of brown-faced lambs as big as their mothers but still nosing for the teat, to a baking pile of stones. So much less romantic than I remember. Again he is ready to turn back, but I insist on leading him up through the oak woods, to see the famed Black Spout.

It is cool and dark here in the trees, with dazzling patches where the sun gets through, making it hard to see the loose stones and exposed roots on the parched earth path. Twice I stumble and he has to catch my arm. The climb is making me short of breath. I laugh for no reason, telling him how beautiful the wood is when the bluebells are out, drawing his attention to the lichen that looks like distemper painted on the deeply-grooved oak trunks. He lets me chatter, keeping a careful eye on the route we take,

126

not sure I will be able to find my way back, but I know exactly where I'm going. I stop a few feet from the steeply-plunging gorge. He hears the sound of rushing water but sees only the chequerboard pattern of glare and shadow. I point. He squints through the leaves, shaking his head. I say the trees have grown since I used to come here, but if we move a little nearer the edge I am sure we will have a better view. He tells me it's too dangerous, my father has entrusted me to his care, but I pay no heed. He orders me back to the path, his raised voice setting off a chaffinch's alarm call. I laugh at him. He is angry enough to think about grabbing me and dragging me back, but I'm out of his reach now. And what if he lost his footing and sent us both over?

'I see it!' I say over my shoulder. 'Oh, not so impressive as I remember. I suppose there's less water in the river. But still, it's worth seeing. Come on, it's quite safe.'

When he crosses the platform at Perth Station, he has to steel himself not to look through the gaps in the iron foot-bridge. He knows vertigo is a dysfunction of the vestibular system, but this knowledge is less potent than his fear. He would rather lose a couple of fingers than take a step towards the gorge, but what choice does he have? He needs to bring me back to the path. He can't return to the station master's cottage and tell my parents he did nothing as I fell to my death.

He arrives alongside me. Through the filtering branches, he sees the streak of white water dropping two hundred feet down sheer black rock. Brilliance and shadow swarm before his eyes. His stomach turns over.

'Hold me,' I say.

He doesn't know what I mean. He is incapable of thought, mind and body rigid. I take his hand and wrap it around my waist, then reach for the other hand, making his arms a loose belt around me and turning away from him to face the falls.

My body cants forward and he is forced to take my weight as I lean out into empty space.

He cries, '*Arabella!*'

The air in the station master's cottage is too stifling to eat inside. We drag the table into the garden and dine in the perfume of roses and honeysuckle. The trout Uncle George caught is so fresh it hardly tastes of fish. After, we eat the tiny, tart raspberries, sugared and floating in the creamy milk the dairyman brings us each morning. Tomorrow we return to Perth. The doctor has not asked for my hand. When I pulled his arms around me he was stiff as a clothes horse. He said nothing on the walk back to the church. I hoped the roaring water would rouse his passion, but instead it has turned him cold.

Dusk falls late at this time of year. Imperceptibly the clear light fades, the distinctness of every leaf and flower grows mottled. The sky is mauve at the horizon, shading into a layer like strawberry jam, then up through antique gold to a pure pale lemon that is also, mysteriously, a kind of blue. The doctor leaves us. We glance at each other, bemused. Ten minutes later, he is back with a borrowed violin. He pulls his chair away from the table and plays a plaintive air with astonishing sweetness. I never guessed he had this music in him. When he finishes the tune Aunt Nellie tries to applaud, but he plays over her, starting another. And then another, and another. Hilda retires to bed. George and Nellie follow, and Mama and Pa, until at last I am alone with him in the soft, scented dark.

When he lowers the bow, he says, 'I will never let you risk your life like that again.'

Exultation thrills through me, but I answer quietly, 'And how do you propose to stop me?'

SEVENTEEN

'I hope you haven't let him examine *you*,' Hilda drawls.

I look at her.

She shrugs, 'It has been known.'

Bill should never have told her.

She's in my room, riffling through the letters in my writing desk. At last she finds what she's looking for.

'Such a manly hand. Can I read it?' Already she has it out of the envelope.

'No!'

She puts it behind her back, out of my reach. 'Are you sure you haven't given him a little something on account?'

'He hasn't even asked.'

Telling her this is a mistake. Her cat's eyes gleam.

'Not a kiss?'

'Yes, of course.'

'Lips open or closed?'

'*It's none of your business.*' On the brow. Until this moment I didn't know it bothered me. I've seen that look in his eye, I don't doubt him, but he almost never touches me.

'He's certainly made a hit with Mama. I'm not so sure about Pa.'

'He'll come round when we give him a grandson.'

She tosses the letter at me, suddenly bored by my fiancé and what we might get up to together. 'So when's the joyous occasion?'

'December fourteenth.'

'*December?* You'd better make it sooner than that, or Mama will marry him herself.'

Now he is back at the prison, he calls on me Tuesday and Thursday evenings, and Sunday afternoons. It seems to him the proper balance. We will see each other every day soon enough. With the question settled, he keeps me in the back of his mind. It is more for my sake than his that he writes to me on the days we spend apart. Slightly stilted letters about his work, or the war's latest turn, or a meteor shower he saw last night. The last line takes him as long to compose as all the rest. *And so, good night, my dearest. Sealing this with a kiss.* He grimaces, scoring out the conventional phrases, replacing them with *Yours respectfully, Hugh.* In his mind's eye, my lips pucker in amusement. Again he strikes a line through the words.

Yours, ever the same, Hugh.

We fall into the habit of making an expedition on Sunday afternoons. Scone Palace; Drummond Castle's classical gardens; windswept Dunsinane Hill; my mother's lost family seat, Balhaldie House in Dunblane. One day we take the train to Dunning and a pony and trap to Trinity Gask church. It's a pretty spot, with its view across the fertile strath. In the tiny graveyard dark yews guard the modest, white-walled kirk. My grandfather farmed a couple of thousand acres here, as well as Balhaldie, and other pockets of land across the county. I point out the roof of Lawhill farmhouse, where my mother was born. He likes the fact that one side of my family is gentry; that they came from nothing and amassed great wealth and lost it all again in the space of a hundred years; that we are both of farming stock, and the Richmonds' luck – good and bad – is only a throw of the dice away from the Watsons'.

We are standing above the lair where my grandparents

are buried. I hope he will find it touching, their bodies lying together for eternity.

He frowns at the inscription on the polished granite stone. Donella Anna. Grandmama's name, and Mama's, and mine. 'I thought he married again?'

To Catherine Stewart Allan, a very old lady now. She lives in Birkenhead.

'Did they not agree?'

Now he has drawn my attention to it, it *is* odd that Grandmother Kate did not have him buried in a double plot in England, where she could join him one day. I shrug and say I never knew him.

He nods at the date, 1898. 'You were eight years old when he died.'

Each time he sees me I am different from the picture he holds in his head. If he could pin it down to my eyes or nose or chin he could adjust his expectations, but it's a matter of . . . innocence, for want of a better word. Like looking into a dark pool and discovering it is a puddle. He drags the unwieldy burden of his feelings towards me and finds something disconcertingly other reflected back. Yet there are things about me that please him greatly. My smallness, always holding myself very erect so I seem queenly at a distance, until my face tilts up at his. The sparkle in my eyes. That way I have of being absolutely open to him one minute, and remote the next. He is learning how to bring me back. The look, the tone of voice, that will make me yield to him. And he loves the airy, exhilarating fact that I was born in America.

He notices I am never hungry. He can't stop trying to fatten me up, bringing me fiery purple radishes, plump gooseberries, warm brown eggs. I tell him, love fills my stomach, but still he urges the fork to my lips. For a long time I tolerate it, because it seems to give him pleasure, but I don't understand.

131

If I comply, he'll have no reason to tempt me, the game will be over. Am I meant to eat, or not? Finally I tell him: *stop*.

And glimpse a side of him I have not seen before.

We are in the drawing room at Balhousie Bank. Aunt Nellie has had Agnes bring us a light supper of shortbread and cheese. A great treat. I know my uncle has had his eye on that cheddar, so I have good reason to refuse. And it's true: love has quite banished my appetite. The doctor cuts a slice of cheese, raising it to my mouth, and I have the queerest sensation, a stirring as I anticipate his fingers touching my lips and, in the same moment, violent revulsion. '*Don't*,' I hiss, mindful of Uncle in his study next door. He persists. I grab his hand in both of mine, but he's too strong for me and, dropping the cheese, he pinions my wrists in his painful grip, forcing them down into my lap, while his free hand seizes my jaw. I have a bolus of fear in my throat and, at the same time, this feeling, as if he has slit me open from breast to belly, this craving for . . . I don't know what.

Hilda walks in.

I almost laugh at the surprise on her face. Though it's no laughing matter, of course.

'Something in my eye,' I say, 'thank you, Hugh, it's gone now.'

One Sunday he asks me to tea at his house. For propriety's sake, Hilda comes too. Her eyes bulge at the nearness of the gaol. Like living under a great black cliff. The first time I saw the cell blocks, the fierce blue sky gave them a diabolical glamour. Today the sky is dirty-white. The gaol looks like a factory. And so it is, I suppose. A place to turn the raw material of crime into despair.

The doctor's house is opposite the Governor's. Smaller than the Governor's, but clean and adequately proportioned. He asks me if it will do, and I say *very well*, sliding my eyes away from Hilda's satiric look. He tells me the furniture

132

belongs to the prison. He has not bothered to make changes, having no interest in such matters. He understands women feel differently, I shall have money to replace anything I don't like. I nod, and say that's very generous, but all I can think is *please let us not live here*.

When he goes to fetch the sandwiches and scones prepared by his housekeeper, Hilda whispers 'There's still time to call it off'. For a moment, I imagine it. The scandal, and relief, and the lifelong regret at my own cowardice. I love him. If I'm the only one of my season of debutantes to be marrying into a prison, well, let it be a matter of pride. This is when the idea of helping him in his work first comes to me. Aesthetically, yes, living next to a prison is depressing, but *he* is not depressed, having a role here. Instead of fussing over swatches of wallpaper and upholstery fabric and net curtaining to veil the dreadful view, I could be of genuine use to him. It's my first lesson in wifehood: selfish unhappiness can be turned to shared joy. But my future husband does not see it that way. Prison is no place for a woman. There are women staff and inmates, I say. *And you are neither*. Hilda is watching with her cat's eyes. I pour the tea and bide my time.

He says no, but I keep asking. Is it fair to expect me to live by a gaol, virtually within its grounds, and have no notion of what goes on inside? There are prisoners in cells, he says, what more do I need to know? A tour, I suggest, so I can meet the staff and acknowledge them if we pass on the street. He doesn't want me hobnobbing with wardresses: I have no idea of the kind of people employed, some of them little better than criminals themselves. But that's just it, I say! I have no idea, and ignorance leaves me prey to worry. My days will be that much longer if I cannot picture him with my mind's eye. After a couple of weeks of this, he gives in. It's not unprecedented, the Governor's wife has been shown around. And a little knowledge now will limit the need for explanation later. What else are we going to talk about when he gets in from work?

When the day comes I dress carefully. Remembering the whistling soldiers around the patriotic barrow, I take no chances, choosing my longest skirt and a shirt from the days when the suffragettes had us all dressing like men. Hugh seems startled by my appearance but, when I enquire, says I look perfectly suitable. The gatehouse reminds me of a cardboard fort of Gordon's I coveted when we were children. The guard eyes me suspiciously. Hugh takes out a heavy ring of keys, explaining that every door must be unlocked and locked behind us again. It seems nothing to cross from freedom to captivity, a single step, but as the iron-clad door slams shut behind me, a weight presses on the back of my neck. I watch the grim set of Hugh's lips as he turns each key. First anticlockwise. The rusty clicking of the tumblers, the grating sound of metal dragged across stone, that awful echoing *clang* as the door slams shut again. Then the clockwise turn. There is violence in this sequence, the brute force of the men held in the gaol, and the equal and opposite force required to constrain them. It excites me, but frightens me too. The inner yard is completely deserted. We cross the stone flags, skirting a black octagonal tower, its lancet-shaped recesses holding not glass, but stone. I wonder if the prisoners are watching us from the cell block windows. A pain, at once dull and precise, declares itself behind my eyes. In through a locked door, across a corridor, and out to an empty yard marked with three concentric circular paths. Mowed grass. Queer little wooden sentry boxes for the guards. Walls within walls: the inner topped with metal spikes to keep the inmates away from the perimeter. The weight on my neck spreads to my shoulders. My eyes ache. If only I could sit down . . .

He tells me this is one of two exercise yards. Each prisoner is entitled to thirty minutes a day. At the appointed hour, eighty-eight inmates walk round and round these paths, exactly nine feet apart, hands behind their backs, pacing and stopping at the barked command of the guards. How desolate it is. I look up at the leaden clouds, so hot and still. In the distance, a roll of thunder. Hugh looks at me with the same startled expression he wore when I arrived, then says it's going to rain, we should go inside. More unlocking and locking. More creaking and scraping. However unfair it is to expect him to be conscious of an activity he performs fifty, sixty, times a day, his automatic gestures disturb me. For the first time, I consider the obvious fact that he must be hated by the men locked up in here.

It is cooler in the block. Stone corridors run off the lobby in three directions, each sealed by a barred gate. There is a roof over our heads, yet it feels more like outside than inside. As if whoever built this place had tried to get rid of every sentimental association with shelter.

'What's that?' I point through the window at a two-storey building.

'The women's hospital,' he says.

Carbolic mingles with a smell of damp, and something more disgustingly animal. He won't expose me to contagion by letting me see the patients on the ground floor, but there is an empty ward above. Climbing the stone stairs, I hear another roll of thunder, nearer now. Hugh shows me into a long room lined with unmade beds. The door clangs shut behind me. The key grinds in the lock. The pain behind my eyes throbs. A vibration high in my nose, like needing to sneeze, and yet not. Since the gatehouse we have not seen a living soul. This ward is just one more unpeopled space, but different enough to trigger the thought that we should not be shut in a room together.

I turn to find him looking at me. The pain is worse, a metal filament spearing me between the eyes. I sink down on one of the mattresses, waiting for him to ask what's wrong, am I unwell? But he just stares at me. Outside the window the sky has darkened. The approaching storm feels like two thumbs pressing on my eyeballs. The filament twists. *Lie down*, he says. But it doesn't help, the walls turn around me, my vision flares and dims. I sit up again, holding out my hand so Hugh can pull me to my feet, but he misunderstands and pushes me back down onto the bed. So ill I can hardly speak. *Lie still*, he says, his hands on my shoulders, his weight forcing me. A flash lights the shadowy room. The thunder directly after. I start to struggle. It's like drowning, his weight pushing me down, and some force in me, some buoyancy, bringing me back to the surface. Now he's lying on top of me. His eyes as blind as the windows of that tower. I say his name. His fingers buried in my hair, his lips kissing my brow and cheeks. A great thrill rips through me. My sore head, my shrieking sinuses, are nothing to this. His hot hands and fervid lips, his body hard on mine. All the old feelings awaken. The cleaving in my chest, and below. The fusing of our two bodies, moving together, the key turning, tumblers clicking . . . *Stop!* A voice in his brain. Quite clearly I hear it. At last our eyes meet. His head rears back, his weight lifting from me. He apologises. Offers a hand to help me up. On my feet again, I squeeze his fingers, whisper '*Soon*' in his ear.

He loves me.

HILDA

All day every day. They jaw about nothing else. Lilies or roses; white satin or silk; Highland or morning dress; the nineteen-fourteen Heidsieck versus the nineteen-fifteen; partridge or ptarmigan; oysters or lobster; until Hilda is ready to scream *who cares?*

'It's the most important day of your sister's life, so try not to spoil it, Hilly, will you?'

Dodo came south in late September. A brisk peck on the eyebrow from her beloved at the railway station? Or did he shake her hand? Two and a half months is no time at all to arrange a society wedding, m'dear. The guest list stands at three hundred and fifty, and rising. The extended Atkins and Richmond clans, all the debs Dodo came out with, and their families, and the matrons from Mama's season (but not the spinsters: too depressing), and Pa's business chums, and Gordon's Cambridge pals who are home on leave, and the *people we know* in Devon, and anyone the Doc cares to invite, of course. Some third parties (Hilda, for one) might find all this expense rather bad taste in the middle of a war. Which just goes to show how wrong a girl can be: holding a really splendid wedding is the *least* we can do to lift everyone's spirits at this dreadful time. And it's hardly your sister's fault that she has fallen in love when the Kaiser's being so beastly. After which the conversation reverts to corsages, cake recipes, court trains, and trinkets for the bridesmaids.

Still, they're back in London until the New Year.

Uncle George will do the honours in Saint Cuthbert's, a

137

cod-Medieval cod-cathedral with compound pillars and cherubs and stations of the cross and every shade of veined marble, and the most hideous artsy-craftsy copper lectern, and a clock on the wall just like a railway station! It doesn't seem to have occurred to anyone (except Hilda) that all this Anglo-Catholic, smells-and-bells palaver might not be to the taste of a Kirk-christened farmer's son.

The bridegroom arrives with Aunt Nellie a week before the wedding and is given a scratcher in Earls Court Square, while Dodo is stowed round the corner at Mrs Curtice's private hotel (because heaven forfend they should spend a night under the same roof before being chained in matrimony). The Doc happens to be bunked across the hall from Hilda, so of course she's going to make the effort of getting to know her future brother-in-law.

He pretends not to hear at first, but she knows he can't be kipping, he's only just turned in. She taps again, soft but persistent, ready to continue for as long as it takes. The door opens a crack. You should see his eyes pop at her nightie, though only a couple of buttons are undone. He's quite the buck in his shirtsleeves. There's some tedious argy-bargy about the lateness of the hour and won't-it-wait-till-morning, but in the end: open sesame.

She stalks the room, peering out of the window to see what sort of view he has, fingering his hairbrushes (wood, not silver-backed), unscrewing and sniffing his bottle of bay rum, opening his top drawer and finding – crikey! – the most enormous sporran she has ever seen. It weighs an absolute ton when she puts it on over her nightie. Though she can see he's not happy, he raises no objection, the spoilsport. She says they should get better acquainted. There's been no time today, and it'll be twice as frantic tomorrow. He must be simply done in, poor him, padding the hoof round London from Earls Court to Kensington to Regent Street and back. She has noticed no one asks *his* opinion about the arrangements. The guests

138

getting blotto on all that pricey fizz, and him a bun-strangler. He smiles to himself in a way Hilda finds most discourteous. As if he knows her game, when she doesn't have a game, or rather, she has several, and she hasn't yet decided which to play. There's the game where he thinks she's trying to seduce him, and she tells him he couldn't be more wrong. And the game where he admits to the collywobbles – or even to second thoughts – and she tells Dodo. And a similar game where she doesn't tell because they become fast friends, and Dodo never guesses that Hilda's is the invisible steadying hand on her marriage. And the game where he tries to kiss her and she shoves him away and remains coldly aloof ever after, and Dodo never knows why.

He tells her he's glad not to be running the show. And your kin, she says: how do they feel about bending the knee at a nuptial mass? Two of his brothers are fighting in Turkey. The rest of the family is needed on the farm, and the school can't spare his teacher-cousin Jeannie for the three days she would have to be away from Glasgow, so his only guests will be a couple of retired schoolma'ams, a poobah from the prisons hierarchy and one Professor Browning, at whose name he seems to think Hilda should bow down in awe. *Four guests*. Hilda surprises herself by taking the hump. What on earth will people think? Does Mama know? She must have had an absolute fit. And now the penny drops: he's a Russian vine, a fast climber, and he doesn't want the peasants dragging at his roots. Won't his chums in Perth hold it against Dodo – he does *have* chums, doesn't he? How's he going to keep her entertained in that dead-and-alive hole? She can't spend every afternoon with Aunt Nellie. He's going to have to get himself promoted toot sweet, engineer a move to fashionable Edinburgh. She closes in, walking her fingers up his shirt front: Dodo may worship the ground he treads on at the minute, but bored wives have a habit of looking elsewhere for amusement.

139

Or won't he mind that, if he's going into the thing quite heart-whole?

He turns away from her and opens the door. Very rudely. But she smiles and wishes him a gracious goodnight.

Hilda has never known Dodo so dizzily distrait, but even the bride-to-be notices that relations between her fiancé and her sister have cooled. And they were pretty tepid to begin with. The next afternoon, between ordering the hothouse roses and rehearsing the page, she draws Hilda aside. 'You haven't been telling tales, have you?' What tales, Hilda would like to know? 'It's not funny, Hilly.' Ah, but it is. So funny that Hilda wouldn't dream of spoiling the jest too early. Not that she has positively decided to tell him, but she may allow herself some delphic hinting when Dodo is around.

The day dawns, shiversome but bright. The groom, Uncle George, Aunt Nellie, Pa and Hilda have brekkers in the little morning room on the ground floor, so the servants can rig up the wedding feast. Everything else has been done. It feels positively skivey, sitting here with no tasks to discuss. Mama has disappeared to Mrs Curtice's to steady Dodo's nerves. Hilda has been warned to steer clear. 'Keeping a lookout for Gordon' is the preferred euphemism. The Engineers have given him a five-day pass. The Doc takes another slice of toast. Aunt Nellie passes the marmalade. No one can think of anything to say. 'The lull before the storm,' Uncle George intones, which only makes the silence more deadly. The door-bell rings. A maid patters down the hall.

'I say, is this the wedding party?'

'Is that Argemone?' Aunt Nellie asks, while Hilda shrieks '*Billy!*' And after that she has the most whizzing time. Billy takes her up to dress in her moss-green velvet, and tells her about the Front, and the wounded Tommies always ready with a quip, and the awkward Frenchies, and the Fritz who was so bamboozled by the shelling he didn't know he'd walked into

140

the enemy's camp, and how the Major was going to shoot him as a spy until Billy talked some sense into him. Hilda is laughing so much she doesn't hear Aunt Nellie tapping at the door, so Pa marches upstairs to bellow that if they hang about for one more minute they're going to be late.

When they take their pew, Billy whispers 'Splendiferous, eh?' and Hilda can only agree. The resiny scent from the ever-green branches framing the door, the pillars wound with holly and ivy, the rood screen crowned with pine cone and mistletoe and hellebore, the guests glowing in shades of amethyst, sapphire, emerald, ruby. A murmur ripples through the nave and every head turns to the back of the church. The bride drifts down the aisle in her white Guinevere dress, a winter sacrifice. The Doc's eyes shine like a child's on Christmas Eve. He's quite the mythic hero, with that dagger down his sock and his barbarian's exposed knees. Uncle George seems nervous before the titled congregation, but rises to the occasion like the old limelight-hogger he is, and the choir sing the *Exultate Deo* like angels, and when the groom places his ring on the bride's white hand, even Hilda's sharp eyes blur with a tear.

Then the newlyweds are out on the pavement, being pelted with white rose petals as they climb into the car, where they're strangely silent but grinning like Cheshires. The guests toddle back to Earls Court Square for speeches and toasts and a spread that would feed five thousand. The next hour or two are lost on Hilda, she and Billy are in a world of their own, until Mama brings Grandmother Kate across and she has to submit to being quizzed about her beaux, with Billy raising a knowing eyebrow, so it's all she can do not to burst out laughing. And then – *gawd blimey, Billy* – the Doc crosses the room to shake her hand and call her sister, and it would be too rude not to introduce Argemone ffarington Bellairs, though it's obvious he disapproves. You can practically hear him thinking 'invert'. Billy's rather tickled, and drops her voice another octave as she clasps his hand and tells him he's a lucky chap, Do's a delightful gel, known her for years. So he's a doctor, is he? She has the very greatest respect for the members of his profession she has met at the Front: so tireless and resourceful and, well, *courageous*. The Doc half-suspects he's being ragged, but can't quite believe Billy would do it at his wedding. Then Grandmother Kate comes to the rescue, asking him to chum her back to her chair. And they all – well, all except the Doc – drink a lot of 'poo, and say *how d'ye do* to everyone they haven't seen since the last wedding, and at least ten people tell Hilda *you'll be next*, and Billy cocks her wicked eyebrow as Hilda replies that she might yet surprise them, and suddenly they're on their feet because the happy couple are about to depart for the hotel where Dodo will finally, irreversibly, become Mrs Hugh Ferguson Watson.

EIGHTEEN

I thought about Hugh every minute of the ten weeks we were apart before our wedding. How handsome he was, how decisive, how brusquely masculine sometimes. I liked to see him angry, knowing his fierceness turned mild with me. When Mama told him I'd been ill, and he took my pulse, I felt the desire he fought down. Banking the fire till we were wed only made it more exciting. I liked to tease him, biting my lip when I looked at him, breathing in his ear when he stooped to kiss my cheek. Thinking my shameless thoughts, waiting for him to read my mind. When his eyes burned at me from across the room it was all I could do not to groan. I wanted to offer myself like a goblet, or a banquet, have him taste all my flavours. As I longed to taste his. I couldn't understand all those Shakespearean lovers lamenting the torments, when love was all pleasure and enchantment. The songs he played, the letters he wrote, the smell of the rain that day we walked up Kinnoull hill, the rabbits we surprised, the sunset flashing gold off the monastery weathervane, the bats flickering over the river at dusk . . .

When the day comes, I think I will die from happiness. Mama forces me to swallow my porridge, unless I want to spend the first hour of married life dizzy with champagne and the next four being sick in the lavatory. She dismisses the girl and dresses me herself, as she used to when I was a baby. No one fit to hire as a nursery maid in that godforsaken country. Besides, she wanted me to know I had a living, breathing mother. Unlike her own bleak start. We're both close to tears

143

when Mrs Curtice knocks to tell us the car is waiting. 'There now,' Mama says, giving my veil a final tweak and moving away from the long glass. I hardly know myself. *Every bride is beautiful*, Hilda will say to me after the ceremony, *so where do all the ugly old wives come from?*

I know from all the hours of planning that the church is dark with evergreen and glittering with candle flame, but I see nothing and no one but Hugh, standing at the altar. The most beautiful man in London. Out-dazzling Uncle George in his gold-embroidered cope. When he turns and looks at me with his blazing eyes, my heart bursts in my chest.

Many waters cannot quench love, neither can the floods drown it.

Twelve months ago I was an old maid with fifty empty years to fill. I would develop a passion for gardening or appliqué work or visiting neolithic sites. Everyone would say how marvellous I was. Today I too can pity old maids, and compliment them on their pointless hobbies. I am married to Hugh. He is here at my side, his hand's pressure on my waist, his lips soft on my ear as he murmurs *How long before we can leave?* 'Not yet,' I smile, nestling my head into his shoulder. There are the speeches to be got through, and the toast to our life together, at which he tilts my chin and kisses me on the lips. When the hubbub resumes I send him across to Hilda, she has been monopolising Bill Bellairs for long enough. She and Hugh are brother and sister now, and must make their peace before they can progress to the sort of spiky badinage Hilda inflicts on everyone she loves. The next time I look he's in earnest conversation with Grandmother Kate, which is good of him, because she's eighty and half-deaf these days. And then he's gone. Five, ten, fifteen minutes later he is still not back. Gordon finds him on the pavement, in the dark, and I don't know what is said but my brother's face is flushed when he returns. He shakes his head. I can't go out there, everyone would look, so I beckon to Bill and, a few minutes later, she re-enters the party with a man who wears my husband's clothes but is otherwise quite unrecognisable. When I lean into him, his chest feels like stone.

'What's wrong?'

'Can you not guess?'

'No.'

'Have a wee think about it.'

Bill is back beside Hilda, the two of them laughing. What a tremendous jest. I ask Hugh for a private word in the next room. He snorts. I'm ready to weep, to fall on my knees and plead for his forgiveness, but how can I in front of three hundred and fifty guests? He says the time for explaining was before we were married, and how can I deny it, but the truth is I'm still *intacta*: I thought he'd never find out. The last hour of the wedding celebration is as miserable as the previous three have been joyous, but I have to pretend I've never been happier, smiling and raising my glass when I would like to smash it on the table and drag the jagged edge across my wrists. If that's what it would take to make him pity me. When at last we're alone in the privacy of the car, after the throwing of the bouquet and our grim-faced dash through the smiling guests, I blurt out:

'It was just girlish curiosity. I'm not like Bill Bellairs.'

For one terrible moment he looks bewildered. And then everything becomes so much worse.

What Mama reads in my tear-bloated face when I burst into her room next morning is the shocked discovery of human biology. She assures me it gets better. Perhaps she should have warned me, but she didn't want to put me off. It might all have gone swimmingly. I am twenty-six years old. I have known the ins and outs of sex for so long I have forgotten who told me. It takes a while to convince her that her fears are groundless. That their very groundlessness is what is amiss. She laughs in relief: many men suffer first-night nerves.

It's understandable, even honourable, a good omen for our future happiness. I look into her generous, loving face and understand that, among the many transformations of the past twenty-four hours, I have moved beyond reach of maternal comfort.

The plan is to honeymoon in London, showing him the Tower and the ingenious bridge next door; St Paul's and Wren's smaller, prettier churches; all the famous squares. A couple of landmarks a day, a concert and a Barrie play, and many private evenings back at the hotel. We stick to the sightseeing. Out on the busy streets, our civility seems appropriate. Surrounded by strangers, we are even affable. It is those long hours cooped up in a room together that expose the essential coldness of our marriage.

But he will not speak of his feelings. Not a word. And so I keep smiling, keep touching him and watching his face freeze, telling myself it will pass, it's as my mother said, he has lived a celibate life for so long, he respects me too much, I just have to wait until he gets used to me. Until he can accept that a single sapphic indiscretion does not mean he has married a tart.

The Strand, Pall Mall, Piccadilly: these famous streets. He says he can think of a dozen thoroughfares in Edinburgh and Glasgow their equal in grandeur, but secretly he is thrilled. Like stepping into the pages of a book. Everything more vivid: sounds, sights, smells, the rich women's clothes, the brown leaves big as dinner plates shed by the plane trees. He searches the faces walking towards him, as if the thing he has longed for is about to happen. Now. Or *now*. A tall woman with luminous skin, a mass of dark hair, those succulent lips. Their eyes will lock. And then she will notice the woman at his side.

Every night he retires to the daybed in our dressing room. Every morning I try to greet him with a kiss. The way he looks at me will never leave me. The bitterness in his silence. What's the matter with me, do I want to force him to the needless cruelty of spelling it out? He will honour his obligations, support me, live under the same roof, but we will never share a bed. Why can I not accept it? Why must I smile at him like this, and stand so close, and touch his clothes? If it is not stupidity – and I am not a stupid lassie – then it is stubbornness, wilful misunderstanding. I have tricked him into marriage – what else? I have only myself to blame, but still he might find it in himself to pity me, if only I would submit.

On the third morning I take him into the fenced gardens across the street, slipping my arm through his. No one else in sight. He is trapped by our seclusion, and his simultaneous awareness of being overlooked by at least a hundred windows. I pass some innocuous remark about the day – cold, leafless, with that ceaseless train and traffic noise he hears even in his sleep – then, after a few seconds punctuated by the clip of my heels on the path, I say his name. Sensing his impulse to draw away, my arm tightens on his. I want to know if there's anything I can do to make amends. I realise the triviality of my fault is not the point. I hid it from him, and I am so, so sorry. I know I must work to regain his trust. I understand that he feels estranged from me. I respect his refusal to make light of what has happened. However painful this is to me, I see it as an investment in our marriage. And a lesson. I will never lie to him again, even by omission. We will emerge from our present difficulties with a strengthened affection and, on that day, we will know the happiness my foolishness presently denies us. A wave of heat comes off him. He wrenches out of my grasp. In a trembling voice, I ask where he is going? Back to Scotland, he says. The honeymoon is over.

NINETEEN

Perth in December. Day has hardly dawned before the light is ebbing. I'm out of doors by ten, whatever the weather. 'Getting to know the town.' A mostly profitless trip to the butcher's. Assuaging my loneliness by smiling at mothers out with their children, who stare back at me with wondering eyes. I could gain some acknowledgement on the North Inch, but word would soon spread that the doctor's new wife is making eyes at soldiers, so I make do with patting dogs and stroking cats, if I find them; watching blackbirds pulling worms from the vegetable beds. Walking for miles. I'll need new shoes before long. An excuse to visit the shops and talk to a saleswoman. By half past four I'm feeling my way along walls in the blackout. Home to the prison.

Aunt Nellie says I must get involved with a charitable committee or two. I agree, before changing the subject. How can I enter a room, discuss the welfare of the needy, when I'm drowning in self-pity, when it's all I can do not to burst into tears? And sometimes it is fury that keeps out the cold when I'm walking. How dare he pretend he loved me? I would not treat my worst enemy as he treats me now, so coldly polite. I have tried to broach the subject, steeling myself against humiliation, asking him if he would rather I had loved a man, if it is giving my body to a woman that so revolts him? He turns and leaves the room. When I follow him he asks, have I no self-respect?

I can't stand another silent meal. The tick of the clock. The clink of cutlery on plate. The hurricane roar of my own breath in my ears. Is this it, for the next fifty years? Yet it is worse having to smile and chatter and pretend on Christmas Day. Uncle George admires Hugh. They have been to concerts together at the City Hall. They retire into Uncle's study to discuss the war. Before lunch, Aunt Nellie drew him aside to ask his advice about the Sick Poor Nursing Society. They know nothing of our troubles, but still I feel my own relatives have turned against me.

With January comes the snow. A thaw, then a long hard freeze. The streets are like glass. Impassable. Through the window I glimpse Mrs Grant, the Governor's wife, collecting a pail of snow. My own taps are still running. Although never formally introduced, we have nodded to each other in passing. Her maid-of-all-work is laid up in Luncarty with a broken ankle. She won't hear of borrowing Mrs Hendry, but consents to a cup of tea, so long as we agree not to tell our husbands. She gives me a conspiratorial grin I am sorry to be too clueless to return. A nice woman, even if she smells of Parma violets. Over the next two years, she will prove a good friend to me. And a mine of information.

February brings two developments. A Peterhead prisoner, John Maclean, is transferred to the gaol, and my husband starts talking to me.

The new convict is a Glaswegian firebrand, a self-styled revolutionary Socialist sentenced for making speeches against conscription. He has many followers, and not just in Scotland. Convinced the prison is drugging his food, he refuses to eat. The government is anxious that he remain in good health. It seems Hugh is a specialist in treating those who starve themselves. Without the intelligence passed on by my secret friend Mrs Grant, I might have suspected him of infidelity. His colour is better, his eyes bright. One morning, passing the bathroom door, I hear him whistling in there.

*

149

Maclean is a potato-faced fellow with a shrewdly-assessing gaze. Highland stock. Thirty-seven years old, five years the doctor's junior, quite apart from his status as convict and his ignorance of medicine, and yet he shows no deference. He addresses everyone – doctor, warders, Prison Commission officials – as his equal, socially and intellectually. The warders don't like it.

'You know why you're here?' the doctor asks him.

'A police officer lied.'

'Why you're here *in Perth*.'

'I caught them tampering with my food in Peterhead.'

'Why should they do that?'

'To discredit me.'

'So the police lie about you, and the warders contaminate your food?'

'And you will certify me mad.'

'For what reason?'

'Because your imperial masters don't like me speaking against their war.'

'I thought the police lied.'

'They lied in the particulars. The law requires exactitude to masquerade as just. I oppose the war, like anyone with a head on his shoulders.'

'You don't think we should honour our treaties and alliances?'

'Use your brains, man. Who is this *we*? Not you, not me. If the workers withdraw their labour in protest, they're forced to work as soldiers. What does that tell you?'

'That resistance is futile.'

'The game's rigged against us. Capitalism is rotten to its foundations. I see it. They see it. That's why they put alcohol in my food.'

'And I'm a part of this conspiracy?'

'They don't have to take you into their confidence. You do their bidding, no questions asked.'

150

'You're very sure of me, on less than an hour's acquaintance.'

'I know you inside out. A yeoman with an education. A class traitor who thinks he's bettered himself. They're laughing at you, man.'

'They tell me you lost your job as a teacher.'

'I'm a teacher with or without their job.'

'You made allegations against your headmaster. An enquiry found them baseless.'

'He's bedding her. An infant teacher sharing the duties of a dominie? It's wrong, and they know it. So they cover it up, like every other abuse of power in the system.'

'The warders say you masturbate several times a day.'

'Tell your peeping toms to mind their own business.'

'It's making you irritable, suspicious, prone to delusions.'

'So that's to be your diagnosis, is it: I'm a sex maniac?'

'You'd be happier if you abstained.'

'Would I?'

'You lost a stone in Peterhead, you can't afford to lose more.'

'I can't afford to let this place turn me into a gelding—'

So far the prisoner's gaze has been fixed on the doctor's face. Now it loses focus. He is thinking.

'—It's a fair question: why turn inwards, to your own pleasure? Are the women the same? Don't tell me you don't know. It's natural to dwell on what you're deprived of, I suppose. But there's more to it. Power. One will forced on another. Disgusting – but exciting too, eh: refusing every decent human impulse? Oh aye, the Devil has some good tunes. Not so good for me, on the other end of it. My body's no choice in the matter, but my mind's still free. I can put myself in your skin, the same as you can put yourself in mine.' An amused breath. 'Aye. I see it in your face. Oh you're ashamed, but you know what I'm talking about. We're two sides of the one coin, you and I. What do you do with it, take it home to your wife?'

'You go too far.'

'Or maybe one of the wardresses, eh?'

I remark to my husband that he seems more animated these days. Is he enjoying his work? He replies that he is not paid to enjoy himself. A difficult case has been placed in his hands. A dangerous man? Not a murderer, but yes, dangerous to our country and its security. He will require treatment for some considerable time, but there is reason to think he can be cured.

And so our silent dinners come to an end. Two months of misery is over because my husband wants someone to boast to. Not that I'm not grateful. The battle of wits between doctor and prisoner is interesting. There's the new light it casts on my husband's character, the vanity I hear when he speaks of his notorious patient, the superior tone, and yet the trace of admiration. Feeling some sympathy for this schoolteacher with whose intimate habits I am so fully acquainted, I ask my husband, is onanism always unhealthy? Surely all men indulge before marriage. Surely Hugh does still.

The look on his face frightens me.

'I mean, since we don't . . .'

'The last thing the world needs is another idiot child.'

The mystery begins to unravel. Bill and Hilda are blameless. It is Grandmother Kate I have to thank for the misery of my wedding night. What he tells me – eventually – is so grotesque, it can only be an old woman's fantasy. So I write to my mother, the most embarrassing letter I will ever have to compose. Her reply is curt, no less embarrassed. I am to speak to Aunt Nellie.

Nellie is delighted to see me. George is out visiting his parishioners. She receives me in the drawing room, seats me in the wing-backed chair, tells Aggie to bring the leftover Christmas cake with our tea. Am I quite comfortable? A cushion for my back?

152

She thinks I have come to break the news that I am pregnant.

Just for a moment, I am tempted to tell her everything. To be pitied and petted in my comfortable chair, knowing she will confide in Uncle George and that, after much discussion, they will feel duty bound to tell Pa and Mama. And then what? I am a grown woman. I chose him of my own free will. I can't be the only wife in the world who did not get what she bargained for. So I put a decent face on it: my husband's very natural concern, after speaking to Grandmother Kate. He has some experience of asylums and the wide variety of circumstances that lead men to be admitted as patients, no one is better placed to understand, but he must know the full facts of the case.

Auntie's eyes fly everywhere but my face. There is nothing she can tell me that Dot does not know. But Mama is down in England, I say; perhaps it is not a matter to be imparted in a letter? This seems to strike home. She bites her lip and quits the room, to return a couple of minutes later, having given Aggie instructions that we are not to be disturbed. Sitting down again, she takes out a handkerchief and rubs at some insignificant mark on her skirt. I catch her eye. She sighs, 'I only went there once.'

Haltingly at first, she tells me the whole story.

The asylum is set in a hundred acres of parkland. A plain old crowstep-gabled house, shouldered – bullied, it seems to twenty-four-year-old Nellie – by newer wings, so the whole is an ugly agglomeration of cliff-like walls topped by gables and turrets. The Superintendent seems to think this ugliness can be disguised with a profusion of rhododendrons. He is a great believer in the morally elevating properties of fresh air. There are two secure courts where the inmates play bowls and shuttlecock, and walk about, and garden. When it rains, they take carriage drives through the grounds, safe from the inquisitive gazes of strangers. He prescribes an excursion a week for his melancholics, the speed quite restoring their animal spirits. Of course, cases of mania like Mr Richmond's require more protracted moral treatment. Uncle John returns a curt nod, the way he does when the seedsmen try to haggle with him in front of his nieces. He's of the old school, holding that women should not be sullied by talk of business, but the fact remains: the sweeping lawns, the strident blooms, the comfort and elegance demanded by patients of higher ranks, all these have to be paid for.

It is 1888.

Nellie wonders how many visits it takes to achieve the indifference her uncle shows to his surroundings. She has eyes for everything. The ornate ceilings and gleaming floorboards, the damask and brocatelle and button-backed upholstery, all these empty chairs. Where is everybody? Shivering in the airing courts? Locked away in their rooms? The silence is eerie. But now, as they climb the great staircase, she hears a noise, a sort of lowing, as if the Superintendent has stalled his cattle on one of the gracious upper floors. She feels a tug and looks down to find that her sister, Dot (who will become my Mama) has grabbed a fistful of her skirt and is holding on for dear life. A maid in drab approaches with a mop and metal pail. Her eyes dart to the Superintendent's and some wordless communication passes between them.

The Superintendent knocks twice and a bold-faced man of about Nellie's age appears in the crack between door and jamb. When he sees the Superintendent, the boldness turns to deference. The door swings wide. A hunched figure is sitting by the window. Nellie takes in his sunken eyes, the yellowish skin stretched over his hollow cheeks. His frock coat seems cut for a bigger man. The hands protruding from its sleeves are skin and bone. So changed! Yet how could he not be, in this place?

What choice does she have but to advance into the room, crossing the polished boards to sit on the Chesterfield beside

154

him? He recoils from her nearness, shuffling his skeletal frame into the sofa's padded arm. They remain like that, side by side, Nellie regarding his profile while he stares straight ahead. It is only now that she notices a man of about fifty sitting in an armchair on the far side of the room. His distinguished leonine head is quite grey, but still recognisable. A flush sears her chest, spreading up over her neck and face, as she rises and makes her way towards him.

Dot gets there first, flinging her arms around his neck. '*Papa!*'

A lump forms in Nellie's throat at the unforced joy in her sister's cry. She is his little *Prinzessen* again, as if the past eight years were a horrid dream, and now she has awoken to a view of mountains and a breakfast of *brioche* and *Schokolade*. How is it that Nellie remembers so perfectly the way Dot used to behave with him? She too must have taken a habitual tone, smiling in a particular way, but for the life of her she cannot retrieve them.

The door opens and a third man comes in, a fidgety fellow in an extravagant Paisley coat whose teeming threads coil like her own anxious thoughts. How does it feel to be mad, she wonders? Is it quite senseless, like a child's scribble when he first holds the pencil? Or is there some pattern to it, a thread of meaning in the maze, until the eye blinks and the attention fails, twisting away into another looping path?

Ask anyone who knows Nellie and they will describe the serious young woman who took over the mothering of her sister so capably after they returned to Scotland. But there is also this other, whose sympathy is a form of pride, a refusal to be shut out from the world's distress. Her eyes lift from the mesmerising Paisley to the face above. No hair at all on the crown of his head, but great woolly clumps around his ears. His hands move busily, the pad of each thumb rubbing over and over his fingertips.

'Your waist is thicker,' he says in a reedy voice, 'your nose longer, you lack her fresh colour, yet the family resemblance is strong. How unfortunate that she should be so fair and you so plain.'

Tears of shame prick Nellie's eyes. At the same time, there is a curious balm in hearing spoken aloud what everyone sees and no one can say.

'I am as God made me.'

The Superintendent will not let this answer stand, but must rebuke his patient, quoting the house rule that those who cannot behave as society expects will forfeit the benefits of society. The attendant ushers the man away. And yet if anyone's manners are at fault, it is the Superintendent's. When is *he* going to withdraw? He seems to think they have come all the way to Edinburgh to see him and his marvellous establishment. What do they care about the second parlour on this floor, the billiard tables, baths and douche, day room and gallery? On and on he boasts. His asylum is run according to the most enlightened principles. Trained nurses and ladies of the educated classes are employed to exert a calming influence on the more excitable inmates. Seclusion and restraint are seldom used, and only as a last resort. Kindness is the method, and congenial society. He and Matron go to great lengths to ensure that the gentlemen sharing each set of apartments are of complementary tastes and habits. Uncle John gives another discouraging nod. Nellie wonders what Papa might have in common with a tactless popinjay and a breathing corpse.

Now her embarrassment has subsided, she finds the courage to study him. He seems well. If anything, a little fatter than she remembers. His complexion is clear, but his face has undergone a change, as if some invisible servant had draped a dust sheet over his features. He never used to have those flaps of skin over his eyelids, that sagging jawline and bull-frog throat. He meets her gaze and she notices a peculiarity in one – or both – of his eyes, the pupils of different sizes.

'Hello old girl.'

'Hello Papa,' she says.

'Have you brought Mrs Richmond?'

'No, Papa.'

He smiles, as if she were ever forgetful. 'Next time.'

Does he not remember what happened eight years ago?

As far back as she can recall, he was scared of the dark. When her mother was alive Lawhill was ablaze with lights. Even the cowshed. Pails of water everywhere in case the straw caught fire. In the kirk on Sundays he prayed without closing his eyes. Her mother used to say he even slept with one eye open. But her mother died, giving birth to Dot, the daughter who bears her name. Papa had the joiner cut two holes in the coffin lid so she could see out. What was that but madness? Tom disagreed: how could he court Kate Allan so soon after, and marry her, and father three sons with her? No woman marries a madman, even if she is thirty-five. It was grief that had him shouldering the turf-cutters aside that awful day, grief that had him down in the clay trench clawing at the coffin. And perhaps it was. But Nellie was the one who sat by his bedside nine years later, after Doctor Balsiger had given him laudanum. She heard him sobbing in his sleep, begging Grandma Richmond to unlock the cupboard door.

What he loved best about Switzerland was being bathed in white light. Even at midnight, the mountains reflected the moon. The high passes held no fear for him. If he wasn't drinking Kirschwasser in the Wirtshaus or buying trifles for Dot, he was walking in the snow. They would see other hikers in low-brimmed hats, and even tinted spectacles, to shield them from the glare. But not Papa. No one was worried the day he was late back. They dined without him. Nellie was just finishing her soup when there was a commotion outside the window. The Belgians at the next table left their plates to look. Papa was being led through the hotel gardens, weeping, stumbling, turning his head frantically this way and that.

157

The physician had treated many cases of snow blindness. Papa cursed and fought when they bandaged his eyes, so they bound his wrists and his thrashing legs. You could hear him all over the hotel. That first night, his wife kept watch. He begged and begged her to loosen the binding that was chafing his wrists. Nellie will never forget being dragged out of sleep by her stepmother's screams. The marks showed on Mrs Richmond's neck for days.

Among the hotel guests was an alienist travelling with his wife and sons, a conscientious Austrian who spoke heavily-accented English in a low, measured voice. Nothing surprised him. Was that why Nellie answered his questions so fully? Mrs Richmond blamed her, even when she'd found a way of turning the situation to advantage, but Nellie only told the truth.

Not that Papa seems so very mad today. If anything, he's too calm, lacking that mischievous spirit Nellie remembers, his way of turning the most humdrum activity into a game. Dot loved this in him. She was never disconcerted by his exuberance. And in return, he let her take liberties Nellie would never have been permitted. Riffling through his pockets. Playing with his moustaches. Even now, perched on the arm of his chair, she holds his big Richmond paw between her small hands. From time to time she strokes it, like a kitten.

'Nellie is to be married, Papa,' she says.

And all at once Nellie grasps what her younger sister seems to have understood all along. They are here to seek his blessing on her happiness. To launch her on the long voyage of the rest of her life.

Papa's face brightens with amusement. 'Who's the lucky fellow?'

Just what he would have said in the old days. A great weight of dread lifts from Nellie's shoulders.

'George Farquhar.' She hears herself omitting the middle names Georgie sets such store by, and for a moment she glimpses the life that might have been. Georgie taking tea at Lawhill. And later, Papa mocking the nervous swipe of his tongue over his dry lips. Remarking that most men use two names, or three if their mothers are well-born, but he has never met a fellow so grand he needs *four* just to say how d'ye do. She explains to Papa that, since Willie Farquhar is set to inherit Pitscandly, Georgie has entered the Episcopalian church. She would like to say more, about the strange workings of fate, how if her stepmother had not reinvented herself as a Piscie, she and Georgie would never have met. But the less said about Mrs Richmond the better.

'Are you wanting me to give you away?'

The question catches her off guard. In truth, this is the last thing she wants. Papa in the cathedral. Praying open-eyed. Winking at Lady Cheyne.

'I'm afraid it's out of the question, old girl,' he says, when dismay is already written across her features.

Out of the corner of her eye, she sees a smirk visit the Superintendent's face.

'Why?' she asks.

The Superintendent starts to speak.

'I would rather hear from Papa,' she says.

'I might catch a chill. The sneeze is a dangerous uncontrollable urge. Many men have been sent mad with sneezing.'

Dot laughs and Nellie understands that Papa is teasing.

'I have not suffered a violent paroxysm for eleven months now,' he adds. In earnest, as far as she can tell.

'You're recovered?'

Papa looks at the Superintendent.

'He has benefited from our regimen and the quietness of his surroundings.'

Papa says to Dot, 'It was the stitching that cured me.'

'Stitching, Papa?' She was never happier than when being the foil to his jokes.

159

'If we rend our garments in our despairing passion, we're obliged to sew them back together again.'

Even Dot can't find this funny.

'Do people really tear their clothes?'

'To shreds sometimes.'

A silence falls.

The offer is not Nellie's to make, or not hers alone, but still she says 'Come home, Papa. We'll look after you. You can live as quietly as you please, among people who love you.'

The Superintendent coughs, 'I could not in conscience sanction that.'

Papa's cheeks redden, his mismatched eyes grow bright. 'Live with you and your Georgie Porgie?'

'Or with Dot, if you prefer.'

He smiles. 'With Donella.'

'Near Uncle John,' Dot says, 'in Brickhall.'

'And what about my wife?'

'Mrs Richmond lives in England now.'

But the words taste bitter in Nellie's mouth. Is this what madness is: being lied to by those who lay claim to sanity?

'And she may not wish to see you.'

The bony, yellow-skinned man on the Chesterfield looks up at the ceiling. Dot follows his glance. Nellie looks to Uncle John, but he's half-deaf from forty autumns on the grouse moors. Again it comes. The lowing they heard on the stairs. A human herd, moved by a single impulse. Excitement? Discontent? Or just a bovine urge to make noise? It seems even stranger to her now, more terrible: the thought of Papa sharing a house with men who moo like beasts.

The Superintendent excuses himself.

'What *is* that?' Dot asks.

Papa touches a forefinger to his lips, waiting until the door closes behind the Superintendent. 'Poor tormented souls,' he says.

Nellie wonders if living with so many lunatics has shocked

160

the madness out of Papa. Or was he never properly mad? If snow can make a man blind for a week, why should it not scramble his wits temporarily? And there was the Kirschwasser, of course. Why was everyone so sure of his insanity? She is afraid she knows the answer. Mrs Richmond saw a way of saving her sons' inheritance before there was nothing left. Tom wanted to go back to Scotland. Nellie was tired of standing in the shadow of her younger sister. And the alienist had spent so long among the mentally bereaved, he saw madness everywhere.

'It's time to light the lamps,' the bony man announces in a fluting Highlander's voice.

They all turn towards the window. A layer of cloud has blotted out the afternoon sun, but dusk is still hours away. The man rises from his seat and stamps across the wooden floor. Nellie's chair trembles. A vase of yellow irises rattles on a table. Reaching the door, he raises a fist and hammers on one of the panels.

Nellie comes to his aid, trying the handle. The door opens.

'Go away,' he says, pushing it shut and resuming his knocking.

Papa winks. 'Andrew has no intention of going out. He wishes Jacob to come *in*.'

There's no point trying to conduct a conversation over this bombardment. They must sit and wait until the attendant arrives with a burning spill. Andrew stamps after him, around the room, but offers no assistance with the tricky business of removing the glass shades while protecting the flame from draughts. The creamy radiance inside each globe makes little impression on the daylit room, but Andrew seems the easier for it.

Loudly enough for Nellie to hear, Dot whispers 'Why does he stamp like that?'

'Andrew? He was driven mad by love.'

Dot frowns and Nellie knows she is thinking of Norman

161

Atkins and what he would have to do, how far he would have to go, to separate her from her wits.

'It is common enough in this place,' Papa says, 'though not so common as those sent mad with grief. Men *and* women. Otherwise we keep to our separate maladies. Women go mad with birthing, and praying, and looking in the glass. Men with dissipation, or being swindled. Or with pride, or the shaking sickness, or sunstroke, or self-hate, or sitting hour after hour without moving, or moving too excitedly.'

'Or with drunkenness,' Nellie says.

Papa nods. 'It's carried in the blood.'

Nellie's dread returns.

Dot too looks stricken. 'But we're not mad, Papa.'

He seems to search her face for corroboration. 'I thank God for it,' he says at last.

Dot is looking at Nellie. She is the elder sister. It's her duty to ask the uncomfortable question.

'Are you saying your madness waited within you all the years you were well?'

'So they tell me, old girl.'

The attendant brings his lighted spill to the lamp by Papa's elbow.

'*Fiat lux,*' Papa says.

Nellie would not dream of lighting a lamp before seven o'clock in late spring. It is a question of not wasting God's good gifts. And Uncle John might think the less of her – Uncle John, who has said and done nothing since they arrived, unless she counts studying his boots. He, too, had reason to wish an end to his brother's spendthrift ways. Silk waistcoats and neckties. Jewelled stick pins. Kid gloves so soft they made her shiver. To Papa these were necessities. It occurs to Nellie that the asylum, with its Rococo sideboards and gilt-framed panoramas, its Ormolu clocks and Persian rugs, is perfectly suited to his tastes.

'Are you happy here, Papa?'

'Of course.'

'You don't feel imprisoned?'

'No more than any spy,' he says in such a reasonable tone that her mind flails like a landed fish, trying to find the sense in his words.

'Why spy, Papa?'

He leans forward confidentially, 'They've not told you?'

She shakes her head.

Again he brings a forefinger to his lips, 'I'm here in disguise, to ascertain how these pour souls are treated—'

She looks at him, fascinated, appalled.

'—We care for all our subjects. Even lunatics.' His lower lip shines wetly through his mutton-chop moustaches. 'The Queen sent me here on a special commission.'

'No, Papa,' she says gently.

'My wife, the Empress Victoria.'

Dot giggles, but Nellie does not think he is joking. And neither does Dot, deep down.

'You're still married to Kate Richmond, Papa.'

'Oh yes. Her too—'

Uncle John heaves a sigh as if wearily familiar with this line of talk.

'—I have five hundred wives.'

'*Papa.*' Dot shoogles his hand as if to shake some sense into it.

'Don't be jealous, Donella,' Papa says, kissing her full on the mouth.

TWENTY

Syphilis.

That is why he won't lie with me. He believes I have inherited my grandfather's taint. That if we coupled I would pass it on to him, and our child would be a cretin. His heartless silence has been husbandly discretion, protecting me from his terrible knowledge. The price of my innocence was to be his lifelong burden: I would never need to know, so long as I posed no danger to others, so long as he kept me chaste. But he is not equal to the task. He cannot watch me every hour of the day. Already I have tried to conceal my friendship with the Governor's wife. And so it is better that I know.

My God, I say.

He presses my head into his chest.

It's overwhelming. The shock. The grief. Being held in my husband's arms. The smell of him. My complete misunderstanding of every day for the past two months. Not sadism but compassion. How my bitter thoughts have wronged him.

At the same time I'm thinking, he never met my grandfather. How does he know for sure? A second-hand description of a man's eyes and he relinquishes all his hopes. His hopes and mine. What gives him the right to decide? I'm not a child. My judgement is as sound as his, and I don't believe it. I am not a carrier of disease. This crisis is a convenient conduit for his anger. Why he should be angry I don't know, but I feel it, even as he seems to comfort me.

When I question his diagnosis, his arms drop to his sides. It's not just the disparity between my grandfather's pupils.

His grandiose delusions, the ingenious reasoning to explain his presence in an asylum, his companion's stamping gait, the Superintendent's policy of lodging like with like: it all points in the one direction. He reminds me that syphilis is his specialism. There are only a handful of people in the country whose knowledge equals his. But if I will not take his expertise on trust, if I wish to know beyond doubt, there is a test. He can do it here, at home. All he requires is a blood sample.

No. I won't take his test. His jaw grits as always when I defy him. For a moment I think he might try to force me. But then his lips crimp in that sadder-but-wiser half-smile. And this time I don't beg his forgiveness, or rack my brains for some way of regaining his favour. When he retires for the night, no conciliatory word has been spoken by either of us.

How have I lived to the age of twenty-seven without noticing the monotony of each day? Waking to the smell of Mrs Hendry's porridge. Finding my husband already reading at the breakfast table. I do not ask if he slept well, having heard his snoring from the other side of the house. It amazes me how quickly meals pass without conversation. Ten minutes later he is gone. The Governor comes home for lunch, but Hugh eats at the prison. It is less disruptive to his work.

Why not just take the test? I think about it. My husband coming in to tell me the result. The joy in his face. His open arms. The birth of our children. The months of mistrust overwritten by decades of family life. I picture our postponed wedding night. Approaching the bed in my virginal lace, reaching under my filmy nightdress and plunging a knife into his self-righteous heart.

That is why I don't let him test my blood.

When I speak of symbolic meanings, he averts his face in disgust. The world is so straightforward to him: itself and nothing else. And for me, always this doubleness. My own

165

vision and his, each as real as the other, and entirely incompatible. He would take mine from me, crumple it in his fist like a piece of paper and toss it into the fire. Gone! That's what taking the Wassermann test would mean to me: seeing the world through his eyes forever. *And why not*, I hear Mama say, *if you love him?* Because I thought *he* loved *me*, head and heart, body and soul. But he loved a convalescent girl, weakened by long illness. He loved the way I bent in his hands.

It's not just myself I have to think about, but Mama and Pa and Gordon and Hilda and Uncle Tom's family out in Canada, and Grandmother Kate's sons, and Aunt Nellie and Uncle George. All of us with the same sentence hanging over us, the possibility that a filthy disease is eating into our brains. My husband hopes it is. Yes, really. For him Grandmother Kate's news came as a reprieve. Why else was he single at forty-two in a country awash with unclaimed women? Oh no doubt a part of him was bitterly disappointed, but how easily that loving, loyal part accepted defeat. I look for him in my husband's eyes, that are always sliding away from mine. In his hands, that never touch me. In his voice, that never speaks my name. What has happened to the man who serenaded me in the honeysuckle-scented garden?

The sheets hanging on the line are more intimate with him than I.

He eats as if his life depended on it. And there is nothing *to* eat. Mrs Hendry makes the most of the prison farm, and her sister's eggs, and I bring back whatever I can find in the shops, but one day's corned beef and boiled greens is indistinguishable from the next. And still he puts on weight. It seems an act of will, as if he is burying the boyish man I fell in love with, walling his lean bones in a prison of flesh. His face is quite different now, his once-expressive features trapped in great slabs of cheek and forehead. His eyes have shrunk, his mouth is a withholding slit. He gets the barber

166

to shave his hair. Those coppery filaments that once caught the sun are now just pig's bristle. He looks every one of his forty-three years, moves with the same blunt, brutish walk as the warders. Is it to punish me, this systematic destruction of his beauty? It's too late now: even if he consented, even if that iron self-control were to relax for one night, I will never know the man I fell in love with. And still I wonder how it would feel to be pinned under this other's weight. To have his bull's head bear down on me, that tight mouth opening to mine. Is a man's fat softly giving and smooth to the touch like a woman's, or coarse and hard? I imagine it, alone in bed at night. Stroking the stubbled back of his neck, kissing those neat ears, finding the man under the layers of flesh. Even his smell is different now. Not that I am allowed near enough to inhale his skin, but sometimes when he has left for work and Mrs Hendry is safely occupied downstairs, I investigate his dirty linen. When I bury my face in his shirt, I can still smell the soap Mrs Hendry used to wash it, and the wind that blew it dry, filling the sleeves that punched and flailed so wildly I envied their abandon. Deep in the cloth is my husband's own animal scent. Not the salty, smoky, earthy smell I remember from Pitlochry, but sweeter, slightly rancid, like preserved meat. The smell of our unhappiness.

It's surprising how little trace of himself he leaves in the bathroom. Pa's whisker-flecked shaving lather was part of my childhood, but Hugh's toothbrush and razor are always stowed in their leather case. His habits are regular. He evacuates his bowels before breakfast, leaving the window open to clear the air. He bathes on Tuesday evenings, never leaving so much as a stray hair in the bath. His towel is always neatly folded and quarantined from mine. I once found a fingernail paring on the linoleum and keep it, wrapped in a handkerchief in my top drawer, knowing there is a good chance it is Mrs Hendry's.

He makes his own bed every morning. Much as I would

love to shed my clothes and roll in the last of his warmth, I do not trust myself to replace the covers with undetectable precision. But there's the wardrobe with his Harris tweed suit, his heavy winter coat, the kilt he wore to marry me, a Homburg I have never seen on his head, and a cheap sack coat far too small for his swelling girth that must date from his student days. Am I wrong to search his things? Are we not one flesh, joined in the eyes of God and the law? But still I start at a tread on the stairs. Mrs Hendry. Carefully I shut the wardrobe door. I cannot be caught in here. Better to come out with my head high. She nearly jumps out of her skin. She must know we are not like other married couples, but we all pretend. Several days pass before I manage to search his chest of drawers. Shirts, collars, handkerchiefs, ties, flannel pyjamas, socks, woollen drawers. I'm hoping for a journal, with keepsakes slipped between the pages: an ox-eye daisy I plucked and threaded through his buttonhole in Pitlochry, a ticket from the concert we attended at the City Hall. Nothing. Until I think to look beneath the newspaper used to line the drawer and find an envelope. Inside it: a twist of hair the same colour as my own.

One evening he announces that we are going to Ayrshire so I can meet his parents. We will stay two nights on the farm where he grew up, and spend an afternoon with his old teachers.

'Why now?'

'You have more pressing business here?'

'You know I haven't. I just wonder that we've not been before – have they not been curious until now?'

'It has not been convenient. Of course they wish to meet the woman who married their eldest son.'

'The mother of their grandchildren?'

'Unless you're cruel enough to rob them of that hope.'

'Isn't it more cruel to let it persist?'

'Disabusing them would require an explanation. They would never forgive you.'

'Because it's my fault?'

'If you wish to have this argument again, I do not.'

'Then don't – let us not. Can we not find some compromise? If we were . . . close, as other husbands and wives, I'm not saying I *would* change my mind, but I might. If I could feel I was granting a request made out of love. There are ways of coupling without bearing children.'

'Not ways practised by decent folk.'

'But if needs must?'

'What *need*?'

'My need not to be entirely sacrificed to your needs.'

'I don't have time for this.'

'No time for your wife?'

'For arguments about nothing. You may have inherited a disease. There is a scientific test which would end the uncertainty. You refuse to take it, depriving us of the chance of a normal married life. However you try to dress it up, those are the facts.'

'*Your* facts.'

'God in heaven!'

'And if I take your test, and I carry the disease, what then? Will you let me into your bed, if we take precautions to ensure you're not infected?'

'I didn't marry to bed my wife like a whore.'

'Even if I wish it?'

'Are you offering to take the test?'

'No!'

'Then this conversation is finished.'

As the train approaches Mauchline I begin to understand why we have not been before. He says the soil is perfect for grass, the belted Galloways that graze here produce the richest milk in Scotland, but it is working land, I shouldn't expect the picturesque. I say it looks pleasant enough, so very green. He tells me it is not so pleasant in the driving rain, the prevailing conditions three hundred days a year. But the sun is shining today, I point out. He replies that I needn't look for shade: every tree has been felled to make way for pasture and to prop up the coal mines under our feet. Everything I say seems to irk him, but refraining from comment is taken as *looking down my nose* at the place. I tell him I've always wanted to visit Burns' county. He says the man was a waster and a drunkard. Better he'd never set pen to paper, than to allow every Scotch sot to claim a poet's soul.

And yet, when we are met at the station by his brother, John Neill, there is no mistaking his pride in me. From the way he hands me up, you would think I'd never sat in a trap before. John Neill dusts the seat with his cap. It's embarrassing, and funny, but I sense that laughter would never be forgiven, and so I play the gracious lady and feel a perfect ass. And that, more or less, is the tone of the visit. Meal times are a torture, with everyone cocking their pinkies and cutting their meat into absurdly dainty morsels. I have a vision of Hilda breaking wind at table just to see the looks on their faces, and have to stifle my amusement in a cough. How can I tell what they are really like? If they're behaving half as unnaturally as I am, they'll be unrecognisable to themselves. John Neill is painfully reserved with me. Disapproval or awe, I cannot tell which. His other brothers are still fighting overseas. I wish we had saved this first visit until their return, when I might have glimpsed the mischievous laddie in Hugh, the puller of pigtails and looter of nests. To his younger sisters, he is a stranger to be addressed with respect. And, oddly, to his parents too. They treat him like the factor, suspending their conversation when he enters the room. When we're alone, I ask if he minds this. To my surprise, he doesn't take umbrage at the question. His father is a proud man, he says, and proud of his eldest son's achievements, but the fact remains that he opposed the decision to become a doctor. Hugh will never be forgiven for proving him wrong.

This exchange takes place in our room. When Mrs Watson first shows us in, my heart leaps at that double bed. I cannot believe he has let this happen by accident. Surely this is our chance to undo all the unhappiness? The first night he sleeps on the floor. Or rather, does not sleep, and spends the next day wincing and rolling his shoulder. The following night I insist on taking my turn on the wooden boards, and of course he will not permit this, with the result that we share the bed, placing the bolster as a barrier between us. This time I am the one who does not sleep, but lies all night pressed against the wall of feathers, listening to his breathing.

On our last day his cousin Robbie arrives at the farm, to be greeted with teasing and backslapping and even some friendly rough-housing from Hugh's young nephew, all of it very different from the stilted cheer the Watsons have shown to my husband. Robbie is a burly dairyman with thinning hair and snaggled teeth, but likeable enough. When he offers to take me up to the coppice where Hugh and his brother are shooting rabbits, I readily agree. On the way, we talk about Hugh's nephews and nieces, the red-haired girls who speak a private language, John Neill's eldest laddie who has just been up to Glasgow Fair. Grinning, he says I should ask Hugh about his visit to the fair. 'Oh yes?' I say, 'do tell'. And after a little more persuasion, he does.

So my husband was once a boy like any other. God help me, it gives me hope.

Later, when Robbie stays to keep John Neill company, and Hugh and I are walking back to the farm, I make the mistake of joking about it. Hardly even a joke: one smiling reference. He stops dead on the path. At first I think he is annoyed with his cousin, and perhaps he is, but this incandescent anger is directed at me. What sort of hypocrite do I take him for? Oh

171

yes, he knows what I'm insinuating. Do I honestly think he'd set such store by me taking the test if he was already poxed?

I stare at him, too bewildered to defend myself.

And at last my face convinces him I haven't the faintest notion what he is talking about.

He moves off, ahead of me. It seems entirely possible we will reach the farmhouse in silence and never allude to this again. But after a while he allows me to catch up and, once we're walking in step, he starts to speak.

Twenty-three years after he met the tinker girl at Glasgow Fair he was a doctor. Not yet qualified, but competent enough to work in Riccartsbar Asylum. He had been assisting the Superintendent in the male wards for a month when the women's wing went down with rubeola. It was the first time he had been in that side of the building, though he had seen the female lunatics gathered on the benches outside. Like old men in skirts, wizened and balding and hairy-chinned, smoking their clay pipes. He had wondered once or twice where the younger ones were?

He was thirty-five and could have passed for twenty. She was, what – forty? Maybe not so old, but not so very different from those hags puffing on their pipes. That once-slender body shapeless as mashed tatties on a plate, her hair greying, both her top front teeth gone. His first thought was that he'd happened on her mother, the twice-yearly absence that had puzzled him throughout childhood. But there was something about the smiling way she held her head, as if she still remembered what it was to be beautiful.

When she stamped across the floor towards him, he knew what was wrong with her. It starts with the riot of the senses and ends with kinaesthesia. General paresis of the insane, the tertiary stage of syphilis.

'Is it yourself, Shuggie?'

Her voice shook in the standard symptomatic way.

'Kitty.'

172

'Caitlin,' she corrected him: she was married to Finn MacCoul. Grandiose delusions are a feature of the tertiary stage. She drew his hand towards her, forcing it inside her dress against the flaccid breasts. He tried to pull away, but her grip was like a vice. She lifted her gaze to his, and they were the same laughing eyes, under those drooping lids. He must not worry: her husband understood that her passions were more urgent than one man, even a giant, could satisfy. She moved closer, trapping his arm between their two bodies, her breath in his face, the salt smell he suddenly, mortifyingly remembered now identified as unwashed genitalia. 'I've missed my Shuggie and his brave soldier, so quick to stand to attention.'

By now he was almost desperate enough to strike her. The other patients were nudging each other and grinning. One of the female attendants had to come to his rescue.

'Ho! Kitty! Put the doctor down.'

She was dead within six months.

He has timed it well. We are entering the farm gate as he finishes this account. So many questions in my head. Did he pity her? Did he pity that lost boy, the twelve-year-old Hugh who had loved her? Was Glasgow Fair the only time? Was this poor wretch the only one, or were there others after her, other black-eyed lassies with easy country morals? Did he take the test himself? But of course he did. And so, after thinking it over, I ask him nothing.

HILDA

London in wartime is not the city Hilda loves. The Empress Hall is a balloon store now. You can't get Cavo's ice cream sundaes, or beef Wellington at the Trocadero, or take an arc-lit evening stroll beside the Thames. There are Belgian refugees everywhere you look, and Zeppelin raids, and too many nights hugger-mugger with the servants in the basement of Earls Court Square. Thank God for handsome strangers in the blackout. Handsome voices, anyway. For a few months, Fritz stops paying his calls. The skies are clear. But in June, just when a girl is feeling safe again: an air raid in broad daylight. Planes, not Zeppelins. Such a novelty that people pour out of the buildings and stand in the street, gawping, as the bombs rain down on them. In July it happens again. Hilda is walking up High Holborn and a hundred-pounder drops right in front of her. The pavement judders under her feet. She's sure she's bought it, she can feel the pressure squeezing her skull, but it's a dud. What a fluke! Mama just about hugs the life out of her when she gets home, then packs her case, dashes off a note to the Doc, and puts her on the chuffer to bomb-free Perth.

Where all is peaceful. Or at least, there's no threat from the Hun. But something's up in Prison Cottage. Dodo looks five years older, her eyes ringed with violet. She has acquired a new habit, a darting glance to check the Doc's reaction. *Oh-ho*, Hilda thinks, but she bides her time until next morning, when he has left for the clink. Dodo suggests a walk along the river but Hilda would rather stay indoors and have a good old confab.

She lifts Dodo's hand and inspects her fingernails. Chewed, as she thought. 'Marriage doesn't suit you—'

Dodo glances towards the door.

'—He's gone.'

She whispers, 'Mrs Hendry.'

'Is she his spy?'

But this is too much. Dodo gets that hoity-toity look Hilda knows of old, 'Of course not.'

'It's too late to start faking now, Dodie—'

Dodo crosses to the sideboard and rearranges a perfectly serviceable vase of fresias.

'—I'm worried about you.'

'Needlessly.'

'All right then: say it. Say, *the Doc and I are blissfully happy.*'

Dodo gives her another fish-eyed look.

Hilda tries a new tack, 'Do you want to know what happened last night, when he gave me the once-over for shell shock?'

'Not really,' Dodo says to the fresias.

'Weren't you jealous, all on your ownsome, your pretty sister and your handsome husband out of sight upstairs—?'

Frowning, Dodo extracts a wilting stem.

'—You weren't, were you? Are you sure you don't want to know what he said?'

'Quite sure.'

'Any sign of a sprog yet?'

'We've only been married seven months.'

'Thought not. So what's it like, sporting in the marital bed?' Hilda flexes her eyebrows, 'You could be at it every night. Twice on Saturdays and Sundays.'

That does it. Dodo doesn't buckle, not yet, but her face loses its snooty cast. 'All right, what did he say?'

'He told me not to breed.'

'*Oh.*'

She starts to blub, and it all comes out. Grandaddy Richmond being a depraved lunatic. The possibility that Hilda and Dodo and Gordon have inherited Cupid's itch. The way Doctor and Mrs Ferguson Watson live. Eating together, sleeping apart. They have never seen each other naked.

'Then you're not really married. You can get out of it.'

'He would never agree.'

'He doesn't have to agree: he's welshed on the deal.'

'He would die of shame.'

Hilda would quite like to slap some sense into her elder sister. Instead she says, 'So you're still gone on him.'

Had Mama sent a missive before despatching her north, Hilda is quite sure the Doc would have said no. But here she is, claiming sanctuary, only to find herself in the middle of a war. No prizes for guessing whose side Mrs Hendry is on. Interesting, that 'Mrs': since when did Scottish housemaids get so ritzy? The Doc behaves as if Hilda herself were an unexploded bomb. No sudden moves or loud noises around her. Smiling at her. A constipated sort of smile, but more than he gives his wife. She hardly knows what to think: her superior elder sister in such a fix. Everyone should know what a catastrophic blunder Mrs Atkins' favourite daughter has made. But then she'd be poor Donella again. Better to leave her to her fate. Once a year, someone will say *d'you ever hear from Dodo?* And Mama will sigh *she lives so far away now*. And it will serve her jolly well right. But here's the shocker: it breaks Hilda's heart to see Dodo so cowed by that red-faced prig, and still putting some lemon into her retorts, telling herself she's holding her ground, when anyone can see she's dying of loneliness. Crikey, she's only twenty-seven. What is life, if not verve and laughter: a rag to be danced at double-quick time? You can't say Dodo is *living*. She might as well be locked in one of the cells.

The house is every bit as hellish as it was last year. The

camel-back sofa, all that pompous mahogany. She has changed nothing, which tells Hilda she has been hopeless from the start. What do people think when she entertains? Dodo looks shamefaced. '*What, never?*' She gives a defeated shrug: whom would she invite? Hugh has no friends. Apart from Aunt Nellie, and if she ever crossed the threshold, she would surely smell a rat. This is when Hilda hatches her plot. A dinner. Uncle and Aunt and three more guests, to make the numbers even. Dodo shakes her head, so Hilda scales it down: surely she can find *one person* in the whole of Perth? What about the Doc's former assistant, didn't she hear his nibs say he's home on leave? If he's medically qualified, he must be half-way civilised. Never having met him, Dodo can't say. That settles it: Doctor Lindsay is coming to dinner. Hilda is determined to let some fresh air into her sister's marriage. And if that air happens to include a good-looking sawbones, so much the better.

The Doc says no, as Hilda knew he would, so she traps him in the drawing room, while Dodo is having a gingerly reproving word with Mrs Hendry. The Ancestors are agog for news of their eldest daughter: how is she settling in to married life, has she found a place in Perth society? She has always been so gregarious. They will be coming north in three weeks for their summer spree with Nellie and George. It would put their minds at ease if Dodo could tell them of a dinner she gave 'just the other day'. He says he will speak to Lindsay, but Hilda's not such a chump as to leave it at that. She posts the invitation, and Doctor Lindsay accepts in writing. Dodo is transformed, prone to sudden gusts of laughter, spending hour after enraptured hour poring over her recipe books. They visit every baker and dairy in the town, every grocer, greengrocer, fishmonger and flesher. Hilda is appalled by the empty shelves, the smelly cheese and stringy pigeons Dodo pounces on so gleefully. Could the shopping not be done by Mrs Hendry? Dodo looks quite crestfallen. This is the most fun she has had since she was wed. Passing the licensed victuallers, Hilda remarks that a gin fizz before dinner would help things along no end, but Dodo says the Doc would never permit it.

Hilda wears her scarlet Fortuny, a head-turner even in London. She's not going to get herself up like a frump just because the porridge-eaters are barely out of crinolines. Dodo takes one look at her and goes back up to change into her pleated silk, so it's almost like old times: the Atkins girls cutting a dash in their snazzy plumage. The Doc's face is an ominous shade of puce, but Nellie and George are delighted to see their nieces *brightening up this dreary war*, so he has to agree that they look 'very nice'. The crying shame is that the other guest should be so unworthy of their fine feathers. Doctor Lindsay turns out to be baby-faced and prematurely balding, with an off-putting whiff of unwashed trouser. Completely smitten by Hilda, of course. He seems to think he has been invited to flirt with her, to hold her gaze with his pink-rimmed eyes. She finds his presumption rather killing. Along with her brother-in-law's obvious disapproval. And there's another amusing detail. Although the Doc calls himself *Ferguson* Watson, and Dodo has taken both barrels as her married name, Doctor Lindsay addresses him as plain old common-or-garden 'Watson'.

They talk about how expensive everything is, especially bacon. When you can find it, that is. Hilda wonders if this is coded absolution for the revolting scoff on the table, but the topic seems endlessly interesting to everyone but herself. What they could buy for ten shillings before the war, now costs them a pound! At long last, Uncle George spots her less than riveted expression and changes the subject, asking Doctor Lindsay where he's stationed. (Nowhere near Billy Bellairs, alas.) Their guest bangs on about the Front for a while, then tells a repulsive tale about field amputations which

178

turns poor old Uncle G quite green. Dodo brings up Hilda's miraculous escape, and she gets to tell her bomb story, playing up the peril to make Aunt Nellie shudder, but it's rather tame after Doctor Lindsay's lip-smacking reminiscence, so she has a bit of fun: 'Hugh says I've suffered no ill effects.' She smiles naughtily, her glance circling the table, 'I felt heaps better once you'd examined me. You really have the healing touch.' Doctor Lindsay's tongue makes a brief appearance on his lower lip. After a moment's silence Uncle George observes what a boon it is having a doctor in the family. Dodo puts her knife and fork together and informs the table that her husband had a very interesting case this year, a Glaswegian revolutionary who wouldn't eat.

Doctor Lindsay chuckles at this news. 'You soon settled his nonsense, I'll be bound. Like old times, eh? I wish I'd been here to lend a hand.'

Doing what, exactly, Hilda wonders.

Her brother-in-law leans forward, making it plain to the rest of the table that he has merely tolerated the conversation thus far. Now, at last, they have a subject worth discussing. 'Political self-starvers are generally intelligent, but neurotic. My method is to treat the neurosis by talking to the prisoner, gaining his confidence . . .'

'Or hers,' Lindsay interjects.

'. . . persuading him to accept the only logical conclusion.'

'Which is?' enquires Hilda, who is on hunger strike herself. At least, until the pudding.

'That he'll be more comfortable eating his supper than taking it by stomach tube.'

Uncle George asks, 'Were you here when those suffragettes were making such a bally nuisance of themselves?'

Hugh is about to reply, but Lindsay beats him to it. 'Indeed we were, sir. It was a regular siege. Thousands of them shrieking outside the gate. I went to Glasgow to collect a woman who'd tried to blow up Rabbie Burns' cottage.

179

There was a handover at the railway station. The hoydens got word and followed me. With all due respect to your sex, Miss Atkins, I've never been so windy in my life. Turned out the prisoner was Lord Kitchener's niece. We were feeding her by tube, and worse. Of course, we'd no idea. They all used false names. There was the devil to pay when the Commission found out. That's why we had to let the other one go. *She* was a handful. Pretty girl . . .'

'I'm sure Miss Atkins doesn't want to hear our old stories,' the Doc says, abruptly.

'Oh but I do,' Hilda purrs, 'it sounds *fascinating*.'

Which is all the encouragement Lindsay needs. 'She was tall for a lassie. Hair your sort of colour, Miss Atkins. And yours, Mrs Watson. In fact, it gave me quite a turn when I walked in here tonight—'

For the first time Dodo gives him her full attention.

'—what was the girl's name? Fought like a tiger at the start, but the doctor tamed her.' He taps the tablecloth. 'Isabel? Annabel . . .?'

'Arabella?' Dodo suggests.

Hilda's brother-in-law turns white as a ghost. Perhaps he has bitten a piece of lead shot.

'That's it,' Lindsay says, '*Arabella*. I wonder what became of her.'

The Doc tells Dodo her uncle would like some more pigeon pie, a suggestion George is quick to refute. 'Though it was delicious, Donella.'

Midway through the evening, Dodo leaves the chit-chat to fend for itself, and turns her attention to her better half, but not with the sort of moithered glance that so disheartened Hilda on her arrival. This is more of a long, cool, interested stare, which somehow her spouse manages not to acknowledge. Hilda knows this has something to do with Doctor Lindsay's suffragette, and does all she can to revive the subject, but Lindsay has finally noticed his old boss looking daggers at him and won't be drawn. Instead, the conversation turns to their hostess. Aunt Nellie wants her to put her brains to use on a charitable committee. Dodo says she has approached the Society for Combating Venereal Disease. Doctor Lindsay snorts into his napkin. Uncle G just about chokes on his gooseberry crumble.

The Doc gives her a look that would turn milk, 'And when was I to hear about this?'

Hilda leans back in her chair to enjoy the show.

'I'm telling you now,' Dodo says. She smiles at the rest of the table, 'My husband is an expert in the field. I don't have his extensive knowledge, but I fancy I have something to contribute.'

'We'll speak of this later,' he says in exactly the tone he would use to dismiss a servant.

Dodo flushes, 'We can speak of it, but my mind is made up.'

'*You are my wife and will do nothing to disgrace me.*'

An electric thrill of embarrassment visits the table.

'Of course,' Dodo says in an impressively offhand voice, 'but ours is a modern marriage, is it not? We each have our private domain. My committee, your . . .' She shrugs, as if plucking the words out of the air at random, 'your Arabella.'

'A patient I've not seen for three years.'

'But you've thought of her.'

Over the past week Hilda has witnessed the arid talk in Prison Cottage and drawn the obvious conclusion: her sister's marriage is a desert. But now she understands that every stunted exchange is lush with implication, with unspoken responses and ramifying consequences. Their life together is a silent conversation so choked with allusion that everyone else is shut out.

The Doc's knife and fork clatter onto his plate. He throws down his napkin, pushes his chair back from the table. 'I'll walk you to your lodgings, Lindsay.'

The evening seems to be over.

181

TWENTY-ONE

It is very late when he comes in. He was hoping I'd be in bed, but finds me sitting in the drawing room. Without my sister, he notes thankfully, albeit with the dusty bottle of brandy he keeps for medicinal purposes. He understands that my desire for alcohol is secondary to the need to defy his wishes.

'I was beginning to think you might not come back,' I say.

'Where else would I go?'

'To Arabella's perhaps.'

He cannot prevent that flash of blood in his cheeks, but he keeps his voice neutral. If I am determined to quarrel, he is no less determined to deny me. 'You are labouring under a misapprehension.'

'Am I? What misapprehension is that?'

'That I am guilty of infidelity.'

I give a laugh that makes his teeth grind, though he will not show it. 'Actually I think you're extremely faithful. But not to me.'

'And that is a misapprehension.'

'It's just an accident that you call me by her name?'

Alarm flares in his gaze. 'When?'

He thinks I'm going to tell him he has been talking in his sleep.

'The day we met, and the day you asked me to marry you.'

'Twice in thirteen months?' In his relief he forgets his resolve not to goad me.

'So it means nothing? There is no reason why it pops out

of your mouth in moments of extreme feeling, this name and no other?'

'It rhymes with yours, it's a slip of the tongue.'

'It's a slip of something—'

The clock on the mantel chimes the hour.

'—your unconscious desires.'

Contempt crosses his face. 'Are you a Freudian now? I would advise you to read his tosh before you start bandying words like *unconscious*.'

'You love her.'

'You're drunk. Go to bed.'

'You love her – as far as you are capable of loving anyone. It may be a poor enough passion, but it is more than you feel for me.'

He blinks as if I have hurled the brandy in his face. (It did occur to me, after his gibe about Freud.)

Why doesn't he speak?

He ducks his head, a very slight and, yes, unconscious, gesture. The grown man at a loss, moving aside to show a glimpse of the little boy. I have hurt him. Too late now to say I did not mean it, that I am a little drunk after so many months without spirits, that I said the very worst purely to make him deny it.

'Hugh.'

He looks at me from a thousand miles away. 'Don't feel obliged to get up with me in the morning.' He turns to leave.

I think of all the days, weeks, months that have had to pass before I grasped this chance to speak honestly. Any other man would see that the very least he owes me is an honest reply. But not Hugh. 'All right, then: go,' I say. 'Sleep well. I'm sure you will, now you can tell yourself I'm in the wrong: your drunken wife who disgraces you in company. You retire to bed with your frigid passion and think about how much happier you would be with her, how much more dignified she is, how she would never drink a thimbleful of brandy *once* in seven months. So why isn't she your wife: did she prefer someone else, or did she just not care for you? Did she find your judging silences uncongenial, perhaps? Tell me, I'm curious. Or do we have more in common than I have guessed? Did she too make the mistake of loving you, and open her heart to you only to discover that your blood runs cold . . .'

The door clicks shut. I hear his footsteps climbing the stairs.

It is not the end of us. Marriages are not so easily unmade, or they weren't then. I have no further contact with the Society for Combating Venereal Disease and Arabella's name is not mentioned again. But something changes after that evening. A stranger has witnessed our marriage. He has not seen anything like the worst of it, but enough to make me understand that the way we live is shameful. I have tried, however clumsily, to talk to my husband about what is wrong between us, and he has refused. That night I lie awake for hours in my solitary bed, while the pigeon takes its revenge, and by morning I am resolved. Hugh and I are at war. If I pretend otherwise, I have already lost. From that day I stop biting my tongue and make it a point of honour to speak my thoughts. It does not always please him, but I am no longer in the business of pleasing. He finds a thousand ways of fighting back. Many a night he must hear me weeping. An objective observer might come to the conclusion that relations have taken a turn for the worse, but that is not my view. The chief casualties are my uncle and aunt. They can't understand how a marriage cannot be happy, how I can tolerate that unhappiness being plain for all to see. And I suppose Uncle George takes it hard, being the one who joined us in God's sight. I regret that, but feel no compunction towards my husband. Whatever the situation, he would have salvaged unhappiness from it. He has had forty-three years to mend his character: what can I hope to do?

The months pass. The Kaiser abdicates. Germany signs the armistice. The streets are lit again, flags flying from all the buildings. Flu has closed the schools and there are children everywhere, ringing bells and setting off firecrackers. Hugh and I go out to watch the show, and I am struck by a thought no less strange to me now than it was then. We understand each other. Certain sights move us to the same sceptical smile, we share coded glances, even one or two sardonic jokes, and still we are enemies.

The Governor dies and his widow, my friend, moves away to live with her sister. The following month I see servants unloading boxes outside their old house. When a car draws up I go out to welcome my new neighbour. I will charm the Governor's replacement before my husband queers the pitch with his sour looks. And if there is a wife to become my new conspirator, so much the better. The last person I expect to see emerging from the car is Doctor Lindsay.

We clasp hands before it occurs to us that we lack the history to justify such warmth. Still, I am glad to see him home safe from the war, and he is glad of this sign that my husband is sanguine about the, *ah*, awkwardness of his position. Awkwardness, I ask? The fact that Doctor Lindsay will resume his former duties as my husband's assistant jointly with acting as Governor. I laugh. After a moment's uncertainty, he joins me. The more we think about it, the more hilariously unfortunate it seems, and though I did not care particularly for Thomas Lindsay the evening I had him to dinner, from that day onwards we are friends.

Thomas was no longer the smirking braggart I had met in 1917. He had lost almost all his hair and, even without that, he had watched too many young men die not to feel old. I had never had a male friend, and I have had so many since it is hard to remember all the skills I had to learn.

185

To hide the tenderness I felt. To crowd the would-be quiet moments with words, ideas, pawky observation. Even at my most sexlessly cerebral, to remember that very different feelings might be stirring in his breast. Maybe I should have slept with him, as I would sleep with a fair few others ten years later, but it did not even cross my mind. My youthful indiscretion was forgotten. The minute I discovered my husband did not care, I became the wronged virgin wife. I was not about to throw that away on a hasty encounter with Doctor Lindsay. And besides, my sexual longings were still for Hugh.

White bread and prunes are back in the shops, but food is still scarce. Thomas has the groundsman make an allotment in the prison village garden, and since our strips are side by side, it can happen that he and I are hoeing or sowing at the same time. Who could begrudge us passing the time of day? We talk about potato blight and cabbage root fly, the meals we will eat if our tender shoots survive, the dishes we have not tasted since 1914, and how the salty rations they ate in the field hospital had all the patients begging for water. I tell him Hugh cannot abide the smell of fish in the house, so I have had to reconcile myself to a lifetime without kippers. We muse over returned soldiers with both legs blown off who seem to be living cheerful lives; and others, shell-shocked but intact, who have not spoken in three years. I wonder if Thomas agrees with Hugh that the influenza epidemic is nature's way of purging the weak? Gradually it becomes clear that what interests us both is medicine, the bloody detail no less than the discovery of new cures. He lends me books that I read in my bedroom. I do not consciously keep this new hobby from my husband, but nor do I discuss it with him.

In the autumn of 1919 Hugh is appointed deputy commissioner of His Majesty's Board of Control. I hope we might move to Edinburgh, but his fiefdom is lunacy, and all Scotland's criminal lunatics are held in Perth. Still, the promotion eases the friction between him and Thomas, a hostility that has nothing to do with me. Hugh has no inkling of the hours I spend with the Governor. There is no one to tell him out of friendship, and no one who would take such a risk maliciously.

TWENTY-TWO

Uncle George caught influenza in 1918. He was one of the lucky ones. Like everybody in Perth, I know of at least twenty others who did not survive. Hugh treated George and several of Doctor Stirling's patients and took it for granted that he was immune. Now it is high summer and his lungs are creaking. He stops eating. Headache. Sore throat. Pains in his bones. So far the prison has been spared. He gets me to send word to Thomas through Mrs Hendry: our house is to be quarantined. Meat, milk, vegetables, eggs should be left on the doorstep. No one is to cross the threshold. In or out. Mrs Hendry goes home to her sister. I could go to stay with Aunt Nellie, but then everyone would know that I am no more intimate with my husband than our cook. So I stay. For the first time in our marriage Hugh and I are alone. I become his servant, companion and nurse.

I am terrified he will die and take me with him. How could I not be? And yet I feel strangely calm. I know we are doomed, and I trust we are not. A miracle will save us. But before then, at his lowest ebb, he will turn to me and beg forgiveness and we will be reconciled. The illness will do what our stubborn wills cannot. Make us one flesh, man and wife.

It doesn't quite happen like that.

He is a difficult patient, demanding, always at me to smooth the sheet under him or plump up his pillows, or remove his disgustingly clogged and sodden handkerchiefs. The virus makes him sweat. Years since I have touched his hand, and now I have to remove his soaking pyjamas, lean across his

188

naked chest (hairless, quite different from my imaginings), work my hands under his rump. He snaps at me when I try to feed his arm into a fresh jacket: what's the point of clean clothes if he is dirty? So I must bed bathe him too. What a performance I make of it, scared of being too intrusive. He has to tell me to wash his genitals. The first I've seen. I take his scrotum too roughly, have no idea the foreskin can be pulled back. We are both close to tears by the time I have finished. But I think about it later, that peeled pink prawn in its nest of copper hair. He is too weak to get out of bed. I try helping him up, but he must weigh two hundred pounds. When his bowels move, I manage with the same hand that twitched my skirt when I curtseyed to the King.

Day and night I sit by his bed. Help him to sips of water, wipe his brow with a cooling cloth, spoon mutton broth into his mouth. (Not so bad for a first attempt at cooking.) His aching eyes cannot focus on print, so I read to him. Articles in his medical periodicals, Hugh correcting my pronunciation of the long Latinate nouns. After ten days of this I am dog-tired but symptom-free. He sleeps for hours at a stretch, only to wake the instant I rise from my chair. Once I get as far as my own bed and fall into a dead sleep. His terrified cry rouses me. When I stumble through the darkness to his bedside he clutches my hand. His breathing labours, his brow burns, the sweat courses down his face. He does not respond to questions, yet I think he draws some comfort from my crooning reassurance. At first light his temperature drops and he starts to shiver. Dragging the blankets from my bed makes no difference. His teeth chatter, his moans distorted by uncontrollable shaking. I tell him what I propose to do, give him the chance to forbid me. Who can say whether he understands? I take off my clothes and crawl between the sheets, strip away his saturated pyjamas and give him my body's heat, skin to skin.

How can he shiver? It's like a jungle under the covers. Hot,

189

damp, aromatic with his smells and secretions. To think we have been married three years and I've never tasted them.

The shivering fit passes. His body relaxes. He lies, weakened but awake. I sense his growing awareness of my presence, his body's awareness. I understand the basics of anatomy and am not completely astonished by the change in him in that place.

I touch it.

He groans.

I know he is delirious. It would never happen were he in his right mind. I could claim an equal confusion, sleeplessness and emotional strain affecting my judgement. It's not true.

The bliss of easing my aching spine in a stretch. My belly rubs against him. His eyes open. Recognition in his face. I place his hand on my breast, watching his mouth. *Yes.* My lips on his ear, making him shudder. The beard he has grown in bed is silky. This soft spot under his jaw, the weathered skin of his throat, his plump white chest. His nipple a bead under my tongue. The wiry hair on his belly. An unfamiliar scent coats the roof of my mouth, stronger as I move down. Goodness. All I have to do is breathe on it.

I push down the bedclothes, straddle his thighs.

It hurts. The shock of it makes me recoil. A mistake. I can't inflict this on a sick man, or on myself. But as I withdraw he grips me with surprising strength. Struggling, I try to prise us apart. He pulls me in, forces us together. Involuntarily I grunt, which seems to madden him, spurring him to move more urgently, grip more tightly, push deeper into me, again and again, until he gives a great shuddering cry and lets me go.

Next morning the sweats and the shivers are gone. I assume he has slept. I spent the night in my own bed. His eyes are closed when I come in. I pick up his dirty pyjamas, lay a clean pair over the chair, bring him a fresh glass of water. I'm creeping out again when he opens his eyes.

190

'Stay.'

'You sound better.'

'Somewhat.'

'Could you manage some breakfast?'

He looks at me. 'Last night . . .'

My heart gives a guilty jump. 'I shouldn't have got into bed.'

'I didn't want to.'

'I know.'

'It's no excuse.'

'You didn't know what you were doing.'

'I should have had more self-control.'

'You were delirious.'

'What did I say?'

He can't want me to tell him.

'Nothing.'

'Don't lie to me.'

I stare at the wooden headboard. 'You said you would make me pay.'

'Pay?'

'Suffer for . . .' I think better of this. 'You were confused.'

'And what was I doing, when I said this?'

I look him in the eye. 'You know.'

He looks away.

'It's all right,' I say.

'All right?' he echoes, as if I am the source of his disgust.

'I'll make you some toast.'

But he won't leave it at that. 'Are you marked?'

'Not much.'

'Bruised?'

'A little bleeding.'

He looks pained. It occurs to me it is my pain that matters here. My pain, my bleeding, my disgust.

He closes his eyes as if he cannot bear the sight of me. 'I've never . . .'

'Lain with a woman,' I say, 'or forced her?'

'Neither.'

'Not even Arabella?'

He seems genuinely shocked. And as suddenly as I blamed him I feel nothing. Just the need to get this over with. 'You said her name. Then you cradled my head against your chest and wept.'

At last I have shamed him.

'I will take that toast,' he says.

'With some beef tea?'

'Aye.'

'I'll get Mrs Hendry back from her sister's. She'll bring it to you.'

What should I do? Fetch him his breakfast, wash his sticky crotch, as if nothing has happened? Shout, call him names? It was something we did between us. The regret, too, is a shared burden. The shame.

I walk across town to the North Inch and sit watching the river, let the merciless thoughts empty out of my mind. Swallows draw their criss-cross lines above the water. It occurs to me I could be pregnant. A sin to inflict such a father on a child. And yet I have this shaky feeling in my chest, as if I'm teetering on a high wall and could fall to either side. Despair. Joy. We will live away from the gaol, in Craigie. He can afford it. We will find Mrs Hendry another position, and I will hire a girl, the eldest in a large family, good-natured and tireless and used to babies. In a year or two we will make a little brother or sister. His children will be midwives to a new Hugh, playful, tender, grateful.

By the time I next speak to him, he hates me.

He has got himself dressed, dragged himself to his surgery in the prison, drawn a blood sample, isolated the plasma. Negative. My relief comes out in a laughing gasp: then there's no reason why we shouldn't ... He cuts me off. The test

192

shows *he* is not infected. It proves nothing whatsoever about me. And if I am carrying a child? Strangely, this has not occurred to him. The aversion in his face will stay with me forever. In that unfortunate eventuality, he says, the child would be tested. Depending on the result, he would urge me strongly towards sterilisation.

I nod, *yes*, trying to salvage dignity if nothing else. We have reached a limit. Not of anything in him. I see now that the key has always been in my possession. The power to say *enough*.

'What did she do?' I ask, 'your Arabella? Did she curse you, strike you, spit in your face, tear at you with nails and teeth—?'

His face flames. He tells me to hold my tongue, but I talk over him.

'—Did she call you devil, scoundrel, sadist?' He flinches, I've hit the mark. 'Is that what you want from me? Does it seem to you the proper response? What you did to me last night, that animal satisfaction taken by force, was nothing to the daily cruelty you have inflicted on me since we married—'

The idea is born in that moment, but who can say how long I have been pregnant with it?

'—I am going to see a solicitor to have our marriage annulled on the grounds of non-consummation—'

I watch him weigh the damage this will do his reputation. And so much worse if he contests the annulment, fighting me through the courts, obliging me to tell the world what happened last night.

'—or you will pay for me to train as a doctor, and I will remain your wife in name but practice overseas.'

'You haven't the application.'

How I would like to strike him. I can almost feel the whip in my hand, see the line it would cut across his cheek.

'Don't underestimate the strength of my desire to get away from you.'

TWENTY-THREE

It took seven years of study to qualify as a doctor, and yet, looking back, the change seems instantaneous. My every waking moment had been spent trying to guess my husband's thoughts, now the burden was lifted from my shoulders, the worry lines vanished from my brow. I had reason to be thankful for our uncommunicative life: all those unreproached hours with my nose in a book. I smiled more readily, walked with a new purpose in my step.

It made me a better wife.

I passed the entrance exams and went away to Queen Margaret College in Glasgow. I had been so lonely in Perth I had started to shun my own face in the mirror. I would watch people strolling on the South Inch, couples gazing into each other's eyes, mothers and daughters, groups of friends, and wonder what on earth they found to talk about? But now I had an occupation, a subject of endless interest to my fellow students, all of us attending the same lectures, asking the same questions, afraid of or in love with our teachers, desperate to impress. It was like being young again, like the carefree years I spent with Bill. I was so rich with company, once in a while I craved my old solitude. Putting aside my books, I would walk through the Botanical Gardens, delighting in the squirrels that took acorns from my hand, the waxy leaves and trumpet blooms in the humid air of the Kibble glasshouse. There was a sweet terror in thinking how easily I might have missed all of this, the frail web of chance that had saved me.

At the end of my first term, I wept.

*

I am sitting in the parlour of our house in Perth, poring over Osler's Principles and Practice of Medicine. The recess is half over. In a fortnight I will start my second term in Glasgow. Mrs Hendry has gone to her sister's for Hogmanay. There is a knock at the door, a warder with a message from my husband. I am to join him in the prison hospital.

Hugh is dressed in a white back-to-front gown and surgical gloves, his hair hidden by a white cap. He explains that the wardresses he has trained to assist him are marking the holiday with their families. I am to follow his orders without question. The experience should prove instructive, allowing me to compare the cutting of living flesh with the cadavers I have dissected in Glasgow.

The patient is a convict, though now is not the moment to ask his crime. A hairy, suet-faced man of around fifty, he lies on the operating table, dumb with fright. The stink of rotting flesh catches in my throat. The left leg is gangrenous, so swollen the skin is tight. There is an open sore the size of a half crown on the ankle, the source of that stench. Three of the five toes are black, and so shrivelled they look charred. The foot and ankle are purplish, as if stained with bramble juice. Towards the calf, the staining turns nicotine brown. Gently I touch its fiery heat, then the blackened big toe, which is quite cold. Hugh watches me closely for a few seconds, then asks 'Where would you make the incision?' Glancing up at him, I catch a glint of intent behind his neutral expression. Like a cat watching a bird. Avoiding the eyes of the terrified patient, I try to read the limb as I would a page in a medical textbook. At first my mind is blank, my only thought the unfairness of being tested on a subject I have not yet studied, but slowly this gives way to professional interest. It occurs to me a prosthesis will be required. Didn't old Tom Waters, Pa's insurance colleague, have a wooden leg? I remember watching its outline through his trousers.

'The leg should be severed below the joint,' I say, with more confidence than I feel.

'How far below?'

'Six inches.'

'Why?'

'Better function.'

He nods, and for a moment I think I have passed the test.

'So you're proposing to retain dead tissue. Do you think you can work miracles, bring it back to life?'

I look at him.

He raises his eyebrows, 'Well?'

'No.'

'No,' he says, 'so how is the stump to heal?'

'It should be cut above the joint,' I say.

'How much above?'

'Two inches.'

Since I have answered correctly at last, Hugh sets me a new test:

'How will you prepare it?'

This I know. 'A tourniquet above the amputation point.'

He points to a leather strap. A terrible suspicion takes root in me. My heart picks up speed. Surely he would not take such a risk with a patient's life? I am fourteen weeks away from complete medical ignorance. Even under his supervision, it would be madness. I look into his face and all doubt is dispelled: he means for me to carry out the procedure.

The convict is watching us. I tell myself I can refuse, it would be the responsible course. It is my husband who is in the wrong. But if he is looking for proof that I lack the necessary temperament, if he wants an excuse to stop paying my fees, it would be playing into his hands. I have no choice. The exigency is oddly calming. My pulse steadies. If I glanced in the mirror, would I recognise this woman, the resolute look in her eyes? In the years ahead this transformation will become second nature. All doctors do it. Some of us find it

196

so intoxicating, we never return to our fallible human selves.

'The patient must be anaesthetised,' I say.

'How?'

'Chloroform.'

Hugh indicates a trolley behind me. On it stands the bottle, along with a dropper, a wire-framed nose mask, a box of gauze and another of Gamgee tissue. I fit the gauze to the mask and reach for the dropper. I know this look of Hugh's. I put down the dropper and pick up the Gamgee, but for the life of me I cannot think what to do with it.

'Do you want to give your patient chloroform sores?' he asks.

I cover the face and eyes with Gamgee, leaving an aperture over the patient's nostrils. Hugh's expression says it is not the neatest job he has seen, but he refrains from comment. I open the bottle and fill the dropper. Having no idea how much is required, I squeeze a couple of drops onto the mask and look at Hugh, release another two, check his reaction, continuing in this way until he tells me the chloroform will have evaporated if I don't get on with it.

I place the mask over the patient's nose. After a minute or so I tap his swollen leg. He yelps.

'Try not to cause the patient unnecessary pain,' my husband says, 'it will be several minutes before the anaesthetic takes effect.'

We wait. I can tell from his face there is something else I am supposed to do.

'Might it be a good idea to keep the incision sterile?' he asks acidly.

Asepsis. I can picture the word in my textbook, but not the paragraph that surrounds it. 'The instruments?'

'Have been boiled in the autoclave.'

'Gown and gloves—'

He gives me a pitiless look. I rack my brains.

'—the limb. It must be washed and shaved.'

The right answer, thank God. Hugh passes me an open razor.

Shaving the leg takes care and concentration. When it is done I feel more in control. I wash my hands, dress in the surgical gown, hat and mask laid out for me, and pull on a pair of rubber gloves.

This time when I tap the swelling, the patient does not cry out.

Hugh hands me the knife, taking a step back from the table, as if I need reminding that the responsibility is mine.

I move the blade up from the knee, not quite touching the patient's skin, until my husband's face shows a subtle change. 'Here?' I ask, to make absolutely sure. He nods. Heat flashes through me, soaking my chest and armpits under my clothes, and yet my fingers are like ice. I have never cut into living flesh. Even now I hope Hugh will relent, but of course he does not. I take a deep breath and, saying a silent prayer, press down with the point of the blade.

In the dissecting room, the first time I cut into a cadaver, I thought of carving a cold joint of undercooked beef. Living muscle is raw meat, a very different matter: warm, where the other is cold, and elastic, not stiff, harder to cut, shifting under the pressure of the knife. It bleeds, forming a red pool in the incision.

I stop, fearing the tourniquet is not tight enough, testing the strap. I can sense Hugh's impatience, the near-irresistible urge to snatch the knife out of my hand. I almost want him to. But he limits himself to moving round to the other side of the table and applying a swab to the seeping blood while I hack away. I spot a glimmer of yellowish-white amid the scarlet pulp. The neurovascular bundle. What I do next will leave the patient relatively comfortable or condemn him to a life of pain. The stakes are too high for pride.

I tell Hugh, 'We have not yet studied the nervous system.'

'Cut above the amputation site,' he says, 'sew the endings

198

individually into surrounding tissue, away from large blood vessels and areas of motion.'

I find the stitching a relief. Not that it is particularly easy, but at least I am repairing something. Hugh continues to swab the wound, allowing me to see what I am doing. We work together, head to head. When did we last stand this close?

'The quicker the better,' he says, 'or are you trying to make the patient lose as much blood as possible?'

When the nerves are secured, I resume my butchery. Towards the back of the leg I proceed more carefully. Soon enough I find the vein, the walls thin enough to show its red cargo, and the whitish artery, fat as my little finger.

'Tie off the blood vessels,' I tell him, as if he were my nurse, and to my relief he does as I ask. How deft he is. How often I have cursed his coldly pragmatic soul; now I could weep with gratitude. I cut through the artery without a qualm.

Hugh passes me the amputation saw.

If there is an art to cutting through muscle, the severing of bone is a matter of brute force. I have found it stressful enough amid the gallows humour of the dissecting room. Now I am mutilating the skeleton of a living man. Even with my husband keeping the muscle out of my way, it is a struggle. The bone wobbles under the blade. The saw jumps and catches, I have to pull it free and relocate the groove I have made before continuing. Back and forth I push. Hugh must see how hard this is for me. Would it hurt him to take the saw back and finish the job himself?

After five minutes' hard labour I feel a telltale loss of tension under the blade, but my ordeal is not yet over. The rough bone must be filed smooth, the flaps of muscle arranged to pad the stump. Hugh directs me in this, his instructions clear and concise. Finally, the stitching: catgut for the internal stitches that will dissolve over time, black silk on the surface. How tough human skin is, how hard I have to press before the

199

needle breaks through. Hugh watches in silence. As a woman, I should know how to make a neat job of it.

Doubling the last stitch, as I would if finishing a seam, I cut the silk. Air rushes into my lungs. I must have been holding my breath. When I look down at myself, the white surgical gown is mostly red.

This has been the longest, most traumatic half-hour of my life, and yet, washing my hands in the sink, I feel strangely lightheaded. I have successfully amputated a leg. Which of my fellow first years can say the same? And now a new thought comes to me. If Hugh has tested my resolve, he too was put to the test. What did it cost him to stand and watch, to trust me?

It is almost midnight when we return to the house. I make a pot of tea and a plate of buttered toast. St John's clock strikes the first of its twelve bells. Raising our teacups, we toast the New Year.

In that moment I am glad to have kept to myself what I have known for sixteen months. Not, as hitherto, because the knowledge gives me power over him, nor out of fear – because he would never forgive me for knowing – but because allowing him his secret is the one thing I can do for him, my last gift as a wife.

The morning Hugh recovered from his bout of influenza, I knocked at Thomas's door. He was both pleased and alarmed to see me there in plain view of anyone passing. He picked up a trug and we made for the garden to harvest his tomatoes. How was Hugh, he asked? Excellent news, Mrs MacNeill had also recovered, it might be the virus had mutated to a less deadly strain. The look on my face silenced him, but he showed no surprise at my question. He had been waiting for me to ask ever since we became friends.

'The first time I set eyes on you, I thought: *I'll be damned, he's made an honest woman of her.*'

200

TWENTY-FOUR

On July 10th 1914 the King and Queen arrive in Perth to open the town's new infirmary.

The streets are lined with loyal subjects dressed in their gayest clothes. Brass bands and pipers, High Constables and Atholl Highlanders, children belting out the National Anthem. Floral garlands, streamers, flags and banners, three decorative arches, a temporary fountain, a dazzle of gas and electric light – in daytime, in high summer! Weeks of preparation, to be glimpsed in a blur as the royal car speeds past. Earlier in the week, Glasgow and Edinburgh. Where are we today again? Every place looks the same when it's painted gold and festooned with roses. Though something catches the eye. That banner unfurling from a second-floor window. *We implore Your Majesty to stop forcible feeding in Perth Prison.* A missile flies towards the open-topped car. *What the devil?* It is twelve days since Archduke Franz Ferdinand of Austria and the pregnant Duchess of Hohenberg were shot dead in Sarajevo. Princess Mary stoops to retrieve a tennis ball slit and stuffed with messages. *Free Arabella Scott!* Fifty extra policemen have been drafted into Perth, but they're not quick enough to confiscate that placard. *Visit Your Majesty's torture chamber in Perth Prison!* A woman dressed in black waits in the crowd at County Place. A bundle of suffragette literature strikes the royal windscreen. She darts forward, trying to climb on board the moving car. In the front seat, the Chief Constable grabs hold of her. She staggers. The crowd gasps. The chauffeur jams on the brakes so suddenly that the car slews in a half-turn. The King finds himself face-to-face with her. How still it is suddenly. George V, ruler of the United Kingdom and the British Dominions, Emperor of India, shrinks in his seat. Such an ordinary man, with his ruddy-whiskery face and his swimmy eyes that slide away from hers. '*Free Arabella Scott!*' The police are pulling at her. She screams, lashing out. The crowd hisses. She is dragged away, only just saved from a lynching.

The vote campaigners of Glasgow and Edinburgh understand only too well why the government has chosen Perth for the feeding of suffragettes. Many have husbands and children, some have jobs. They can't be uprooting themselves to this backwater, it's practically in the Highlands! But nor can they let the King come so close to the barbarity perpetrated in his name without making some sort of protest. And Perth is not at all what they expected. The crowds, the lights, the quiver of anticipation in the air. So gratifying to find the natural history museum, public library and swimming pool all closed for fear of arson. Such fun to saunter around town in a gang with a policeman at your heels, to cast significant looks at the post office or use a tape to measure the prison wall and, glancing over your shoulder, find the constable noting it all down. The town is alive with rumour. That police spies have infiltrated the protesters, that some spectacular act of violence is planned, that government *agents provocateurs* are plotting to discredit the movement. It's all so thrilling. How can they go back to their indoor lives? Dundee Suffrage Society rents a third-floor flat in a tenement overlooking the prison. It becomes the headquarters for those who stay on. They soon learn to recognise the Governor, the two doctors and Matron. You should see them jump when their names are called through a speaking trumpet.

The rallies at the High Street Port and the nightly vigil outside the prison gate attract crowds of three thousand, but always of a certain sort. A plan is devised to reach the more respectable citizens. Groups of soberly dressed women seat themselves in churches and cinemas. No tricolour ribbons, nothing to give the game away. When the minister begins the intercession, when the heroine is kidnapped by her wicked guardian, they rise to their feet.

Thomas thought prison doctoring would be a quiet life. Who cares whether convicts are healthy? But now Perth Prison is front-page news. One evening, after opening a parcel from his sister, he smooths out the brown paper it came wrapped in and draws a man and a woman in a circle, with lines radiating outwards enclosed by a larger circle, like the spokes of a wheel. In his small, neat hand he labels each tapered box. Newspaper readers (scandalised by rectal feeding). Herbert Asquith and his cabinet, at war with – three more boxes – female suffragists, Ulster Protestants and the House of Lords. McKinnon Wood, the Secretary of State for Scotland, whose wife it is said has not shared his bed since becoming president of the Shetland Suffrage Society. John Lamb, his Machiavellian secretary. The Chairman of the Prison Commission (a nice man, many leagues out of his depth). Matron, nursing her sense of grievance. The Governor, slandering the doctor to his masters. Flag-wavers cheering the royal car. Startled worshippers in the Episcopalian cathedral. Courting couples in the Kings Cinema. The nightly rabble at the High Street Port. The hymn singers outside the prison gates and their reluctant audience: the sleep-deprived wardresses quartered along Edinburgh Road. He names a compartment for each one: Florrie, Jeannie, Lizzie, Bella, Greta, Catherine, Mary Jane. Their lives a round of drudgery, petty injustice, marital wallopings, the bairns they've watched die, the hungry days when the bastard rolls in blind drunk. And now they've to put up with those snifty bitches from Edinburgh preaching about equality and going home to have their bloomers washed by

203

some poor slavey. *And aye, all right, the world's no fair, but how come ah'm always on the rough end o' it?*

All this electricity in the atmosphere. And at the heart of it, though apart from it, two people.

The wardresses are flagging. They have not had a day off for five weeks. Just the one afternoon to see the King and Queen. The day shift can get away in the evening but the minute they show their faces outside the gaol the crowd starts booing. Not just those Edinburgh bitches. Locals too. No knowing when you're going to stop a stinking egg. Not that they feel much safer in the gaol. Having to stand like stookies on the landing outside the women's hospital. They can hardly say no to the doctor, but if Matron catches them they'll rue the day.

Florrie Cruikshank cracks first. She is meant to be getting the new one, Prisoner Arthur, into her nightgown. They have been in the cell twenty minutes and she is not even out of her boots. Some cheek, belting out *Scots Whae Hae* when she's in here for trying to blow up Rabbie Burns' hoose. Florrie sings over the top of her. *Green Grow the Rashes-O*. That shuts her tattie-trap. But only for a wee minute. Then she starts into a lecture about forcible feeding. 'As infamous as the sjambok of the South African prison or the bastinado of the Turkish torture chamber. That man who calls himself a doctor is a blood brother of the Medieval skin-flayers, the ghouls of the Inquisition, the witch doctor who sticks red-hot needles into his victim's brain . . .' On and on in that cockapentie voice until Florrie lifts her hand and catches her a great whack across the face. You should hear her yell, fit to raise the dead. But there's no consequences. And even though Thomas is glad for Florrie's sake, he knows it's not right. If they can skelp a member of the quality like that, they can get away with murder.

Prisoner Janet Arthur – real name Frances Parker – is thirty-nine. Short, curly-haired, charming to those she wants to charm.

People tend to remember her voice. Not just because she can't pronounce the letter R. Where the well-spoken Englishwoman swallows her words in a throaty drawl, she booms. Because she's so small? To counter the rather sweet impression of her mangled diction? Whatever the reason, Doctor Watson finds it every bit as aggravating as the wardresses.

She is no fonder of him. He almost killed her lover, Ethel Moorhead, never mind poor Fanny Gordon. And Lord alone knows what he is doing to Arabella and Maude. But at least they are convicts. Prisoner Arthur has not even been tried and he is depriving her of visits and letters, forcing the feeding tube on her. She won't stand for it. Is there due process of law in this country or not?

It is old-fashioned influence, not the law, that will save her. But not just yet. Janie Allan, suffragette organiser and Glasgow shipping heiress, lets it be known that Prisoner Arthur is the niece of a very distinguished person, is determined to die in prison, and the government can expect trouble if she does. The authorities neglect to pass this warning on to the Governor. They are slow to uncover the prisoner's true identity. Events overtake them. Mistakes will be made.

The prison has acquired another suffragette, Helen Crawfurd, a hunger striker who was liberated from Glasgow and failed to return as licensed. The doctor is not unduly concerned. She is drinking water and could do with losing a few pounds. The Governor feels differently. *Four* of them now! He doesn't have the staff. Especially with Doctor Watson insisting on such unnecessary precautions to make sure Prisoner Scott comes to no harm. The gaol's resources are taxed to the limit. Prisoner Edwards signs an undertaking not to engage in further militant action and is liberated. A day later Prisoner Crawfurd is freed. Anyone can see the Scottish authorities are losing their enthusiasm for force-feeding suffragettes – anyone but Doctor Watson, that is.

The Commission suggests Prisoner Arthur's own doctor might be allowed into the gaol. (Doctor Watson won't hear of it.) If the prisoner shows any resistance, the case should be considered unfavourable for feeding. This broad hint, too, he ignores. Something about her imperious manner rouses his thrawn streak. Who does she think she is? Then there's the target of her crime: Burns' cottage in Alloway. He's an Ayrshire farmer's son who has risen by his wits: how can he not take it personally? She was carrying a bomb. Such a masculine form of destruction. Fire has its own horrors, the low crackle, the inexorable creep building to a roaring, leaping, all-consuming apotheosis, but there is something recognisably *womanly* about its fury. The bomb is cold. One minute everything is normal. Then *boom*! He'll be damned if he'll let her out. Not even when she falls off the chamber pot in a dead faint. Since she refuses to open her mouth, he uses the nasal tube. When this goes badly, he resorts to nutrient suppositories. Preceded by enemas. The wardresses have seen it done so many times that he leaves the procedure to them.

'You dinnae recognise me, do you?' MacIver says.

Prisoner Arthur looks surprised. 'Have we met before?

'Have we met before?' Philp mimics.

But MacIver's the ringleader. 'No socially, as you might say. We werenae introduced. But I ken you, Miss Parker.'

The third one, Cruikshank, laughs, 'Oh aye, she's paying attention the noo.'

And she is. This could ruin everything. At this very moment her brother might be opening a telegram. They could let her out within the hour, and the past five days will count for nothing.

'Do your superiors know my name?'

'No yet,' MacIver says, 'shall I tell them?'

The craven one, Philp, says, 'Mebbe, mebbe not . . .'

They are playing with her as a cat torments a mouse. She tells herself they cannot help it, it's in their nature.

'Still no recognised me?' MacIver says in that needling voice, 'aw, you've hurt my feelings. I thought I'd a made a wee bittie o' an impression.'

Cruikshank shuffles her chair closer to the bed. 'Go on: hae a guess. It's no sae hard.'

Another prison, but which? 'Dundee . . .? Craiginches?'

Philp smirks at her colleagues. 'Nae idea.'

MacIver puts on a parodic toff's accent. 'My darling Fan, I haven't slept a wink since hearing. When I think of your dear curls lying on a grimy mattress . . .'

Ethel. For a moment she is afraid they have caught her, but no: this was a couple of years ago. She remembers now. They discussed it after she was liberated. 'You were the one she trusted with her letters.'

The mood turns. Suddenly there is nothing playful in their cruelty.

'I was the one she bribed.' MacIver sounds angry, affronted.

Philp's tone is vicious: 'But she didnae pay her enough to deliver that filth.'

'So you destroyed them?'

'Oh no,' MacIver tells her, 'I kept them safe.'

Cruikshank leans forward, 'Ye never know when they might come in handy.'

A possible solution occurs to the prisoner. 'Are you asking me for money?'

Maciver sits on the bed. 'I might be,' she croons in a new, soft, insinuating voice, 'I might be asking you for something else.'

'What do you think it's worth,' Philp says, 'keeping your dirty wee secrets?'

The prisoner looks towards the door.

Cruikshank smiles. 'Expecting somebody, are you?'

'The doctor.'

A look passes between the three wardresses.

'Aw, did they no tell you?' MacIver says, 'Doctor won't be coming this morning. He's gi'en us the job o' feeding you.'

Three on one. MacIver lifts her by the hair and drops her at the bottom of the bed. Philp sits on her knees to stop her getting up. Cruikshank kneels on her chest, makes her promise to *behave*. Not that she is strong enough to cause them any trouble: she has not eaten or drunk for almost a week. They offer her a deal. If she promises not to resist, two of them will leave and Wardress MacIver will do what she is tasked with as gently and decently as possible. The prisoner agrees, so there are no witnesses when MacIver rapes her with a metal syringe.

Someone should put a stop to this.

Where is the doctor?

TWENTY-FIVE

Some days Prisoner Scott takes tea, some days tea and toast. The doctor boasts of achieving this by *much argument and persuasion tempered with firmness*. The truth is more complicated.

The protests outside are noisier than before. He worries they will strengthen her resistance but, the louder her supporters shout, the more she withdraws into herself. Each night they give her three rousing cheers. She claws at the backs of her hands. His stomach clenches as if he is the proper object of her raking nails.

'I heard a woman call your name last night.'

'My sister Muriel.'

'"Fight on Arabella. You must win"—'

She makes an ironic sound in the back of her throat. A comment on her sister? Or is it self-disgust?

'—there must have been thousands of them out there. Just for you.'

She shakes her head. 'Not me.'

'They shout your name.'

She says again, 'They're not here for me'.

Lately she seems to talk in riddles.

'Who else?' he says.

'An impostor. She was plausible, even I believed in her, but she is gone.'

'Then who is this?'

'A woman I would not wish on my worst enemy.'

A grain of humour thickens his voice, 'Nonetheless I have you in my care.'

'You do your best, but she is my real punishment.'

'Is she so disagreeable—?'

She looks at him, her eyes full of hostility and yet, somehow, imploring.

'—Because she drinks tea and eats a slice of toast?'

'Because she is weak and vain and treacherous and . . .' She stops herself.

'And?'

'She is a woman no one can love.'

'But Muriel loves you.'

She cuts across him. 'No *man* can love.'

'Ah.'

She looks away with a wintry smile.

'Try to sleep. You'll feel better when you're rested.'

'*Oh God.*'

'What's the matter?'

'Nothing. I commend your honesty.'

'*What are you talking about?*'

She turns towards him and his stomach dips, his bowels loosen. Not an unpleasant sensation.

'The woman they cheer cares nothing for people's opinions, and wins admiration at every turn, while I . . .'

'What?'

She gives him another hard look. 'The woman you see before you uses words like "freedom" and "justice" but has a slave's heart. She cares too much what . . . *others* think of her. And when she shows it, I too am repelled by her.'

Is she saying what he thinks she is saying? And if she is, why so bitter?

Six o'clock. The wardress delivers the tray with its pot of tea and two slices of toast (one for her, one for him).

'A cup and saucer,' she says, 'can I be trusted with china now?'

He is so rarely abstracted with her, she so seldom has the chance to study his face like this.

210

'I was thinking of my sister,' he says.

'Annie or Mary?'

'Jane.'

This is the first she has heard of Jane.

'I had a brother too, Robert. He died before his fourth birthday. Croup. Jane was younger, still talking gibberish, but she seemed so . . .' The skin around his eyes darkens. He is gone again, lost in some other time. Unexpectedly, he smiles. 'She could walk for miles on those wee legs. She'd get herself to the milking shed and stand there, roytering away—'

Who else has Arabella heard him speak of with such affection?

'—the kye all watching her. Such a fierce wee character. The other weans were given tin cups until they were old enough, but not Jane: she had to have china.'

'What happened to her?'

'Drowned. In the trough. They think she knocked herself out.' He blinks twice, thrice, rapidly, 'I was in the haybarn with a book, keeping out of sight. I thought I heard her, but she'd never called my name before . . .'

'So you assumed you were mistaken.'

In the silence Arabella can hear the wardresses gossiping on the landing.

After a while, he says, 'I was the eldest of eight, all my cousins living round about. When a new one turns up, it's just another bairn. When Robert died I hardly noticed. But Jane . . .' he takes a breath, 'I paid her more heed after she was dead than all the months she was running about the place.'

Arabella lays her hand on his.

He looks down at her white fingers, the long, dirty nails.

'She could have been a teacher,' he says.

Arabella used to be brave, constant, her strength of purpose blazing like a beacon to weaker souls. Now she swithers this

211

way and that. Scorn. Self-abasement. Violence. Tenderness. Fury. Need. Each contradictory impulse as urgent as life itself, until overtaken by the next. She hates him for outwitting her, loathes herself for being his dupe. But what a miracle that they should find each other. How unbearable that, having beaten the odds, they should still be kept apart. These feelings drop away, leaving a small hard self like a blackbird's beady eye, watching, waiting. She will weaken on her diet of tea and toast which, when all is said and done, is only bread and water. She will bribe him with intimate talk, flatter him with seeming surrender. His mind will equate a return to forcible feeding with failure. He will not notice her decline until too late, when the tube will kill her. Death will be victory. He will be disgraced.

She loves him.

He has planted a seed in her mind, and his. A life together. Ridiculous. Impossible. They know it. But still it germinates in the dark.

An inmate dies in the Criminal Lunatic Department. A Glasgow drunk, no madder than the rest of his kind, but he had the good fortune to fire a shotgun at a statue of William Gladstone and has eaten three square meals a day for the past five years. Until the infection took hold. No possibility of foul play, but there will have to be a public enquiry in the sheriff court. The doctor must take statements from all the warders who had care of him, making sure their evidence is tidy. No point in muddling the court with loose ends.

For forty-eight hours he leaves the care of Prisoner Scott to Lindsay.

When he returns, she is cold.

'You are busy these days.'

'I have other patients.'

'They've never detained you before.'

'There was an emergency.'

'Of course. Such an important man.'

She infuriates him. Her unpredictable moods, the talkative afternoons that end with him pushing the rubber tube down her throat. *Why* does she make him do it, when what he wants more than anything is to be at peace with her? And yet there's an inexplicable satisfaction in their quarrels. A voluptuary's abandon.

'I think you find me dull lately. You liked me best when I screamed and fought.'

He turns to the wardress, 'Bring two cups of tea.'

'Don't trouble yourself on my account—'

The wardress goes out, locking the door.

'—You pretend to want my compliance, but actually you prefer me to resist. Now why should that be?'

'I don't know why it *should be*, I know it is not.'

'No? Then your visits were merely a means to an end. Having achieved that end – you think – no more visits.'

'I made no secret of wanting you to eat.'

'And when I would not, you resorted to subterfuge.'

'What *subterfuge*?'

'The pretence that you were my friend.'

'God's truth! What is wrong with you?'

'I wasn't the one who suggested a voyage across the Atlantic.'

'What?'

'You heard—'

A knock at the door, the turning of keys.

'—That'll be your tea. I hope you're thirsty. I shan't be touching it.'

'You have been excused one feed a day in exchange for a steady increase in food taken voluntarily.'

'That is your understanding, not mine.'

'You cannot live on one cup of tea and one slice of toast a day.'

'Which is exactly why I agreed to them.'

The wardress sets the tray down and leaves.

A change comes over her. Quietly she says 'Why did you ask me?'

'Ask you what?'

'To go to Canada.'

He could tell her, confess the immense effort of will it takes not to think about her when he is with his other patients. A different story after hours. Medicine taught him all bodies are the same. Working in prison, he has learned that men's minds, too, are depressingly similar. And women's. He remembers how adults looked to him when he was a boy. Their mystery and grandeur. She brings it all back. When he is with her, the world is transformed.

Why did you ask me?

Ask you what?

To go to Canada.

'For the sake of your health.'

It seems he was wrong: the quarrelsome fit is still upon her.

'And sitting with me day after day, reminiscing about your gypsy love, weeping as you described your sister's drowning: all that was for my health, was it? Until two days ago.'

'*I have a job to do*. Unfortunately.'

'Then resign, if you do not like the work. Leave it to someone who finds it more congenial. Ah but of course, there is no one else. You and the butcher's boy were the only doctors in Scotland willing to violate your oath.'

He turns to go, 'Good day.'

This panics her, as he intends. 'Just tell me what I did.'

'*What you did?* This prison is under siege. I've got lunatics dropping dead on me, the Governor plotting against me, the Commissioners on my back, women shrieking and clinging to me in their neurotic craving for attention . . .'

214

'I beg your pardon, I thought that was one of the consolations. I should have trusted my first instinct: you are a savage, you enjoy inflicting pain.'

They should stop now, he must know it.

'Then what does that make you, who are so eager for the company of such a savage?'

'You are disgusting!'

'And you are a fraud. Oh aye, you're full of passion. A passionate remorse for compromising your hunger strike? No: a tantrum thrown by slighted vanity.'

'You took away my clothes. No man, or woman, not even my sister, has seen me as you have seen me. Nor touched me as you have. If I resisted, you used force. I was completely alone.'

'You're not a child. You put yourself in this position.'

'But I had not reckoned on the cruelty of my worst enemy masquerading as my friend.'

'I am *your doctor*.'

She laughs, 'It is you who are the fraud, *Doctor*.'

'Meaning what?' He takes her by the shoulders. '*Meaning what?*'

'Hiding behind the skirts of the government. It is your duty. Ha! *You liked it*. Clad in your white overall, handling women stripped of clothes and dignity. Forcing us to submit. Making us weep, and soothing us, only to come with violence again.'

'I take no satisfaction . . .'

'"I have given it up. It dulled the mind."'

'Aye, you are a woman no man can love.'

'You humiliate me?'

'You humiliate yourself. You and your *sisters*. I have learned about women, these past weeks. I never thought to see them behave as I've seen here. Fighting like hellcats, screaming like banshees, barely clad but quite without modesty. I expected shame, a proper aversion. In fact, you cannot get enough of my company.'

215

'By God, when they let me out of here, I will get my father's gun and shoot you.'

Another day she springs out of bed. The wardresses have left their post outside and are gossiping in the water closet. There is no one to intervene. He is heavier, it should not be hard to overpower her, but he is afraid of hurting her. Or afraid of some other urge. He catches her wrists. She uses her head, her feet, the tensile strength in her back but, in the end, she exhausts herself. They stand face to face, hand to hand, sweating, their breathing ragged. She says it again.

I swear I will shoot you.

He has never felt more alive.

TWENTY-SIX

A Captain Parker strikes a deal with the Secretary for Scotland and his sister is released. The pretext is 'obtaining a second opinion of Prisoner Arthur's condition'.

A few days later the doctor is summoned to the Governor's office where he is handed a three-page medical report written by an Edinburgh practitioner in cahoots with the suffragette doctor Mabel Jones.

'You may be interested in page two. Severe bruising on the arms and legs.'

'She had the bruises when she arrived.'

'It wasn't in your reports.'

She received them at the hands of Doctor Dunlop, in Ayr Gaol. He sees the way it will go. A courtesy to his Prison Commission colleague will be made to look like covering his own tracks. And there is worse. *Pain in the genital region; raw surfaces on the mucous membrane; distinct swelling of the vulva in its posterior part.*

Disgust rises in his throat.

The Governor asks 'Could it have been an honest mistake?'

Of all the fatuous remarks the doctor has heard him make over the past four months, this is the most asinine.

The Governor grows pale under his whisky flush. 'You know who she is?'

'A Miss Parker, it says here. Unless that, too, is an alias.'

'Who *her uncle* is.' The Governor's voice drops to a whisper, the old ham. Only this time the drama is justified. Frances Parker is the niece of Lord Kitchener of Khartoum,

217

former commander-in-chief of the British Army in India, the general who delivered victory in the South African War.

'What the hell did you think you were doing? A woman in that condition should never have been in a cell.'

All very well to say that now. Where was this wise counsel when it mattered? The doctor re-reads the first page of the report. Lindsay let his mouth run away with him when handing the prisoner over. It's all here in black and white, much of it untrue. For all the difference that makes, now it has been circulated in triplicate.

'Dr Lindsay says she fainted. Is he lying about that too?'

'I let her sit on the chanty. It was a mistake.'

'I thought Dr *Ferguson* Watson did not make mistakes.'

'I have been under some strain.'

'*Strain?* I have to find the money for seven temporary wardresses, and twenty-six days' leave my own wardresses have not taken so you can be sure Prisoner Scott comes to no harm. This place is like a powder keg. When the staff aren't at each other's throats, they're doing God knows what to the inmates. The Trades and Labour Council has called a meeting on the North Inch to condemn us: no hall is big enough for the crowd they're expecting. And why is that?'

'The newspapers.'

'Aye, the newspapers – but what is it they're printing? *Your* doings. I'll have no more mistakes in this gaol, Watson. You've been allowed to run the hospital as your own private fiefdom. I warned them, but I was overruled. From now on you will take orders from me. The Chairman is coming tomorrow to discuss the terms of Prisoner Scott's licence.'

Bull's-eye. The old bastard knows it.

'Prisoner Scott has eight months left to serve.'

'*Five weeks* has brought this prison to its knees.'

'She will claim it as a victory.'

'We cannot keep her.' The Governor's eyes glint with

218

malice, 'And even if we could, she'll never give you the satisfaction you're seeking.'

The doctor could fell him with one punch. He can feel his body rebalancing to maximise the power behind his fist.

'Tell the Chairman he can find a new medical officer.'

It is out of his mouth before he has time for second thoughts. He pictures his father, who has never said boo to the factor.

'*Oh no*. You think you can create this bloody mess and just walk away?'

'My probationary period expires at the end of the year. I do not wish my position confirmed.'

His head is light with a sort of vertigo. The worst has happened. He almost laughs. The Captain can marry them on board ship. A ten-minute ceremony and then down to her cabin. No need for shame. The two of them free to do everything he cannot let his waking self imagine. Everything his dreaming self has done night after night since he first set eyes on her. The emission a cold patch on his pyjamas next morning. Sometimes more than one.

It will happen in mid-Atlantic, on deck, after many talk-filled evenings under the stars. She will feel the pull between them, night after night of holding her breath for his touch, so that finally, when he lays hands on her, she will shudder with fulfilled longing.

'And what reason am I to give the Commission?'

'Tell them, circumstances that have arisen since I came to Perth.'

The Governor gives him a cockeyed look and for a moment his nerve wavers. He is counting on the Colonial Office finding him a post with a house and a decent salary somewhere far from ice and summer mosquitoes. But what if he is wrong? He is giving up four hundred pounds a year, for what? Has she ever said, in so many words, *I will go with you to Canada*? He could spring her from gaol and never see her again. She could tell the world. His integrity in tatters, the butt of every music hall joke, cartoons in the newspapers depicting him as a salivating lecher.

He turns to leave, but the Governor has not finished. The Chief Constable of Edinburgh telephoned this morning to pass on some intelligence.

TWENTY-SEVEN

Arabella's father took seven years to die. Apoplexy. Heart seizure. Malignant growth. A series of blows from which he rallied less and less convincingly. His face shrank to a skull's concavities. That big soldier's body with its meaty neck and barrel chest dwindled to a bundle of bones. She glimpsed him once without his pyjama jacket, when her mother was washing him. The blueish ball and socket of his shoulder was like a five-year-old boy's. But it was his mind's dwindling that afflicted her most. He became, not someone else – even that might have been endurable – but no one. A scarecrow's head stuffed with leaves and straw. He knew he was dying but didn't take it personally, while she sat by his bed, exhausted with the effort of willing him to be himself.

Now she knows exactly how he felt.

Random words rise to her lips, phrases divorced from any conscious intent. She knows it is important not to voice the babble in her head, but sometimes the stale hospital air seems to ring with the echo of her thoughts. Has she spoken aloud, or is it a figment of her brain? She has acquired the knack of not hearing the wardresses' gossip. Once in a while she will catch them staring, as if waiting for her to answer a question or react to a taunt. How strange it is to smell their greasy hair and sweaty armpits, the particular stink of an unwashed uniform ironed into yet another day's service, and to feel so detached.

And then she hears his footsteps. Ah God, how good it will

be to clash with him, to feel strength re-entering her limbs, anger firing her blood. To become *real* again.

I have hated her for fifty years. I have thought of her so often it's hard to remember we have never met. I feel closer to her than I did to Hilda. We both know how two hearts can yearn to beat as one and still every word spoken leaves its scarring of hate. At least they had an excuse. Or was it not like that for them, did she take him by the hand and lead him to a place where he could let himself be loved?

The prison swelters in the grip of a heat wave. When Thomas ventures out, the town is stricken. Lassitude in the empty streets, pavement strays prone and panting, blinds three-quarters drawn to protect the shopkeepers' wares. Back at the prison, the doctor's face shines with sweat, but he will not shed his frock coat and walk about in his shirtsleeves like a labourer. On any other day he would be doing the rounds of the Criminal Lunatic Department by now. This departure from routine irks him but cannot be helped. He has twenty-four hours. It must be settled before the Chairman arrives to start haggling over her release. She must be told how to play it, what to ask for: her passage to Canada and the wherewithal to make a new life. She will not like the idea of taking their money. He will convince her of the necessity. But first, he must declare himself.

He has been adding meat juice to her feeds. It makes her less drowsy, but more argumentative. Her eyes flash when he walks in. The wardresses know this mood of his. They scramble off their backsides and out into the corridor.

'Up,' he says.

'What?'

'On your feet—'

She stares at him.

'—don't you want to?'

222

'Of course I want to.'

He extends a hand to help her off the mattress, but she ignores it, using the bedframe to lever herself up.

He smiles.

'What?' she asks.

'You look different, standing. When you're not in a temper.'

'I may walk about?'

He nods. She takes a step and staggers. He steadies her. Her legs are weak after so long in bed, but she won't give up. She tries again with his hand supporting her upper arm. Reaching the empty stretch of floor in the middle of the ward, she gives a gasping laugh.

'You can't imagine how I've hungered for this. Sharper than hunger. It's movement the body craves, more than food.'

This is his chance. All he has to do is keep hold of her arm and, with his other hand, draw her waist towards him. He even has the words to breathe in her ear. *This is what I have hungered for.*

He is unnerving her, standing there with that queasy simper. Smiling is not part of his repertoire, unless she counts the occasional sarcastic grimace. Something has happened. She should have paid more attention to the wardresses' gossip.

'Yesterday . . .' he begins.

'You insulted me.'

'You said you would kill me.'

'I said I would shoot you. I did not say I was a dead shot.'

'Your friends would kill me. That mob out there.' He pauses, 'The police have word of a plot to bomb my house.'

Ethel. She knows beyond doubt. Who else would think up such a crack-brained scheme? Under the noses of the authorities: what a coup for the cause! She has a history of outrageous stunts. Three grand houses in upper Strathearn

223

in a single night. They say the blazes lit the sky. She is not squeamish about human targets either, marching into that schoolmaster's classroom to attack him with a dogwhip. He had strong-armed her out of a meeting. What might she do to a doctor who almost killed her with the feeding tube in Calton Gaol?

He watches her closely, 'It is to happen at night, when I'm in bed, asleep.'

'But you'll sleep inside the prison, now you know.'

'I wouldn't give them the satisfaction.'

Her stomach turns over. He will be blown to pieces out of stubbornness. Ethel will be hanged. 'The Governor will overrule you.'

'The Governor would like nothing better than to be rid of me.'

'Then don't give *him* the satisfaction.'

She seems worried. He did not foresee the annoyance mixed in with her alarm, but still, this is promising.

'I knew what I was taking on. I didn't expect to be popular.'

'*They're going to blow up your house.* You think they're not capable of it? Don't be too sure.'

'They?'

'Whoever it is. We do not always fail.'

'You side with them even in this.'

'We've never killed anyone.'

'But for me they might make an exception, eh?'

She looks away. 'Accidents happen.'

'They might kill me *by accident*?'

Her voice cracks, 'It's not funny.'

'Not for me, perhaps, but what is it to you?'

Her eyes are lowered. Only the shallowness of her breathing gives her away. He waits. Will she touch him? Plead with him? Weep for him?

'I don't want anyone's death,' she says at last.

224

'Not even mine?'

She lifts her eyes to his.

Seven days from this moment she will be released. Tomorrow she will meet with the Chairman of the Prison Commission and the horse-trading will begin. The texture of her encounters with the doctor will change. This giant who has blocked out the light, dominated her thoughts, coloured her dreams, will shrink to man-size. Their volatile intimacy will end.

But today, in her ignorance, she wants to write a letter. To warn Ethel. And to protect him. His neat ears, the freckled backs of his hands, his precious flesh.

He says no. She argues with him, a tremor in her voice, her hands reaching towards him, before dropping to her sides. A thrill in his blood as he refuses, like the pleasure he felt toying with Prisoner Edwards, but with the complication that Arabella's desperation is for his sake. And so at last he says yes. But he will not let her use the pen. They sit side by side on the bed, eyes fixed on the notebook in his lap, both of them remembering that other letter he wrote at her dictation, both thinking how far they have come since then. As always, she is naked under her nightdress. He takes off his coat. The smell of her skin. His breath on her cheek. Her hair brushing his ear. It has to happen. Why else let her stand and walk about? He is changing the rules, letting her know that what was forbidden is now possible. Desire can be acted upon. She may bite him, strike him, claw at him, or open her mouth to his. The choice is hers. She pretends not to know, but he can see her palpitating heart through the cotton of her gown. She wants the letter to name him, to forbid his harming above all others'. She turns her face towards him. Their eyes, mouths, inches apart. Her soft lips. Who closes the gap? The pen drops from his hand. She moans, yielding. Is it now? Do they lie down on the bed?

Thomas could not tell me.

225

TWENTY-EIGHT

Doctor Lindsay takes a day off to visit his parents, and when he returns the doctor tells him he will be more useful in the men's hospital. His daily contact with the prisoner and the wardresses who attend her is at an end.

Almost everything I know he told me that day in the prison garden. I have gleaned a few details from newspapers stored in public libraries. My friend Patrick in the Colonial Office pulled some strings and got me a glimpse of the Scottish Office files. But what passed between them from Tuesday to the following Sunday, when she was released, is not recorded.

It is like being locked out of my own life.

Yes it was so long ago, and almost everyone is dead and it can't be so many years before I'm among them, but for now it still matters. I walked down the aisle to become the sort of smiling woman whose home smells of warm biscuits and rings with children's laughter, and that hope turned to ashes. Yes, I had adventures. Egypt, Syria, India, the Gold Coast. I saved so many lives, and found a man to spend the rest of his days with me. I would not want to have missed any of that. But the price of making a new life was exile. I had to train as a doctor in Glasgow, then turn my back on Britain, leaving behind mother, father, brother, sister, uncle, aunt, all the friendships I had forged since leaving Perth. And I had to turn my back on him, too. My husband.

Half a century has passed and I still don't know whether he was done for before we met; whether his heart was already

226

claimed, or smashed; the exact quality of his regret; whether another wife, more selfless and forgiving, or ruthless, or vainglorious, might have redeemed him. Whether the love story pieced together in these pages is mine, or hers.

Some things I do know. He could stare at her with his eyes full of wanting but, unless she pushed the moment beyond ambiguity, nothing would happen. The crucial question is, what was *she* capable of?

I have read about prisoners kept in solitary confinement. How it erodes the personality. The way they come to depend on their captors. The demoralising effects of harsh treatment interspersed with kindness. Far worse than unstinting brutality. But Arabella is a political prisoner. Even as she suffers, the soldier in her sleeps with one ear open.

'What if I said you'd had all you could take—?'

She squints at him.

'—the prisoner has been on hunger and thirst strike for the past five weeks. She does not appear any the worse for her treatment . . .'

'I am very much the worse for it.'

'. . . at the same time, it seems desirable some cases should not be fed in this way over too long a period.'

'Why?'

'All good things come to an end.'

She does not even think about it. 'No—'

He looks at her as if she has taken leave of her senses.

'—I won't go.'

'Why not?'

'It will be made to look like surrender.'

'*For God's sake!*'

She wavers. Will she look back on this moment and curse her wrongheadedness? He seems well-disposed to her today, almost fond. But when has he acted in her best interests?

227

'This comes from them, not you. You do what they tell you to.'

'I've resigned.'

He should never have told her. The soldier's ear pricks up. 'Why?'

Does he admit it: 'You'?

She laughs. His eyes fill with dismay. The woman softens, but the soldier says *wait*.

'What will you do?'

'Whatever it is, it will be nothing to do with politics.' He swallows, 'I might go overseas.'

Canada. She blushes as if they are saying aloud the words she hears in her head:

You spoke once of taking me there.

And you never gave me an answer.

Why not, she wonders now? Because it seemed too much like a dream, or a trick. Or because, even as the woman was tempted, the soldier knew this day was coming. He would not risk raising the subject if there was the slightest possibility of losing face. They are willing to let her out. She sees the agony in his features and her heart strains towards him, but she bites her tongue. Discretion was ever the better part of valour.

Besides, there is the question of power. Hers returning, his diminishing. *I have resigned.* If it was done to win her favour, he made a mistake.

When he has gone, she sends word to the Governor via a wardress. If the Prison Commission is minded to release her, she will hear what they have to say.

Next morning she is given a bath. The Chairman himself enters the hospital. A balding, pouchy-faced fellow with a nose like something fashioned out of orange peel. He takes a fatherly tone, letting her sit up, patting her hand, which she tolerates because she has a schoolteacher's forbearance with those less intelligent than herself. He wants her to break with

228

the Women's Social and Political Union, to give her word she will not organise or incite illegal acts. She refuses with such finality there is nothing more to be said. They sit in silence. He does not get up to leave. She nearly laughs aloud. Her tea and toast suppers count for nothing. She has beaten them.

The Chairman returns the day after, having taken instruction from the Secretary for Scotland. He tells her he is her friend. Not everyone wishes to see her liberated. The prison doctor, for one, argued against it most vehemently. She tells him they can hold her until she is a hundred, she will never give up the cause.

What can he do? The authorities want rid of her: no more questions in the House and headlines about indecent assaults on the nieces of national heroes. Whatever she says or refuses to say, they think it unlikely Prisoner Scott will return to militant action. They are prepared to release her unconditionally. At this news, she gives up her hunger strike.

The doctor brings her a tomato. Firm, still green around the scar where it was so recently plucked from the stem. She sniffs it, holds it in her hand. Almost too beautiful to eat. But in the end, she bites. The skin bursts, spraying seeds down her chin.

They laugh.

She could be let out that very evening. Or the next day. The newspapers are predicting it. The wardresses are stood down. Muriel takes a posy of sweet peas to the prison gate. Within the hour, Arabella buries her face in their silky fragrance. She is out of bed all day, walks twice in the prison exercise yard, eats three good meals.

The doctor assigns the rest of his duties to Thomas Lindsay. Time is short. All her talk is of liberty, the pleasures she has missed. Playing the piano. Visiting the theatre. Walking the shoreline at Gullane, opening her arms to the wind. The sea is in her blood. Great Aunt Charlotte was married to a harbour master. She takes her middle name from her. She pauses, distracted by a thought. Where does his middle name come from, that Ferguson?

Does he answer? Would he lay himself so open to her?

'I made it up. To lend me distinction.'

Can he truly believe they will see each other again once she has left the prison? Does he imagine taking the train to Edinburgh, knocking on her mother's door? *'Come in, come in, delighted to meet you . . .'* Or is he reduced to childish fantasy? A fairy-tale coincidence many months later. Seated in the concert hall, half-drugged with Schubert. Glancing up to find her face, her shocked look reflecting his own, that same shaky smile. *My God.*

Does she give him hope, let him hold her, touch her, murmuring promises between their kisses? Is she cruel enough to pay him back like that?

There is one other possibility. They both understand this is all they will ever have. These two days locked away from the world.

She is liberated discreetly at ten forty-five on Sunday morning. He makes one last physical examination, finding no mark on body or limb. Muriel and Ethel come in a cab, taking Arabella away to a dentist's house on the moneyed side of town. The dentist's daughter has become a good friend. That afternoon, the Trades and Labour Council hold a rally on the North Inch to condemn forcible feeding. Thousands cheer the prisoner's release.

Sun, air, pollen-drunk bees, the chatter of friends. A sister's hands to wash her hair. Feather pillows, laundered sheets, warm scones with this year's strawberry jam, as many hot baths as she cares to take. These dear women hanging on her words, gasping and exclaiming.

Doctor Mabel Jones arrives to examine her. Does she

stiffen, insisting 'No need'? But her physical condition must be checked: who knows how that brute might have damaged her? Pulse, temperature, her chest. And now a departure from the familiar routine. Her petticoat is lifted. '*No! You may not!*' Mabel assures her she will be very gentle, nothing like the assaults inflicted on Frances Gordon, Maude Edwards and Fanny Parker.

'Assaults?'

They explain.

Arabella writes a letter to the newspapers. It is printed in the *Glasgow Herald* two days after her release.

It is very clear that forcible feeding was inflicted upon me in order to extract an undertaking, and further on account of the part I played at the by-election in Ipswich, when Mr Masterman was defeated. To try to force a person to yield her opinions under pain is torture, and nothing else. The only effect it has had upon me is to strengthen my principles.

Unlike most of respectable Perth, which favours the Edinburgh paper, the *Scotsman*, the doctor is from the West. He reads the *Glasgow Herald*.

He likes to breakfast in the kitchen, as he did as a boy on the farm. While Mrs Hendry makes his porridge, he reads the paper and drinks a cup of strong, sugary tea. Even in summer he cannot abide it less than scalding, the thought of tepid liquid makes his gorge rise. He hears the porridge sucking and dimpling as it comes to the boil. An advertisement for liver pills catches his eye. These damned mountebanks! Mrs Hendry says something about the weather being set to break. And now he sees it. A letter to the editor. His heart bucks in his chest. He spreads the paper across the table, on top of plate, cup, cutlery, butter; sends Mrs Hendry to the shops. 'But the porridge, sir?' '*Just go!*'

A message from her. His quick eye has taken it all in, but he reads it again, lingeringly, hearing the words in her voice, trying to squeeze some new meaning from them. There is none. A draining feeling in his arms, his fingers, the adrenaline ebbing.

His tea goes cold. The porridge solidifies in the pan. He has not felt like this since his sister died. This bruised sensation around the eyes, the dull ache in his throat. But the tears won't come. What has she done to him? He is still sitting there when Mrs Hendry gets back. She takes one look at him and turns around, claiming she has forgotten the bread.

To gull him like that. After everything they have been to each other. Oh aye, she pulled the wool over his eyes. Had him mooning after her like a lovesick calf. Those damn fools at the Commission: they had to insist on letting her out, had to cave in to the Governor's bleating about the cost and the strain on the staff. Did he not warn them they should keep her? He wasn't so drunk with her he forgot his duty. They can't lay that at his door.

He writes to David Crombie, Secretary of the Prison Commission, his nib slicing across the paper. She has returned to militancy, as he predicted all along. He said from the first she would never give in. He told them she should remain in prison for as long as possible. He knew she would defy all authority the minute she got out. She is about to do something desperate, of that he has no doubt. She is practically an anarchist. She believes every act of destruction draws attention to their cause. Should anything very serious happen, they may be certain it is done by the hand of Arabella Scott.

He pauses, imagining it. Waverley Station ablaze. St Giles Cathedral. Holyrood Palace. They will catch her red-handed. She will come back to him. Raging, weeping, insulting him, writhing under his hands. It will begin again.

All at once he pictures Crombie's face, those bushy eyebrows lifting. He will need to go carefully if he is to retract his resignation. Is the letter too intemperate, even unprofessional? Will a copy be circulated to the Commissioners? And if to them, then to the Governor, who will take the opportunity to pass on who knows what low gossip from the wardresses?

I have formed such opinions by allowing her to have her own say over long periods when I put the wardress out of hearing but never out of the hospital.

He reads it through again. What has he to be ashamed of? Aye, he sounds angry – is he not entitled? He will not tear the truth up and drop it in the wastepaper basket. They have let her win. He alone stood up to her. Let them hear it. He addresses the envelope, attaches a stamp, then, at the last moment, scrawls across the top of the letter: *though I offer this opinion I give it as a private man.*

She sets no fires. Within a week the nation is at war with Germany. The suffragettes suspend their campaigning and are granted an amnesty. Arabella goes to France as an officer in the Women's Army Auxiliary Corps.

It is over.

HILDA

If she had to prise her old bones out of Chelsea for six months, Hilda would have chosen Paris or Barcelona or Buenos Aires or New York. But no: it had to be South Yarra, where the art scene is all sausage-fingered Aussies brawling over *figs* or *abs,* and Billy can't drink in the bars in case she starts a fight, so it's night after night at Maisey's or that old poofters' coffee lounge, or back to the suburban box with its swing seat, barbecue and car porch.

But that's a subject best avoided for now. It doesn't do to criticise the love nest, with the bowerbird not yet cold in the ground. Who would have thought it: the cosmopolitan Billy Bellairs swilling lager and swapping blue jokes with the convict stock in South Yarra? The famous artist's business manager and bed-warmer. True love, Hilda has no doubt. Billy would have stared at that revolting wallpaper, going quietly doolally, for the next twenty years, if she hadn't arrived to take charge. Weeding out the paintings to be kept, getting a contract drawn up so the gallery can't flood the market with the rest. Selling the house and most of the furniture. Shipping the bed. She's not completely heartless.

Hilda liked Jan Cumbrae-Stewart well enough, but there was just too much of the Edwardian soap advertisement in her portraits. Those rosy-skinned, golden-haired nudes (so often painted from behind) that met with such acclaim, while Hilda had her hopes raised so cruelly by being shown in the British pavilion in Venice in twenty-four, and afterwards . . . nothing. Or worse: a badly-lit side room off a couple of Jan's shows in Australia and a yawning paragraph tacked on to each of Jan's gushing reviews. One critic noted the hard-edged quality in Hilda's etchings, finding it not stark or unflinching but 'rather unpleasant'. As if she had sneezed over the soup. As if art had to *please*, when she was capturing the moment, and doing it rather better than Jan Cumbrae-Stewart, if truth be told. Of course, the fact that Jan was decades out of date was just what they liked about her. Along with that broad hint of the bedroom, the fireside glow, the coy provocation of all those turned shoulders and plump young buttocks. Public taste was ever base.

And to prove it, here they are at this Sunday painters' jumble sale in Sydney. Mountains and seascapes. Vases of flowers. Still lifes. Soulful-eyed cats, for Christ's sake. And this oddity, an abstract, crudely executed but with more feeling in its slashing diagonals than all the pretty-pretty figuratives put together. Just look at that bloody carmine, the bilious green, the sheer force in that line pushing down from the upper right hand corner. Hilda squints at the typed card, the old peepers not being what they were.

'Body Politic,' says a voice behind her. Scottish, if she's not mistaken. 'Rather pretentious, I'm afraid, but it sums up what I wanted to say.'

She has all the marks of age, ivory teeth, mauve-tinted skin, fleshy grooves and folds, but it's still an astonishing face. A quiet intelligence that says *I am a person of consequence, if only to myself.* 'Arabella Colville-Reeves.' They shake hands and Hilda's heart gives a little thump, though she hasn't gone home with a stranger in fifteen years, and Billy's just the other side of the room, having her grief stroked by one of you-know-who's many admirers. She turns back to the canvas. *The body politic.* She sees it now: oesophagus, stomach, intestines, painted with such anger. Those poor bloody queers in Soviet loony bins, being cured of what ails them. Aversion therapy. Electric shocks. But surely they'd leave the Brits alone?

'I'm so sorry,' the woman says, 'I wasn't trying to upset anyone. Let me find you somewhere to sit.'

A return to civilisation is what Billy needs. England, where they drink proper beer and the spiders don't bite and the sun doesn't fry your brain in your skull. A fresh start in London. Or Surrey, if she must, but near the station, no more than an hour from Soho and Shaftesbury Avenue and old friends. In South Yarra, Billy conceded the wisdom of this but, now that they have landed at London Airport and are stuck in a very English queue, she is having second thoughts. Thank Christ for Dodo! Sweeping through passport control against the tide with a nod that says *I know perfectly well I'm not supposed to do this*. The years overseas have left her with an old colonial's arrogance. Who can refuse that frizz of white hair, the sparkling gaze, the blend of sweet-old-lady charm and steely command? ('It's *Doctor* Coubrough.') She has found some lackey to escort her into the arrivals hall with an empty wheelchair. Billy spots them first, tipping Hilda the wink to play up her limp. '*Hilly!*' '*Dodo!*' Hilda gives the smirkers an icy stare. Of course she's a fossil, but she had the best of it, being young when the Modern carried a whiff of blood and madness, not refrigerators and drip-dry nylon. And being old's not so bad when you're whizzed through customs with your smuggled bottle of scotch and out into the blessed drizzle of good old Blighty.

'*Well.*'

Always this moment when the sisters stop and take a gander at each other. A few more liver spots on the backs of Dodo's hands. *Sun spots*, apparently. And she'll have to watch that stoop, it's halfway to a dowager's hump. Meanwhile Dodo sees what: the cripple's walk, the tippler's complexion? (But then, they both like a stiffener before lunch.) Perhaps just age. These days Hilda looks the older sister. Not that it matters any more, except with Dodo. The only person in the world

Hilda still needs to best, and the fact that Dodo doesn't feel the same only makes the struggle more compulsive.

Billy knows exactly what's going on and springs to the rescue with gallantry all round. The only thing better than spending time with one of the Atkins gels is being in the company of both. A celebration is in order! A late lunch at the Ritz? Or is the old place in Sloane Square still open? Hilda quite fancies the Gay Hussar, but Dodo is wearing the colonial smile that brooks no contradiction. They're going back to Langstone Manor where the daily is cooking roast lamb and apple pie. A weekend of sea air and good English food (and drink) to recover from the flight. Beefy will drive them back up to London on Monday.

And talk of the Devil, here he is: waiting outside in the Consul. Beefy Bill Coubrough. If it's sausage fingers you're after, he's your man. Hands like shovels. Big head, big shoulders, big feet. Probably big where it matters, too, but Hilda finds these Frankenstein types utterly sexless. No nuance. The booming voice and hearty guffaw. Not so different from Billy B at first glance, but with Billy it's ironic. Beefy spent thirty years yelling at the natives in words of one syllable before coming home to play lord of the manor. Plus fours and an alcoholic bulldog. A *character*. And a bit of a bully behind closed doors. The way he growls at Dodo sometimes. To marry one overbearing oaf may be regarded as misfortune. To marry two looks like perversion. Not that Hilda would say it. At least, not outright. Though who knows where the conversation may wend once she passes on her news?

Design a hideous home for returning colonials. A Rayburn under a shelf of brass preserving pans; twelve-seater dining table; crewelwork curtains; fire dogs either side of the roaring grate. A Jacobean settle opposite a grandfather clock with an echoing tick and a chime like the knell of doom. All inside a redbrick villa built for the local brewer in 1904.

Beefy's a parvenu. Forever bragging about growing up in Old Ballikinrain. (And so he did, in the staff quarters.) A Tory, like all those *I pulled myself up by my bootstraps* types. Still, he's not stingy with the drink. Hilda has stayed with them before, she knows the form. Down to the pub at eleven so Bobby the bulldog can have his beer; gin and tomato juice at lunch; whisky in their afternoon tea. They'll all be three sheets to the wind hours before they sit down to the serious drinking at dinner.

And so it goes.

The lamb is burned and the mashed potato lumpy, but it soaks up the booze. Beefy delivers his party piece: *faint heart never won fair lady*. How he was turned away by the houseboy, though he knew damn well Dodo was in: he could hear her in the bath. Did he get to be inspector of works for one of Africa's biggest public building programmes by taking no for an answer? He did not. Crawled under the house, found a hatch to climb through. Planted himself on the end of her bed. You should have seen her face when she came out of the bathroom! Hilda has heard this tale at least three times, and finds it more sinister with every retelling, but Dodo twinkles with wifely satisfaction, says she had to marry him, just to bring him under control. Which is Beefy's cue to ask when Hilda is going to settle down with a nice chap? 'I'm waiting for Dodo to tire of you, Bill.' Laughter all round. Then that revolting dog tries to roger the ginger cat, and Billy B tells a couple of the riper stories doing the rounds in South Yarra, to much *ho ho*-ing and table-slapping from their host. Dodo clears the table. Hilda picks up the gravy boat and follows her out.

'How're the legs?'

Poor old Hilly, never the same after that hit-and-run driver. Give Dodo a symptom and she'll be off, airing her knowledge of tibias and fibulas because she's a medical professional, not a failed painter living on Mama's legacy, and so Hilda has to

238

answer 'Right as ninepence,' when in truth her knee is killing her.

Odd, the way she can feel so overshadowed and still bask in Dodo's reflected glory. It doesn't hurt a girl's cachet, having a sister who has met a witch doctor and delivered black babies in mud huts. Does Dodo ever boast about her little sis the bohemian, palling around with spies and deviants? What Hilda wouldn't give to find out.

Watching her kick drunkenly at the wheel that makes the Rayburn hotter, she feels a sudden stab of affection. How marvellous it was when Dodo left the prison of her first marriage and they were the Atkins girls again, gadding about London, working up a glow on the Kit-Cat dance floor, vying for the affection of Billy Bellairs. What larks! Then Dodo hooked it. Toronto first, then Cairo, Damascus, Borsad, Accra, anywhere but home. Fourteen long years. Hilda missed her so dreadfully that, in the seventeen years she has been back and living seventy miles away, they've hardly met. Why should she have it all her own way, taking off to the ends of the earth and then, just when it suits her, coming home to the welcoming arms of her kin? But who suffers most from Hilda's sulk? Not Dodo. She has her shovel-handed husband, her bookish Oxford professor down the lane, all the friends and neighbours who drop by to drink her gin, and her career (so indispensable she's still seeing patients at seventy). While Hilda has – what? A tenancy in Phene Street and the crowd in the pub across the road. The odd port and lemon in the Gateways, eavesdropping on the latest slang. Bugger, it's good to see Dodo again. But even now, alone together in the warm kitchen, both of them woozy with drink, Hilda can't seem to break through. So many things they could laugh over, so much to say, yet here they are, their small talk petering into silence.

If only Dodo would ask how she is. Not her legs, *herself*. Is she happy with her lot, is she afraid of dying alone, is she still carrying a torch for Billy Bellairs? How many people in her life has she truly loved? Hilda would like to ask these questions of Dodo too.

'Billy's on good form,' Dodo says. Bloody Pollyanna.

'Tonight.'

'Not generally?'

Hilda pulls a face.

Dodo sighs, 'It's so sad.'

'It's always *sad*. You don't get life without death. I would have thought you'd know that, Doctor Coubrough. I met a woman over there who's been widowed twenty-five years. Longer than she was married. She's made a go of it—'

Dodo retrieves the apple pie from the oven.

'—interesting woman. About your age. Travelled around. France during the war, South Africa, Oz. A Scot.'

'Oh yes?' Dodo pours the top of the milk into a jug.

'In fact, she had a connection with Perth.'

Moving towards the dining room, Dodo says over her shoulder, 'Be a darling and bring the cream.'

Hilda had her own brush with the body politic. Stumbling down the hall half-asleep to find a gaberdine mac at the door: was she aware that Guy Burgess and Donald Maclean had flown the coop? Had she helped them? At the time it seemed rather a hoot, being knocked up by MI5 in the middle of the night. She dined out on the story for weeks. But the joke wore thin. Her telephone emitted peculiar whirrings and clickings. Her god-daughter was turned down by the civil service, despite a first in Greats. The off-licence stopped giving her tick. One or two of her more conventional friends simply dropped her.

She learned it pays to be cagey. And yet, settled in a quiet corner of a Sydney tea shop, she found herself spilling the whole story to that graceful stranger with the faint Scots burr. She too had had a police tail, before the Great War. Then she went to gaol. She opened her lovely mouth and showed Hilda her ruined teeth. All that sacrifice, and by the time the government caved in she was living on another continent. She'd had her fill of Britain. Too many bitter memories.

'He was my brother-in-law.'

A long silence. Was she going to get up and walk out?

'Biggest mistake of my sister's life,' Hilda added, lest there was any ambiguity.

Arabella Colville-Reeves regarded her across the Victoria sponge. 'I wondered if he was altogether sane,' she said at last.

It's late but the coals are still glowing in the grate. Beefy has gone up to bed, completely blotto. The grandfather clock lulls them with its ponderous tick. The bulldog snores on the sheepskin rug. Dodo, Hilda and Billy carry their brandy balloons to the hearthside chairs.

'I've been thinking I might go back to calling myself Argemone.'

Hilda doesn't know why this should be so killing, but even Dodo is amused. They talk about Gordon and Gyp and their kids, and Billy's nephews, and Dodo says 'It's funny none of us had children of our own'. Not so very funny, Hilda drawls, with two of us lesbian and the other one not sure. Anyway, there's a lot of barren stock about. This woman in Sydney, too. After a moment's hesitation, Billy says, 'You mean the one who knew Hugh Ferguson Whatsit?' Yes, Hilda says, that one.

Dodo puts down her brandy glass. Hilda wonders if she twigged earlier, in the kitchen. She certainly knows now. There's a green flicker in her eyes that takes Hilda back to when Billy switched allegiance. She is feeling usurped: *she* should have been the one to bump into Arabella Colville-Reeves. She can still write to her, of course, but Hilda would bet her boots she won't get a reply.

241

'Is she very like me?' Dodo asks.

'Maybe once. Not now.'

'So she's . . .?'

'Strong.'

'I'm strong.'

'Intelligent.'

'And I'm not?'

'You married him.'

'Did he ask her?'

Billy says 'Come on, Do: ancient history.'

But she won't be put off. 'Did he?'

'He tried to get her to go to Canada.'

'Where he sent me,' Dodo says in a small voice.

'But with her, the idea was he'd come too.'

'Hildegarde,' Billy says warningly.

'All he had to do was ask me to stay. It was ridiculous, taking off because of someone he knew before he met me. If he'd said one word to stop me—'

Billy looks at Hilda.

'—Did she see him again, after they let her out of prison?'

Hilda didn't ask. She could bluff it, of course, but what would be the right answer from Dodo's point of view? Perhaps she would rather her sanctimonious first husband had been a secret rake.

'Someone sent her a picture of him cut out of the newspaper.'

Dodo jumps on this, 'And?'

'He'd got fat.'

'But did she love him?'

'Steady on, Do.' Billy gives Hilda another meaningful look.

'If she did,' Hilda says, 'she didn't tell me.'

They stare into the fire. Hilda feels like an actress who has fluffed her big scene. A chance in a million, and what did she learn from it? Just one thing: even as an old lady, Arabella has more sex appeal than Dodo.

242

'He wrote to congratulate her when they gave women the vote. She was long gone. Her sister came across the letter in a drawer, took it over when she visited Oz. This was about ten years ago, too late to write back—'

Dodo looks up.

'—he was dead by then.'

Dodo's mouth frames a word, but no sound comes out.

Hilda drains her glass. 'Just after the war, she said.'

TWENTY-NINE

Four months since I'd left the Gold Coast and still I woke every morning feeling cold, missing my old breakfast of paw paw with lime juice, fruit bats hanging in the trees above me, women cooking fufu on the street below. Charcoal smoke and orange blossom and the oddly comforting stench of drains.

Glasgow smelled of damp. It rained all day every day, as it must have when I studied medicine there, though my memories were all sunlit and laughter-filled. We laughed in 1943, too, but my shoes still let in water. Why had we come back? *To make an honest woman of you, old girl.* I could see Sheila and her friends thinking 'you can't marry him' the first time they met Beefy, but they warmed to his jokes and nicknames and booming voice. Warmed to his warmth.

You would have thought Scottish hospitals would be clamouring to employ someone with my experience. Evidently curing the natives didn't count. With nothing else to do, Beefy and I spent every minute in each other's company. We had a ball, despite the powdered egg, and the mouse droppings, and the stony looks each time I walked into a bar (too old to be a tart, so what was I doing there?). Despite the dean at the Episcopal cathedral who found out I wasn't yet divorced and wouldn't marry us, no matter who my uncle had been.

Anyway.

We were lucky to find those digs. The tenement was on a corner, with a broad potato bed between us and the other side of the road, so we didn't look directly into the building opposite. The ceilings were high, our fellow boarders friendly, our landlady took the brass ring on my finger at face value. As far as she was concerned I was already Mrs Coubrough. And Sheila was just up the road in Marchmont Terrace with her ruthless mouser and her black-market coal and a cook who worked wonders with the ration.

As soon as we were married, Beefy and I planned to get out of Glasgow. I was applying for jobs in England, as far south as we could get, as close to Europe and temperate winters and summer heat. We had love, and his pension to tide us over, we'd be all right. But first, I had to get a divorce.

I never thought he'd want to see me.

Beefy was determined to come too. If I wouldn't let him meet the blighter, then he'd wait in a bar and escort me back to Glasgow. It took the best part of a day to dissuade him. And now I was shivering at Waverley Station in my pre-war musquash, with every other woman on the platform bare-legged or in uniform, and every other poster asking *Is Your Journey Really Necessary?*

Tommies loitered by the newsagent's counter, each one burdened with an enormous kit bag and strap-on hessian packs fore and aft. I felt tired just looking at them, but they were lively enough to whistle at those WAAFs running to catch the Kirkcaldy train. Sex was everywhere in those days. Couples kissing in broad daylight. Gasps and moans in the blackout: so many girls with their pants round their ankles and their backs to the wall. I always hoped the man was a Yank. They said the Army gave them rubber johnnies.

Turning my head, I scanned the crowd. A surge of adrenaline sharpened my eyesight. Over there. Brown homburg, tweed overcoat, that hawk's gaze. I hadn't expected to feel like this. So desperate to get away.

He stopped a few feet off. A porter walked between us. The hiss of an engine about to depart. A platform announcement, the Inverness train was late.

245

It had been sixteen years.

'Hugh,' I said.

He stepped forward.

A moment of confusion, as we wondered whether to shake hands.

He cleared his throat, 'You look well.'

'So well you didn't recognise me,' I said drily, wondering whose voice this was. Not mine.

He gestured towards Waverley steps. We carved two separate paths through the people descending from Princes Street.

The North British Hotel was next door to the station. Gilt-framed crags and stags, Edwardian mahogany, black Vitrolite from the twenties. Notices in copperplate script regretfully informing patrons of this or that decline from their exalted pre-war standards.

'We can get a cup of tea here,' he said.

God, I needed a drink. How had I spent so many years of my life with a teetotaller?

Without his hat and coat he looked younger than sixty-nine. The heaviness I'd found so ageing when we were married had stopped the clock. His head was solid as wet clay. A faint craquelure around the eyes, but his brow and cheeks and jaw still plumply taut. Meeting him for the first time, you might have taken him for a sensualist. Until he looked at you. Who was feeding him these days? Had he found a companion to share his retirement, a wife-in-waiting to trim the hairs in his nose and listen to the radio with him at night? And later, did she warm his bed? Good luck to her. Beefy was fifty-two. The future Mrs Coubrough had the better bargain.

'I'd like a sherry,' I told the waitress.

His mouth formed a disapproving line, though choosing sherry was a concession to his feelings.

'Actually, no,' I said, 'a gin, please.'

Which, when it came, was even weaker than the ones they served in Glasgow. Still, at least they'd found some proper

246

tonic water. The taste of quinine reminded me of all the malaria cases I'd treated in Africa. He listened with that look I used to dread.

'I thought you might manage a professional interest,' I said, surprising him. And myself. I'd rarely taken this satiric tone when we lived together.

After a few empty seconds I refused to fill, he told me he'd retired in thirty-four. When war broke out the Emergency Medical Service had got in touch. They were recruiting a team of volunteers to deal with outbreaks of neurosis in the civilian population: panic during air raids, rumour-spreading, hoarding food, anything that could undermine the war effort.

'And has there been much of this neurosis?'

We both knew the answer to this.

'Not as much as was feared,' he said.

Outside, dusk was falling. Two waitresses circled the room, lowering the blackout blinds, until we were sitting in complete darkness. A brittle *click* and we were revealed again. That same yellow light you found in hotels the world over.

Weak as it was, the gin did its work. I shrugged off my fur, warmed all the way through. Across the lounge, a grey-haired man caught my eye. Just for a moment. I might have been fifty-three but I'd kept my waist, and my skin had retained enough sun to mark me out from the peeliewallie locals. There was a young woman with him, swollen belly straining against the crepe of her dress, one of the unlucky few whose suffering didn't pass with the first trimester.

Hugh watched me watching them, his hawk's eyes burning into my cheek.

'Who is he, this man you want to marry?'

He had never been one for small talk.

'A Scotsman,' I said, 'a structural engineer. Nearer to me in age. And in other things.'

'He knows you already have a husband?'

'We've no secrets from each other.'

247

'Then he's a scoundrel.'

I raised my eyebrows, took another sip of gin, 'A scoundrel who loves me—'

He released one of his old disparaging breaths.

'—as you never did.'

Colour flooded his face. He checked the nuns at the next table, who hadn't heard. And what if they had?

Studying that beetroot flush, I wondered about his blood pressure, his risk of apoplexy or heart seizure. Many a heavy old man went that way. A moment later I was stricken by the thought, by the words *old man*.

In the street outside, the air raid siren wailed.

I'd come back in June. Queues outside the butcher's, sandbags everywhere, but no trace of the enemy. Doubtless there'd been panic, back in forty-one, but by now nobody rushed. The waitress continued loading dirty crockery onto her tray and carried it calmly out to the kitchen.

The hotel manager walked in, urging us to our feet. We would be supplied with fresh pots of tea after the all-clear. Hugh collected his coat and hat. I took my time, finished my gin.

In the lobby there was a scrum. Chambermaids, porters, kitchen skivvies, travellers too smart for the station buffet, guests flushed from the bedrooms, grandmothers and great aunts giving white-kneed schoolboys a mid-term treat: all of us trying to get down the stairs to the cellars. The manager asked for patience, the taking of turns from left and right. No one listened. Hugh and I loitered at the back.

'I'll not divorce you,' he said in my ear, making me start. The old dogmatic Hugh, though I recalled these diktats being delivered at arm's length. Now the words were flavoured with his tobacco breath. His baritone voice vibrated in my skin.

Someone stepped on a nun's foot. Tempers were rising. Grumbling turned to accusation. Clumsiness, bad manners, pushing-in. Hugh tipped his head towards the room we had just left.

Back to our table in the empty lounge, amid the half-drunk teacups and crumb-strewn plates. *I'll not divorce you.* It wasn't as if the stigma could hurt his career. Besides, I was the adulterous party, the shame was all mine. Why would he refuse?

He lifted a corner of the blackout blind, peering up into the sky. I pictured a fleet of Messerschmitts following the line of Princes Street towards the clock tower directly above us.

'If we couldn't live together, we can still die together,' I said.

And then it came to me: the provenance of this ironic drawl of mine.

He dropped the blind. 'No one's going to die.'

'It was a joke.' In my new Arabella voice, I added, 'There weren't too many of those when we were married.'

'We are *still married.*'

Something in his tone. Looking up to meet his eye, I felt a flutter in my chest. What a fool I was, my vanity would feed on anything. Beefy wasn't the first. Hospital colleagues, embassy staff, a fellow who'd deflected my questions with vague talk of 'import-export'. We'd drive out to the Pyramids, the temple at Dakor, the Wli falls. A late dinner, a moonlit walk. The heady moment when our laughter stopped. That sweet languor, my blood slowing with the miraculous certainty: I was wanted.

I thought about saying it: *I was more married to that diamond smuggler than I was to you.*

A slam as the door to the basement was pulled shut.

'Where are you living?' My words were loud in the silence.

'Montgomery Street.'

'Your own household?'

'Lodgings. Though we've been together so many years we feel like family.'

'A pretty widow, with children?'

He gave me a long, unsparing look, 'I've kept my vows, if that's what you're asking.'

'Because being married to me brought you such pleasure?'
'*Because you're my wife.*'

We both heard the footsteps. Our heads turned. An angular woman in a tin helmet glared at us from the doorway.

'Are youse deaf? Get in that shelter *now*.'

The whitewashed cellar walls were lined with two tiers of bunks. On the lower tier sat the nuns; mothers with children; a few frail, white-moustached old men and their indestructible wives. Everyone else was on the floor. Electric light bulbs dangled at intervals from a cable running the length of the ceiling. Though he was quick to look away, the filaments were seared across his vision, still there when he shut his eyes. A crypt-like smell of underground mixed with the warmer stink of sour breath, unwashed armpits, flatus.

We claimed the last vacant bunk, beyond the glare of the naked bulbs. From the look I gave the grimy blanket, he gathered I had not had much to do with shelters. I asked how long we would be down there, as if he could read the Luftwaffe's minds. He saw I was worried about missing my train. No point getting myself into a state, since there was nothing I could do about it. I bridled, as I always did when he talked sense. Then, shrugging, I relaxed.

Side by side, we watched the people on the floor. The upper bunk made a cave around us. He glanced down at my shoes, my still neatly-turned ankles. Something French-smelling in his nostrils, soap or scent. In a bunk on the opposite wall, the pregnant woman turned away to let her companion rub her back. Hugh had taken him for her father but, now he thought about it, the gap in their ages was no wider than the years between us.

'When you went away to study, I'd listen for the postman. Friday evenings I'd meet every Glasgow train, just in case—'

I turned to him, my eyes filled with amazement.

'—Sundays were the worst. I'd get out to the Sma Glen or

250

the Carse, walk as long as the light lasted, come back and write to you.'

The look on my face. As if a stranger were importuning me on the street. 'I received no letters.'

'I didn't send them—'

He'd planned it last night, how he would put it to me incrementally, nudging me home. But having started, he had to get it all off his chest.

'—I've enough put by to keep us comfortably in a house of our own. Bruntsfield, Morningside. Gullane, if you fancy the sea.'

'Hugh,' I said, with a gentleness he didn't like the sound of.

But if he stopped now it would never be said, so he ploughed on. He could arrange his affairs any way that pleased me. It was his habit to winter in Ayrshire, on his brother's farm, but he'd thole the east coast wind for me if I preferred Edinburgh. I wouldn't be short of invitations. The Royal Society of this or that, the Red Cross ball, dinners at the Surgeons' Hall. He tried to make me see it: the stir I would create. *By Jove, where's he been hiding you?*

I didn't smile or look at him, yet the air between us felt kinder. I sat very still, eyelids lowered, lips slightly parted. My lovely profile. Half in shadow like this, I could have been the girl he proposed to in 1916.

There was one last thing he had to say.

'I know you wanted children. I've no patience with them. I'll play cards with John Neill's weans at Christmas, but you can't have an intelligent conversation . . .'

My eyes snapped open. I sat up, straight-backed.

'I took the Wassermann test,' I said, 'I did it myself, in the lab one lunchtime, my second year in Glasgow. It was negative.'

His face showed nothing. No embarrassment or regret, not even the most basic recognition. He resumed what he'd been saying before I interrupted. 'I paid for it, watching you sail off to Canada with nothing to keep you here. Knowing it could have been different.'

I wasn't letting him away with this. Since I'd had the courage to raise the subject, he could do me the courtesy of acknowledging it.

'Is this the story you tell yourself: that our separate bedrooms were a form of contraception—?'

I kept my voice low, but he glanced round about us. And suddenly all my old resentment flooded back.

'—You never loved me. We weren't even married in the true sense. Other than one night, when you called me by her name.'

His brow furrowed.

'Arabella,' I hissed.

'What?' he said.

There was no mirth in my laughter. He remembered me in this mood. I'd keep at him hour after hour, following him from room to room, as he'd prodded the adder with a stick as a boy, trying to get it to strike. As if I wanted him to roar at me, wanted him to do something I could never forgive him for. God knows he had a temper, but he'd kept a tight rein on it.

'Let me jog your memory,' I said, 'you had influenza.'

He'd barely had a day's sickness until that summer. The relief of giving in to it. His life such a struggle. Every rung of the ladder enjoyed no sooner but despised straight. Shakespeare, was it, said that? He'd buried enough patients to be fairly sure he wouldn't be getting up again. Sore eyes, aching joints, parched throat. Time stretched and shrank. Hour after hour of waiting to hear my tread on the stair, to feel my cool hand on his brow, my care. He talked to me then as he had not before, but was I really there?

All this he recalled well enough, but not what I told him now.

252

It could have been a neurotic phantasy, but I was a doctor, qualified these sixteen years, so he had to consider the possibility. He grued, even as he felt a shameful twitch between his legs.

'I was fevered, delirious.'

I said it was not what he did then, but his determination *not* to do it every other day of our eleven years together that I found unforgiveable. That, and calling me by her name.

'I hardly remember the woman.'

I gave another brittle laugh. 'You remembered her well enough to find yourself a wife who looked just like her.'

'*It was you I married.*' Too vehement. Heads turned towards us. He leaned into the shadow cast by the upper bunk and said it again, 'It was you I married'.

And now it all poured out of him. He'd had years to ask himself why I left. 'Aye, we got off to a bad start, but that's common enough.' He felt such love for me whenever we were apart, yet in my presence felt the very opposite. Not hate, never that, but irritation. Fury, sometimes – though he hid it – and a kind of exasperated pity. Other women were happy enough as wives. He would think of me sometimes as he went about his duties in the prison, and his flesh would ache as if bound by invisible chains. He knew I blamed him. Tense as he found our speechless dinners, they were better than listening to my complaints. When I raised the idea of training as a doctor, there was a pinch of vengefulness in his assent: *let's see how you like hard work for a change*. But I had liked it. The clinical practice no less than the studying. Those weeks between academic terms were the happiest of his life. A pile of books by my elbow, an eager light in my eyes. At last we had something to talk about. But what he'd taken for a new beginning was the beginning of the end.

I didn't know what to say.

It may be he read my silence as a change of heart. He told

me about the framed photograph kept by his bedside all the years we'd spent apart. The presents he bought every July, on my birthday. Brooches, rings, a blue silk scarf to set off my eyes. A dress, one year. The annual pilgrimage to Pitlochry, to the scenes of our courtship. Scouring the Lancet and each new edition of the Medical Directory for news of me. Hours in the public library, reading up on the topography, climate, tribes, language of wherever I was working. Attending medical conferences in Edinburgh and London, seeking out the Syrian or Egyptian or African delegates, hanging on their talk like a dog waiting for scraps to drop from the table. And every week he wrote to me. Stiff, rather formal missives at first, but, as the years went by, unashamedly tender and emotional. Words he had never addressed to any other woman. The letters were mine if I wanted them. He had them in a suitcase under his bed, hundreds of pages spanning twenty-two years.

But I didn't need proof. I believed him. My heart unfurled as if he had reached inside me and touched the love-struck girl who'd accepted his proposal all those years ago. She lived in me yet, alongside the grown woman who saw all too clearly what had happened. He was incapable of loving me, so I left. And it turned out to be the one thing I could do that would bind him to me.

'Hugh—'

It was dreadful to see that loving, hopeful light leave his eyes.

'—I'm going to marry someone else.'

Had we not been trapped in a bomb shelter, he would have got up and walked out.

'I'm sorry,' I said. And I was, a little.

I thought about Beefy, waiting for me on the Queen Street station platform. About the dinner he would buy us at Rogano's later. About the porridge we would eat with our fellow boarders next morning, taking the edge off our hangovers before slipping back up to bed. Giggling under the eiderdown. Squalls of rain against the window. Then out for a quick gin and French before lunch. If the German bombs spared me.

Hugh consulted his pocket watch. I gave him an enquiring glance.

'Six o'clock,' he said.

He'd bought me a one-way ticket to Canada: he would give me my divorce.

Despite the hour, there was a hushed, middle-of-the-night atmosphere in the cellar. Some people were drowsing. Others talked in murmurs. The hotel staff were playing cards. A ginger-haired waitress shuffled the pack one-handed before she dealt. A sharply-dressed young man offered around a packet of cigarettes. Half a dozen heads leaned in to the struck match. A couple of bunks away from us, a mother hummed a meandering tune to the child in her lap. The melody was taken up by the women around her, becoming a softly-crooned sing-song.

I shivered and felt the weight of Hugh's tweed overcoat settle on me. I looked sideways at him, at that crease in the lobe of his still-neat left ear.

Resting my head on his shoulder, I waited for the all-clear.

Afterword and acknowledgements

Most of the characters in this novel are based on real men and women who left a trail in public archives, newspaper libraries and the memories of a few people I was able to question. That trail is necessarily patchy. Where there are facts, I have used them, drawing on my imagination to fill in the gaps. The National Archive of Scotland holds daily reports filed by Hugh Ferguson Watson while the suffragettes were in his care in Perth Prison, but I have found only the sketchiest record of his life with Donella. I know they were unhappy enough for the marriage to end in separation; that within a year of the wedding she was no longer mentioned in the diary of her uncle, the "Perth Pepys", George Taylor Shillito Farquhar; that her grandfather died in a private asylum in Edinburgh; and that Hugh's specialist subject was syphilis. The connection between these four facts is mine alone.

So *A Petrol Scented Spring* is a work of fiction. Most of it is narrated by a character who is herself indulging in tormented guesswork. It should not be read as history. For that, we have the late Leah Leneman's groundbreaking *A Guid Cause: the women's suffrage movement in Scotland* and *Martyrs in Our Midst*. Without her scholarship, I would never have heard of Hugh Ferguson Watson and Arabella Scott.

For those who wish to know more about Arabella, a biography is currently in preparation, based on interviews tape-recorded by her niece, the late Frances Wheelwright. Her family was kind enough to allow me a preview of some chapters.

I am indebted to the late Hugh Ferguson Watson, nephew and namesake of the Perth Prison doctor, who shared vivid memories of his uncle with me; and to Hugh, John, Willie and Jean Watson. John McGie, Donnie Groot, Anthony and Guy Chapman, and Roy Balfour all helped with background information. None of them bears any responsibility for the fictional slant I have placed on the details they supplied.

I am also grateful to Donald Macgregor; Brian Singer; Norman Watson (no relation); the National Archives of Scotland; the AK Bell Library in Perth; Perth & Kinross Archive; the Royal College of Physicians and Surgeons of Glasgow library; Glasgow University archives; the Imperial War Museum; the State Library of Victoria, Australia; Perth Six Circle Project; and the Scottish Prison Service, which allowed me access to the older parts of Perth Prison.

Before writing this novel, I explored aspects of the story in a play, *Cat and Mouse*. Muriel Romanes of Stellar Quines Theatre Company, Kirsty Duncan, and the Gannochy Trust provided invaluable support in developing the script through a series of rehearsed readings.

Finally I would like to thank my agent Judy Moir for her unerring editorial judgement and sheer hard work; my brother Jeremy Close for IT help; my early-draft readers Geraldine Doherty, Siobhan O'Tierney, Fiona Thackeray and Alice Walsh for their insights; and Jim Melvin for everything.